"There is no online magazine quite like *Guernica*; dignified and youthful; serious and lively; a marvelous amalgamation of politics, literature, and enlightened thought. An invaluable forum and outlet for those who care about art, dialogue, and, quite simply, the future of the world.
—RICHARD PRICE,
author, *Lush Life*

Guernica, and its editors, respect the life of the mind with an intensity rarely seen these days.
—GEORGE SAUNDERS,
author, *Tenth of December*

Politics, journalism, art, fiction, poetry—*Guernica* does it all with style. And massive amounts of intelligence. Reading *Guernica* reminds us that there actually is a world out there—and in here. It consistently raises the tone of the political and literary conversation.
—FRANCINE PROSE,
author, *Lovers at the Chameleon Club, Paris 1932*

Hot damn, do I love *Guernica*. It's just one of the smartest and most far-ranging magazines around these days, whether in print or online. Let the crabass folks bemoan the end of magazines, they miss the point entirely. Intelligence and curiosity are vital qualities in any medium and *Guernica* proves both are far from dying off.
—VICTOR LAVALLE,
author, *The Devil in Silver*

In a world where "starting an online literary magazine" often involves nothing more than changing your subheader to read "...*a magazine of dreamers and poets, full of flights of fancy*," the online literary magazine *Guernica* stands out like, well, the intimidating cultural, artistic, and political force it is.... Their first-ever print edition [celebrates] a decade of being the baddest online-only lit mag on the New York City block.
—*BUSTLE*

Guernica, a small online literary magazine that punches way above its weight class.
—NPR BOOK NEWS

For a web-only magazine with the simple tagline "a magazine of art & politics," *Guernica* proved to be so much more to us last year. Covering a wide variety of topics with top-notch writing and unique insight, *Guernica* was another one of those sources that we kept trying to find an opportunity to share with our readers. Last year, it introduced us to ecopsychology and challenged us to rethink the virtues of a green economics and carbon offsets…. *Guernica* makes us excited about the future of web journalism.

—*UTNE READER*

I don't remember the last time I was as excited as I am now by a new magazine. I love the wonderful selection of writers and the wide-ranging points of view. Bringing good fiction and good poetry together with such solid political writing distinguishes your magazine from so many others out there. Bravo!

—BRUCE WEIGL,
poet, *Song of Napalm*

Guernica magazine stalks the boundary line between art and politics. It reports back to us on what it finds there by publishing long-form writing for the digital age, transgressing the borders of conventional wisdom about what can be done—and what is to be done. I can't think of a more provocative, thoughtful place to be than on the edge, with *Guernica*.

—STEVE KATZ,
publisher, *Mother Jones*

Guernica: the place, the event, the work of art. The enterprise of this magazine is wrapped up and inspired by all this powerful iconography of place, event, and work of art, and I am emboldened by it, for to me it means that there are things in our past that are so powerful, their defeat was in reality a pause. Now the pause is no more. I look to reading *Guernica* with a mix of pleasure and disturbance, which for me is the ideal state of reading, and its—*Guernica*'s—existence is important for the foundation it will establish, which means the support it will give the literature that is even now being written by people who remind me of when I started to write and was certain that nobody would like it. In truth, more important than somebody likes it is that somebody writes it. *Guernica*!

—JAMAICA KINCAID,
author, *See Now Then*

Guernica magazine is a fine example that online publication can also carry depth while providing readers media versatilities.

—WUER KAIXI,
student leader of Tiananmen Square protests

Guernica is a rare and wonderful work of art in the age of artless reproduction, a magazine of high aesthetics that pursues politics as if they mattered in our increasingly immaterial world.

—ROGER HODGE,
author, *The Mendacity of Hope: Barack Obama and the Betrayal of American Liberalism*

GUERNICA
ANNUAL

VOLUME TWO

Guernica Annual #2
© 2015 Guernica, Inc.

Guernica / a magazine of art & politics
112 West 27th Street, Suite 600
New York, NY 10001
www.guernicamag.com

and

Haymarket Books
PO Box 180165
Chicago, IL 60618
www.haymarketbooks.org

ISBN 978-160846-537-8

For editorial inquiries: editors@guernicamag.com
For business inquiries: publisher@guernicamag.com

Trade distribution:
In the US, Consortium Book Sales & Distribution, www.cbsd.com
In Canada, Publishers Group Canada, www.pgcbooks.ca
In the UK, Turnaround Publisher Services, www.turnaround-psl.com
All other countries, Publishers Group Worldwide, www.pgw.com

Special discounts are available for bulk purchases by organizations and institutions. Please contact
Haymarket Books for more information at 773-583-7884 or info@haymarketbooks.org.

Guernica is supported by:
The National Endowment for the Arts

Guernica is a proud member of:
The Council of Literary Magazines and Presses

Book design: Nadxieli Nieto / NIETO Books

Cover image (detail):
Alexandria Smith, *The Uncertainty Of It All*
24×24", acrylic/glitter on panel, 2014. Courtesy of the artist.

Printed in Canada by union labor

Table of Contents

3

4

•

Foreword

JESMYN WARD // 2015

W HILE I WAS struggling to write the first draft of my memoir, one of my friends sent me a link to an interview with David Simon that *Guernica* published on April 1, 2011, called "The Straight Dope." The article spoke to issues I'd been trying to confront— but mostly had been effectively avoiding—in my own work. From 2000 to 2004, five young Black men I'd loved, including my brother, had died, and I'd run from the telling of that story for damn near a decade. I come from a poor Black community in Mississippi, and my life and the lives of my family and community have been marked by tragedy for generations: we've sold dope, done dope, gone to jail, raised children alone, lived hand to mouth, betrayed each other, loved each other, and died. I say that I was struggling because I was fighting the memoir: I didn't want to reveal painful personal secrets, and I didn't want to reckon with the big issues. I didn't want to confront systemic racism, and in doing so, to force a reckoning. In the interview, Bill Moyers asked David Simon about drug addicts leaving detox and returning to poor Black neighborhoods, and Simon said: "These really are the excess people in America. Our economy doesn't need them—we don't need 10 to 15 percent of our population.... [W]e pretend to need them. We pretend to educate the kids. We pretend that we're actually including them in the American ideal, but we're not. And they're not foolish. They get it. They understand that the only viable economic base in their neighborhoods is this multibillion-dollar drug trade."

I was floored. Reading this interview changed me: it recommitted me to telling my story, to telling the world about my family's life, my brother's life and his death, to reckoning with all the awful ways being poor and Black made us expendable in the American South. And David Simon's words taught me there were other people in the world who were committed to saying the hard things, to being blunt and frank and honest, to telling stories that were painful and raw. And finally, that *Guernica* was a place of gathering, a forum, a magazine invested in sharing these kinds of stories with the world. That moment was revelatory for me. I've read that women and people of color and queer writers often need permission to write creative nonfiction, to tell the stories of our lives, because the larger culture silences us and tells us in so many ways that our stories are unimportant. *Guernica* gave me permission. *Guernica* told me that marginalized stories, unexpected and painful stories, are worthy, that there is value in sharing our experiences with readers, in meeting in that place where art and politics converge.

Whenever I am struggling with self-doubt or hopelessness, I turn to *Guernica*. I pour through the articles, awash in the chorus of voices, every one confronting the ineffable, the uncomfortable, the unbearable: the war in Syria, the drought in California, girls' education in Afghanistan. I hope that *Guernica* endures, that it continues to provide space for the multitude of dissenters, the straight-talkers, the word-crafters. That it continues to welcome we of the savage tongue and clear eye.

Introduction

MICHAEL ARCHER // 2015

THESE PAGES serve up no beer manifesto, no ode to chicken tenders. If you're looking for a (very) personal essay on finding oneself cuckolded, a meditation on vorarephilia (the desire to be devoured), or undercover reporting on the hottest trend in vaginal-reconstruction surgery, you've landed on the wrong patch of planet *Guernica*. Online, in the magazine's archives, you'll find the above, and lots more.

Eleven years in, I'm learning to live with an awkward fact. *Guernica*'s diversity of topics is my excuse for helplessness when posed the perennial question: "What kind of stuff do you guys publish?"

> "We're interested in anything that falls under the umbrella of art and/or politics."

> —Wouldn't that include everything, everywhere?

> "We publish work that's well crafted, literary but not arcane, and tells a story that's not being told."

> —That sounds like the aspiration of every magazine, everywhere.

In our early, earnest days we worked up this formulation: "A typical *Guernica* piece…is defined by a curiosity that favors the universal over blind nationalism or static notions of community or humanity, in favor of the most honest and radical engagement with the world as topic."

That manifesto carried the freight with partners and in publicity. Not so good at a party or a dinner table, unless the point was to fend off further invitations. Never my objective in the days when cooking meant plugging in the Foreman Grill.

So here I am, again struggling to tie together twenty-five pieces collected as representative of our interests, of our contributors', and those of the year just past. If two years running count as a ritual, this is a ritual I enjoy.

I'll start with the gimmes. There's more than one axis connecting Habibe Jafarian's assertion that to survive in Tehran a woman must co-opt all the conventional attributes of a man and Masha Gessen's contemplation—on the eve of surgery to remove her ovaries, uterus, and fallopian tubes—of gender transition. There's resonance, too, between Claudia Rankine's ze-roing in on quiet, everyday racism and Mano Khalil's opting, in the fight for Kurdish freedoms, to wield a camera instead of a gun. Likewise be-tween Richard Price's account of the past glories of New York City public housing and Zach St. George's reckoning of the sequoias' ominous future. More subtle or implicit is the conversation between John Benditt's quotid-ian deities and Ingrid Rojas Contreras's protagonist, fearful that her father has been kidnapped by the also-missing Pablo Escobar. Reverberations like these are, for me, a big part of what this annual is about.

With collections or theming in mind we do, several times a year, engage in a little gerrymandering. Roughly a third of the pieces here first appeared in *Guernica* special issues, and ran under banners put up by the editorial staff: "Religion in America," "American Empires," and "The Boundaries of Gender." Often, contributors propose those rubrics to us—not as phrases but as topics they're drawn to, pursuing their own interests and ideas. When we noted that many writers were addressing the boundaries of gender, we capitalized the phrase and invited others to weigh in on the subject. A piece like J. Malcolm Garcia's rage-provoking investigation of America's deportation of combat veterans, on the other hand, could have anchored a special issue with any one of three themes—Immigration, Militarism and Justice, or The Boundaries of Grotesque Hypocrisy.

Putting together the annual, we agree on our selection process, then cheat a little. After voting on our favorites—the best, in the view of *Guernica*'s staff, of what we've published in the previous twelve months—we swap out a few of the most frequent picks to include pieces taking up matters the collection would otherwise overlook.

Applying sort criteria proposed by the zeitgeist, the year picks its own topics and issues, and the collected pieces for the annual reveal themes we'd not seen. (Emergent theming! There's a pithy reply to the question I fumble over.) Reading through our mid-2015 selection, I was struck by these two:

Fear. Fear that is, by any rationale, legitimate, and fear that might be construed as paranoia, or the cynical cultivation of paranoia by power. Fear of surveillance, but just as much the fear of not being seen. Fear of what may be lost, along with fear of what may be coming.

Resilience. Resilience in protecting the sacred, as well as in fighting the corrupt. Resilience in staying put, and resilience in journeying home. Resilience in battling both the blatant and the camouflaged.

Fear and resilience. A point-counterpoint for our era? Two of various readings time can test. Will what we now recognize as fear shift toward caution, or toward revulsion? Will today's resilience, seen from a distance, look like exemplary fortitude, or more like blind obstinacy?

A yearbook that prompts us not only to revisit but to reassess earns its shelf space.

Unwanted Alive

J. MALCOLM GARCIA // MAY 15, 2015

*Since changes to US immigration law in the '90s,
many veterans are being deported.*

IN A STOREFRONT on the east side of Tijuana, US Army veteran Hector Barajas spoke to his nine-year-old daughter in Los Angeles a week before Christmas 2014. He wore shorts and a white tank top. Tattoos arced across his back. His shaved head reflected the glow of the ceiling light. A thin mustache drew a dark line beneath his nose. He lay on a cot in the front office of the Deported Veterans Support House, a nonprofit that stands next to an auto mechanic shop and a karaoke bar and assists veterans removed from the United States. Pizza joints and convenience stores lined the main drag, less than half a block away. At night, dogs roamed the streets, toppling garbage cans. An American flag concealed the glass front door.

Through Skype video hookup, Barajas saw the Christmas tree his daughter had decorated. He told her he wished he could be with her.

"It's beautiful," he said of the tree.

Then the video connection shut off.

"I can't see you," she said. "Daddy, I can't see you."

He tapped his phone. She called out to him but he would not see her again unless he reconnected with Skype or she came down to Tijuana for a visit. Like the men he helps, Barajas, thirty-eight, is a deported veteran. He served in the Army from 1995 to 2001 and received an honorable discharge. He says he was removed from the United States in 2004 for discharging a firearm into a car in Compton, a gang-infested city in South Los Angeles County where he spent much of his childhood after

4

his parents moved there from Mexico. He denied the shooting. He says he served a three-year prison sentence before he was deported. He would have been allowed to return to the States in 2024 but he didn't want to wait that long. He crossed back into California the same year he was removed to reunite with his family, got caught, and was deported again in 2009, this time for life.

I learned about Barajas and the support house when I began following the immigration case of a Pennsylvania Army veteran, Neuris Feliz, fighting deportation. An Iraq war veteran, Feliz left the Dominican Republic for Puerto Rico and then the United States mainland as a boy. He enlisted after 9/11. He thought it his duty. He considers himself an American. His paperwork, however, says otherwise: he is a permanent legal resident, not a US citizen.

Feliz is also a convicted felon, the victim of his own ruinous choices and those of lawmakers intent on showing their tough-on-illegal-immigration political bona fides through a harsh, inflexible law passed almost twenty years ago. The 1996 Illegal Immigration Reform and Immigrant Responsibility Act, signed by President Bill Clinton, greatly expanded the classification of crimes that allow for the removal of immigrants, including veterans. To the surprise of the deported veterans I spoke to, their military service had not granted them citizenship. Immigrant veterans can be deported for a period of years or for life depending on the severity of their crime.

Today, in addition to such serious crimes as murder and rape, a great many other offenses, when they result in a sentence of a year or more in prison, can meet the definition of an "aggravated felony" and lead to deportation. The US Immigration and Customs Enforcement agency, better known as ICE, does have discretion over whom it refers for removal. ICE, spokeswoman Gillian Christensen told me in an email, is "very deliberate in its review of cases involving veterans." But the 1996 act does not permit any discretion on the part of immigration judges, who may not take into account a defendant's military service or any other mitigating circumstances once they have been convicted of an aggravated felony. The act can be invoked against an individual at any time, even years after they have been released from prison. Complicating matters further, non-citizens do not have the right to a government-appointed lawyer. They may hire their own if they can afford to.

Margaret Stock, a retired lieutenant colonel in the Army Reserve, is now an immigration attorney with Cascadia Cross Border Law in Anchorage, Alaska. She told me that before 1996, deportations of military veterans were extremely rare. Now, nearly every day, she said, she consults with a lawyer handling a deportation case or speaks to a veteran facing deportation. The day before I reached her recently, she had consulted on five such cases.

"I do not personally know of any honorably discharged military veteran who was deported prior to the 1996 changes to the immigration laws," said Stock, a 2013 recipient of the MacArthur Foundation genius grant.

In June 2011, then–ICE director John Morton wrote a memo suggesting a different set of standards for veterans facing deportation. Morton advised that "when weighing whether an exercise of prosecutorial discretion may be warranted," ICE officers, agents, and attorneys should consider among other factors "whether the person, or the person's immediate relative, has served in the US military, reserves, or national guard, with particular consideration given to those who served in combat." But lawyers for veterans facing deportation question how often this happens or whether it happens at all. An ICE spokesperson said that the agency does not specifically track statistics on how many people removed from the United States have prior military service.

"ICE is driven by statistics to show the public they are deporting criminal aliens," Stock said. "The pressure is on agents to find criminal aliens and deport them. They don't care if the criminal case is more than ten years old. Immigration agents don't get a medal for letting a criminal alien go for being a vet. They get credit for deporting veterans."

In Tijuana, Barajas said he assists about fifty deported veterans and is in touch with more than 200 others in twenty-six countries, including Canada, Jamaica, Trinidad, and the Dominican Republic. These veterans face a host of challenges. Some of them don't speak the language of the country they were deported to because they left it when they were toddlers. Jobs are scarce and pay little. Those who received an honorable discharge are eligible for Veterans Affairs services through the agency's Foreign Medical Program, which covers certain healthcare costs related to military service, said VA spokesman Randy Noller. Still, according to attorneys representing deported veterans, mental health services for post-traumatic stress disorder and other psychological problems are few or nonexistent in most countries. Unfamiliarity with their new country makes deported veterans vulnerable to criminals and corrupt officials.

"Over here, it's the twilight zone," Barajas told me when I arrived in Tijuana. "You see people walking back and forth across the border and you can't."

Deported veterans include those who joined the military and those who were drafted. Many of them, like the "Dreamers," came to America as children, brought by relatives and with no say in the matter. Had they kept their noses completely clean, or committed a different class of crime, they would have been eligible to pursue citizenship, just like any other green card holder. In some states, they would even have been allowed to pay in-state college tuition, just as though they belonged.

But they don't. Last year, ICE removed 315,943 immigrants. Among them, 56 percent or 177,960 had been convicted of crimes as serious as drug trafficking, or as minor as entering the country illegally. The data do not quantify how many of the deportees were veterans.

About 25,000 non-citizens are today serving in the US military, according to a Department of Defense spokesman, or a little less than 2 percent of active duty forces, and approximately 5,000 non-citizens typically enlist each year. In a 2005 study, "Non-Citizens in Today's Military," the Center for Naval Analyses found that "non-citizen servicemembers offer several benefits to the military," most notably, racial, ethnic, linguistic, and cultural diversity. "This diversity is particularly valuable as the United States faces the challenges of the Global War on Terrorism." It also found that non-citizens have substantially lower attrition rates than white citizens—9 to 20 percentage points lower over thirty-six months.

In March of this year, the US Army enlarged a new program that encourages legal immigrants with "in-demand skills" such as Arabic and other languages to join the armed forces "in exchange for expedited US citizenship." The Military Accessions Vital to the National Interest program, known as MAVNI, will seek 5,000 enlistments next year, almost double its current level.

"Because the MAVNI program has been extremely successful in filling our ranks with highly qualified soldiers who fill critical shortages, we expanded the program," said Army spokesman Hank Minitrez.

But any recruits who haven't yet become citizens—or who aren't already in the citizenship process—run the risk of deportation should they run afoul of the law. After serving prison sentences, they are punished further and far beyond what an American citizen would experience for identical offenses. They are being kicked out. Their military service does not entitle them to a second chance.

"You don't have to like them," said immigration attorney Craig Shagin, who represents veterans facing deportation. "They served in our uniform and under our flag. They took an oath to defend the Constitution. If they get shot, no one says, 'They're Mexicans.' They are ours. Why when the uniform comes off are they shifted back to lawful permanent alien? When is it they are not ours and why?"

The veterans I spent time with weren't angels. They had been convicted of serious and, in some cases, reprehensible offenses. But no matter what they did, they served and in some cases fought and risked their lives for the United States, just like citizens.

Stock said she is unaware of a single case in which a deported veteran successfully appealed removal and returned to the United States. Veterans have only one sure way to reenter the States legally. When they die, those not discharged dishonorably are eligible for a full military funeral in the United States.

Unwanted alive, they can return home as a corpse.

In late January 2015, I sat with Neuris Feliz in the dining room of his Lancaster, Pennsylvania, apartment. A late January morning, shades drawn, the gray light of an overcast winter morning barely breaking through. The horse-head profile embossed against the yellow shield of the 1st Calvary Division with which he served in Iraq stood on a desk. Near it, a photo of Feliz in his Army uniform, an American flag behind him.

Three deflating heart-shaped balloons from his thirty-first birthday party the night before sagged above our heads. A poster on the wall behind them read, *Live, Laugh, Love.* Feliz looked younger than thirty-one. Black hair, wide brown eyes, a weary smile. Just he and his wife and a bottle of pink wine, a red ribbon slipping down it. Happy birthday. Perhaps the last birthday he would celebrate in the United States.

"I live here," he told me. "Hell, my favorite sport is football."

But he was not from here. Feliz was born and raised in the capital of the Dominican Republic, Santo Domingo, with a brother and three cousins. Early in his childhood, his mother, separated from his father, left him with an aunt and moved to Spain and later Puerto Rico to find work.

He spent much of his time in the countryside of the Dominican. So free. Not congested like Santo Domingo. He remembers canyons deep and wide, small wood houses, and all types of fruit. There were sheep, cows, horses, sugar cane, too, and coffee plantations. Clouds concealed the tops of mountains and fog descended across valleys at night with the stealth of ghosts. In the morning, he wore a jacket until it warmed.

In 1995, when he was eleven, Feliz traveled to Puerto Rico to rejoin his mother, who had returned there from Spain. Four years later, they moved to Lancaster, where other family members lived. The weighted mugginess of Pennsylvania's humid summers surprised Feliz. The nineteenth-century brick buildings with their sagging wood porches looked ancient. He had never seen so many white people up close.

He attended summer school, enrolled in English as a Second Language classes. Within a year he'd learned the language well enough to participate in classes with American students. His aunt taught him multiplication, slapping his knees with a belt when he answered incorrectly. He fell in love with science. He wanted to be an astronaut.

He grew restless as he advanced into his teens, however, and school no longer captured his imagination. He spent his high school senior year clubbing and drinking. He didn't bother to attend graduation. If he could talk to the young man he was then, Feliz would tell him, If you lose your love for school, you lose everything.

The terrorist attacks of 9/11 refocused him. He thought of the United States as his country. No one had told him otherwise. In 2002, he signed up with the Army National Guard. Within a few months he went active.

"With me, it was, 'You want to join? Sign here,'" Feliz recalled. "I don't remember [the recruiters] saying anything about status. But they did ask for my green card."

One year later in March, while he was walking ten kilometers and carrying a ninety-pound rucksack as part of a three-day war games drill, the United States launched airstrikes against Iraq. Feliz didn't grasp that a war had started. That was part of being in the Army. Don't think, do. He loved that. That sense of purpose. Just do. Civilians stopped and watched him when he walked past them in his uniform. How impressed they looked. He didn't know anything to beat that feeling.

Feliz, a power generator mechanic in the Army's 1st Calvary Division, deployed to Iraq in 2004. He landed in Camp Doha in Kuwait. Three weeks later, the division began a three-day drive to Sadr City in northeast Baghdad. So many people on the street. The convoy inching through jammed markets. Move, move! Get out of the way! the Americans shouted. Some soldiers from the 115th Battalion, including Feliz, bivouacked at Camp War Eagle. The camp would see combat with the Mahdi Army, an Iraqi paramilitary force opposed to the Americans.

Daily mortar attacks became the norm. Feliz rode in convoys and heard the gunfire, the ting of metal when bullets struck his vehicle.

For six months, he pulled guard duty six hours on, twelve hours off. Sometimes, he directed vehicles entering the camp and driven by Iraqis into a large concrete box to contain a blast should the vehicle be wired for a bomb. If it blew up, so would he.

One hot evening in April 2004, Feliz stood by the camp's main gate and heard explosions. OK, he thought, another firefight. Then he saw a truck racing toward the gate. More vehicles came behind it, all of them carrying wounded. He heard someone shouting, Medics! Medics! He responded automatically. He and others of his squad put the injured on litters. Ankles, arms, legs all shot up. Everyone running so fast. Seven or eight people died. He realized where he was. Iraq. In a war. Not a war exercise, but a real war. He told his pastor he had blood on his hands from trying to help the wounded. Not long afterward an IED killed a close Army friend, Leslie Denise Jackson.

She had worked in supply and drove back and forth between Camp War Eagle and Camp Muleskinner in eastern Baghdad. Her vehicle struck an IED. Feliz heard the explosion. He had no idea her vehicle had been hit until he got off guard duty. His squad leader told him. He couldn't believe it, choked back tears. She was only eighteen. He could not get her out of his mind. "I didn't join the Army for this," she used to tell him when a mortar hit and wounded had to be treated. Meaning the killing and dying were getting to her. For days after her death, Feliz kept recalling her words: "I didn't join the Army for this."

He changed. No more don't think, do. He talked back to his supervisors. He didn't complete his work. His superiors, he said, did not suggest he seek counseling, though an Army spokesman said counseling would have been available to him at the camp. Instead, they allowed him a four-day leave in Qatar. From there, he spoke to his family and pastor.

"He was depressed, crying," recalled Cesar Melo, pastor of the Iglesia Poder de Dios en Acción, or Church of God Power in Action, in Lancaster. "He saw parts of the body of his friend after the explosion. He didn't understand why we had to go to war. He didn't want to live. He wanted to go home."

When he returned to Camp War Eagle, he assumed his old don't-think-do attitude. He told everyone he was OK. To all appearances he was.

In 2005, Feliz reenlisted just before the 1st Calvary received orders to return to the States. Once in Fort Hood, Texas, everyone took a thirty-day leave. Feliz returned to Lancaster. He stayed drunk the whole time.

Back at Fort Hood and awaiting redeployment to Iraq, Feliz continued drinking. He did not seek counseling. He did not consider he had a problem. But he couldn't keep himself out of bars. He had an on-again, off-again girlfriend. When they were on he wouldn't let her out of his sight. He didn't want to be alone.

"I was very selfish, very possessive. I was running from my life," Feliz said, describing that time. "I felt very alone."

In May 2005, after a day of drinking, Feliz drove to his girlfriend's apartment at night. A guy stood in the parking lot waiting for her. He said they were dating. When she drove up, Feliz took an ax handle from the trunk of his car and ran up on the guy as he was getting into the car. Feliz began hitting him with the ax handle, swinging like a baseball player, striking the guy four times around his right knee and ankle, the guy screaming and trying to shield himself, the girlfriend screaming, the guy half falling, half jerking himself into the car and slamming the door shut.

Feliz ran to his girlfriend's side of the car and cussed her out as she sped off. He watched them leave. She had her two-year-old son with her. He remembers that. He doesn't like that he cussed around him. He was drunk and angry. He left his girlfriend's place, drove to a strip club, and drank. To this day, he said, he does not know why he had the ax handle or even how it got in his car. For protection, he thinks. But he cannot imagine from what.

That night the police questioned him at his apartment. He told them what happened in the parking lot and gave them the ax handle. The police left without detaining him. A week later, they called and told Feliz to come to the station for more questioning. He didn't. He didn't give a damn. Another week passed and the police called again. This time they told him to turn himself in. He complied. He still didn't give a damn. He just wanted to get whatever might happen over with. He says now he could have asked the Army for legal assistance, as an active duty service member, but instead he went with a court-appointed lawyer. He didn't care what might happen.

Feliz pleaded guilty to aggravated assault. According to court records, the judge asked him if he appreciated that by pleading guilty the United States could choose to "deny you the right to remain in this country, they might deny you the right to apply for citizenship and they could in fact deport you from this country. You understand that?"

"Yes, your honor," Feliz said.

The judge sentenced him to five years. He was twenty-two. Feliz says now that he does not recall the judge speaking to him.

"I just remember saying yes to everything," he told me. "I don't remember much. I was just going with whatever they gave me."

A few weeks later, when we spoke by phone, he reflected on his sentence.

"My lawyer wasn't that much of a——" he began and then paused. "He was court-appointed and didn't do much. He told me I'd get probation and then the day of sentencing he told me the DA was asking for four years. But really, I didn't care too much."

After two days with Barajas at the support house in Tijuana, I took a bus to Rosarito, a town farther south along the coast, to meet deported veteran Alex Murillo.

Murillo, thirty-seven, has thick black hair and an easy manner, liberally dropping the word "dude" into every other sentence. On the afternoon I showed up at his apartment, he was talking on the phone to his eldest son in Phoenix.

"How you doing?" Murillo said to him. "How's school?…All right… Nothing. I'm watching *Planet of the Apes*. The latest one."

Murillo was born in Nogales, the last one in his family to have been born in Mexico. He was an infant when his parents moved to Phoenix. He remembers nothing of his birthplace. He grew up as an American kid. He played baseball and basketball. Didn't care for soccer. He scored As in grammar school and was on the honor roll in junior high.

"What's going on in school…What do you mean?…I thought you were getting good grades."

As a high school sophomore, Murillo started screwing up. Treading that line between dropping out or not. Spending too much time with his girlfriend. He did graduate but his grades had sunk so low he was ineligible for college grants and financial aid. His parents didn't have the money to send him.

In October 1996, after his girlfriend became pregnant, he joined the Navy. Quit screwing up, he told himself. Make your family proud, take care of the baby, and after your enlistment, attend college. Get into law enforcement. Something exciting.

"How's it gone down to Cs, son?…Straight Cs? That's a straight average. How are you going to get into college? What are you having problems with, son? You were getting As and Bs."

Murillo became a naval mechanic. He said he was voted honor recruit in boot camp and graduated top of his class in aviation school in Pensacola, Florida. He loved the Navy but hated it, too. Loved the camaraderie, meeting other sailors from all over the United States, but had a phobia of being swallowed by the ocean and floating away into nothingness.

After three months at sea, he returned stateside for a brief break before beginning a six-month deployment. He started drinking a lot then. Young marriage and baby all at once, away from his family. Twenty years old, he was just a kid. Maintaining equipment, working sixteen- to eighteen-hour days. The job wore him down.

His ship, the *George Washington*, returned to Norfolk, Virginia, in 1998. He drank more and more. He got popped on a piss test for marijuana. He was placed on restriction. One night, he cut his wrists with a razor blade. He doesn't think he wanted to kill himself. Maybe he did. Or maybe he just wanted out. He spent about two weeks in the psych ward. He spoke to a chaplain often and to a doctor a few times. The doctor jotted comments in Murillo's file. He doesn't know what he wrote anymore than he understands how the doctor helped him. When he was released, he left the Navy in 1999 with a bad conduct discharge.

"I'm going to stay on you about your homework. Bring back As and Bs. More As than Bs. I have to stay on you...I know, son...I want to see you. How's your mother doing? I'm trying to get a job."

Murillo returned to Phoenix and continued drinking. His marriage, already rocky from his time away, worsened. He and his wife tried to make it work and had two more children but the marriage didn't last and they divorced. His drinking began costing him jobs: Home Depot, Cox Communications, DirecTV, he can't say how many jobs he lost. He couldn't pay child support. His wife would not let him see their children.

In April 2009, he found another job, the wrong job. He agreed to transport around 700 pounds of marijuana for a dealer and got busted in St. Louis. He was sentenced to thirty-seven months in the federal prison in Lompoc, California. While he was there, immigration flagged his name. In December 2011, after he completed his sentence, a prison bus carried him to the San Diego/Tijuana border.

"I care, son, because I'm far away. You have to move forward. I messed up. I'm paying for it. You got to be a success, son. I see nothing but good stuff ahead of you if you stay on those grades."

Murillo can still see himself getting off the prison bus at about 11 p.m. He had $120 hidden in his prison sweats, gray on gray, his only clothes. Guards unshackled his hands and feet and he walked off the bus. Pitch black out, the air heavy. A guard gave him a cup of noodles, shrimp-flavored. He got one phone call. He tried to reach his mother but the call didn't go through. He stepped forward, his left foot in Mexico while his right foot remained in California until he raised it, too, and crossed over.

He stayed with a cousin and then moved to Nogales. He didn't like it there, felt people held his "Americanness" against him. In September 2012, he resettled in Rosarito.

With the help of his family, Murillo recently started a satellite sales and installation company. He coaches football and freelances as a photographer and videographer. His mother brings his children down for visits when she can. They throw a ball on the beach until they leave. He watches them go, that fear he had of the ocean overcoming him, that feeling of being sucked into nothingness.

"Apply yourself a little more, OK, son?…All right. We'll web chat later? OK. Tell your brother and sister I love them very much. I love you, son. Bye."

He put down his cell phone, slumped in his chair. He stared at the wall. He raised his head to the ceiling and covered his face with his hands. He dug his fingers into his forehead and his face broke beneath his hands into tears.

"I just want to get back home, man."

His voice catching barely above a whisper.

"I just want to see my kids."

Deported veteran Hans Irizarry, thirty-eight, picked me up at the Santo Domingo airport in the Dominican Republic late on a Tuesday afternoon at the end of January. He stood slouched to one side waiting for me. He had a roll to his walk that at times blossomed into a strut. A dragon tattoo encircled his left arm. He wore a baseball cap tipped down the left side of his head.

I came to the Dominican to meet the wife, uncle, and cousin of Neuris Feliz. Before I left the States, I got in touch with Irizarry through Facebook. Hector Barajas in Tijuana had given me his name. I wanted to spend time with him to get an idea of what Feliz would face should he too be deported to the Dominican. I also wanted Irizarry's help with translation when I met Feliz's family.

I rented a car and from the airport we drove to the house of Luis Milanes Mendez, seventy-eight, and Yeimi Mendez, thirty-seven, an uncle and cousin of Neuris Feliz's. He lived with them as a child after his mother moved to Spain.

They remembered him as a normal, calm boy. Humble. He did what he was told. He played baseball and enjoyed swimming. When he moved to Puerto Rico to be with his mother and later to the United States, Yeimi felt his absence. She had regarded him as a younger brother.

Feliz called Luis and Yeimi when he joined the Army. They were so happy, as proud as any father and sister would feel. For him to be part of the US military, the most powerful military in the world, well, that compared to nothing they had ever known.

From Iraq, Feliz wrote to his mother. She sent the letters to Luis and Yeimi and they forwarded them to other family members. He said he missed them all. He wrote about hungry Iraqis and how they reminded him of the poverty in the Dominican. These thoughts made him think of his family and he grew sad and lonely.

Feliz spoke very little about Iraq when he returned, Yeimi said, not even about the death of his friend. He had always been quiet but the pronounced silence that hovered around him could be felt even over the phone. It was like he was missing a part of himself.

Luis and Yeimi did not know what to think when they heard Feliz had been charged with assault in Texas. They didn't understand. They didn't know him to be violent. They felt even more confused about his situation now.

16

Why, they asked, is he facing deportation for a fight? They don't know US immigration law, but how can anyone say that's fair? He risked his life for America and now it wants to toss him out?

If he is deported, of course we will take him in, Luis told me. You have to be careful of everything, he would warn him. You have to know where and what to say, what to do. Everyone carries a gun. Don't get into a fight. Here, they'll kill you. Don't try to be brave. It is dangerous. Step on a person's foot, sorry, and they kill you. That's how bad this country is.

When Feliz called recently, Luis and Yeimi told him not to give up. OK, he said. They did not hear from him again for weeks. That silence again. Already, a part of him had been removed.

After the interview, Irizarry and I drove to the home of Feliz's in-laws to meet his wife, who was visiting her family. We had not gone far when two police officers pulled us over. Irizarry showed them his expired Army identification.

"You're American? You're the boss," one of the officers said.

"No, you're the boss," Irizarry said.

"We're here to protect you," the officer continued. "Anything you can do to help us, we'll take."

"What can I tell you? I'm short of money."

"Anything you consider good, we'll take."

"I need money from you," Irizarry said.

The officers stepped away. There are two kinds of cops in the Dominican, Irizarry told me as he drove off. Traffic cops during the day, like these guys, but after dark it's the badasses. At night, he won't stop for the police. The night cops will tell you to get out of your car and take it. Now, you're walking. Now you're a target.

"I've had police fuck with me," he said. "They see the tattoos and earrings. 'Oh, you're a deportee. We're looking for some criminals. You look like one of them. Where're you from? How long have you been here?' What has saved me is the military ID."

It wasn't always like this. Irizarry was born in Santo Domingo in 1976. Those were different days. Cops didn't shake you down. No bars on house windows to keep out burglars. He could sit in front of his house and not worry about gangs. Every time it rained, he stood outside and played in the puddles or under a gutter overflowing with water. Now kids don't do that.

After his mother and father divorced, his mother moved to New York City in 1990, taking with her thirteen-year-old Hans, his older brother, and his younger sister. Some aunts and uncles were already living there.

They moved into an apartment at 125th and Broadway. Irizarry learned English easily. After school, he and his sister walked home and he would cook dinner. His mother and older brother worked for a tailor late into the evening. When he turned sixteen, Irizarry got his residency card. He assumed that made him a citizen although he didn't really think about it one way or the other.

He attended college and studied computer science. Bored, he dropped out. His mother got on him, What are you going to do with your life? He didn't know. But he always liked war movies. The more he thought about it, the more he thought the Army would offer him a future. He certainly had no sense of direction now. So, on a whim in 1997, he walked into an Army recruiter's office and asked, How can I join? The recruiter did not ask about his status. Four weeks later, he was in boot camp.

Irizarry and I stopped outside a tall, multistoried house that stood behind a concrete wall. Feliz's wife, Carolina Martinez, opened a heavy metal door in the wall to let us in. Yard cats trailed after us into the kitchen and up a flight of stairs. We sat near a balcony enclosed behind bars. A photograph of Carolina's father in a military uniform hung on a wall. A maid brought us orange juice.

Carolina, twenty-nine, had known Feliz since they were children. Then they lost touch but met again in Pennsylvania when she was visiting her sister. He had been out of prison for six years then. He was not a typical Dominican man. He was not macho. He seemed very open-minded. He did not hang out with other women. He wanted children and to grow old with a wife.

After they married, he showed her photographs of dead bodies in Iraq. Very ugly things. He told her Iraq was not easy. He had nightmares. He kept saying he wanted to go back. Before they married, she said, she had not seen that part of his personality that had been affected by war.

Carolina was in Lancaster when customs officials detained Feliz in Puerto Rico. He had called her that morning before he left Santo Domingo for San Juan. She worried when she didn't hear from him the following day. She wept when he finally called and told her what had happened. She still cries about it. She tells herself everything is going to be OK, but she can't be certain.

If he gets deported, he will use his military knowledge to survive, she told me. But that may not help him. People here pick fights for anything. He doesn't know how things are.

The US government should give him a chance, she continued. It should look at all the years he has not been in the Dominican Republic. It should look at his military service. He fought for the United States, after all, not the Dominican Republic.

In 1998, while he was in the Army, Irizarry married. He also was deployed to Kuwait as part of Operation Desert Fox, a four-day US– and United Kingdom–led bombing campaign on Iraqi targets. He unloaded tanks, M-16s, missiles. He spent six months in the desert seventeen miles from the Iraqi border. He carried a gas mask with him everywhere, including the latrine. He almost got himself killed when he drove an armored vehicle into a minefield. He stopped, looked, saw mines all around him, and backed out the way he'd driven in.

He returned to the States in May 1999. That June, while he was stationed at Fort Stewart, Georgia, he notified his sergeant that he was taking his pregnant wife to the hospital for a checkup. His sergeant told him if he wasn't back on base in fifteen minutes he would take his rank. Irizarry, just back from Iraq, wasn't taking his shit, and went AWOL. He and his wife left for New York. Two months later, Irizarry turned himself in to the Army. In 2000, he received an administrative discharge, which he appealed. It was later upgraded to general discharge under honorable conditions.

While the upgrade resolved one problem, a more immediate issue, employment, remained. He didn't like people telling him what to do. He didn't think like them. He behaved as he had in the Army. Tell him to do something, he did it. Just like that, done. What's next? His coworkers would mess with him. Why are you working so fast? Who you trying to impress? Or, I didn't tell you to do that, Izarray.

"You did, too."

"Watch how you talk to me, Izarray."

"Fuck you," and he was gone.

Irizarry and his wife divorced in 2003. By then he had two daughters to support. In and out of work, he wasn't making any money. The bills piled up. In 2004, he ran into an old high school buddy, a drug dealer. If you need money, all you got to do is pick up a package and you'll make $800, he told Irizarry. Irizarry didn't ask what would be in the package. When he picked it up, the police were waiting for him. The package held two ounces of heroin. Irizarry was arrested but got out on bail. However, he would face a judge, he said, who had a reputation of sentencing everyone who appeared before him to fifteen years to life. Irizarry jumped bail and fled to Florida, where his father had immigrated. About a year later, the police caught him. He was extradited to New York and sentenced to four and a half to nine years. He served three and a half because of time served in Florida waiting to be extradited.

"Do you think a good father would have done what you did?" I asked Irizarry as we drove back to his apartment. "I mean, transport dope?"

He stopped the car. He turned and faced me. Speaking in a measured tone, a tight grip on his anger.

"Listen, you cannot tell me what is a good father. You do anything for your kids not to starve. I did everything it took. It was an easy way out. It was stupid, selfish. I went to Iraq. I was a hero. I got caught with drugs, now

I'm not a hero? If I hadn't been caught would I still be a hero? A lot of people have done stupid things and have not been caught. They're lucky. It was a mistake, a stupid, dumb, desperate mistake. You don't know what people go through."

In 2007, while he was still serving his sentence, Irizarry received a summons to appear before an immigration judge. According to trial transcripts, the judge said he could not give Irizarry a break.

"I do appreciate your service to the country. I mean that quite sincerely…. But because of the drug convictions, the way the Immigration laws are written, I'm not—I have no discretion. I'm not allowed to consider things such as how long you've lived here. Your family ties to this country. Whether you've served in the military. All those things that show that you would be a desirable member of society. Because of the seriousness of the conviction, I have no discretion. I'm a delegate of the Attorney General. I have to follow the laws as written and the law—the way the Congress has written it says I can't even examine those things. You're not eligible to apply for any of the applications that would allow me to consider those things."

The judge then issued the following order: "It is HEREBY ORDERED that the respondent be removed from the United States."

On October 13, 2008, after he had exhausted his appeals, immigration authorities escorted Irizarry to a plane bound for the Dominican. When he landed in Santo Domingo, police took him and other newly deported men and women to a police station for registration. A man took their photographs. Another man registered their fingerprints. They stood in different lines identified by the crimes that led to their deportation: drug felons here, possession of a firearm there, and so on. The intake took about two hours. The police taunted him. You're going down, motherfucker. Oh, we got another for drugs. We got you, motherfucker. Irizarry paid a cop $2,000 to delete his registration so when he looked for work no potential employer would know he had been deported.

He found a job in Santiago, about an hour outside the capital, helping a man rent houses. When the work dried up, he returned to Santo Domingo. He works at call centers now, similar to telemarketing, and earns about $180 a month.

"Sometimes I think of going to Mexico and crossing over into the US," Irizarry said. "If I could see my daughters. If I could see my father. He has Lou Gehrig's disease. I can't see him. Believe it or not, some people learn from their mistakes. I've learned. I would give what I don't have right now to see my family."

Irizarry and I left the house of Carolina Martinez and drove to his small apartment: bright yellow walls, tile floor, two bar stools the only furniture. He had a Chihuahua, "Tony." The name reminded Irizarry of New York. Once we were inside, he double-locked the front door. Then we called Feliz's mother, Juana Feliz, sixty-one, in Puerto Rico.

She recalled how scared she felt when Neuris deployed to Iraq. Many times he didn't call. She didn't know from day to day if he was alive or dead. She did not earn much so when he told her he had enlisted in the Army she thought, "Wow. He can have a bright future. The Army can do much more than I can do for him." She assumed the Army would enroll him in school. Instead, it sent him to war.

When he came home in 2005, he locked himself away. She didn't know what had happened over there. Something. Days, weeks he didn't talk to her.

She did not hear about the fight over his Texas girlfriend until two months after it happened. You know how men are with their mothers, she said. Only when he was locked up did he tell her.

She did not understand why the United States wanted to deport her son. She was suffering through what only a mother would understand and taking all kinds of medications for her nerves. Neuris broke the law but she asked for forgiveness as a mother for her son.

"Please keep in mind it is not the end of the world," Irizarry told her. "There are more people here like your son. You're not alone."

"You're in the Dominican Republic?"

"Yes. I'm a veteran. I was deported."

"Oh, my God, they did that to you, too?"

"Yes."

"I'm going to cry."

"Don't cry."

"I'll pray for you."

"Don't feel sorry for me. At least I'm not dead in Iraq. Neither is Neuris. You still have your son."

I left the Dominican the next day and stopped in Miami to visit Guillermo Irizarry, sixty-five, Hans Irizarry's father, at Franco Nursing and Rehabilitation Center. I wanted to ask him about his son but his illness had progressed to the point where he could no longer talk or move. He breathed through a tube in his neck, was fed through another tube in his stomach. The machines keeping him alive made clicking noises. He lay on a bed, hands at his sides, palms down, and stared at me. I didn't want to leave without saying anything. I approached his bed and introduced myself. I told him I had seen Hans. He had a job, I said. He had an apartment. He said to say hello. He said he was sorry for messing up.

His father listened, eyes tearing, roaming my face. He opened his mouth, watching me, but made no sound. I wanted to think he heard and understood me. But there was no way to know.

After Feliz told me about the ax handle assault, I spoke to psychiatrist Judith Broder, founder of the Soldiers Project, a national nonprofit based in Los Angeles that provides counseling for post-9/11 servicemen and women. She was not surprised by Feliz's post-deployment behavior.

A sense of alienation, reliving traumatic experiences, and anger can all contribute to drinking and drug abuse and other self-destructive actions, Broder said of soldiers returning home from war. How much of this behavior has led Iraq war veterans to prison is unknown. Available information is woefully out of date. The most recent veteran incarceration data from the US Department of Justice dates back to 2004, just one year after the Iraq war started. It found that 10 percent of state prisoners reported prior service in the US armed forces. A majority of these veterans served during periods of war but did not experience combat duty.

Few people would dispute that soldiers are often ill-prepared to return to civilian life and that lack of preparation can lead to problems legal or otherwise. A 2008 RAND report, "Invisible Wounds: Mental Health and Cognitive Care Needs of America's Returning Veterans," found that 300,000 veterans who had served in Iraq and Afghanistan suffered from PTSD or depression. In addition, about 320,000 may have also suffered traumatic brain injuries.

Symptoms of PTSD include aggressive, hyper-alert behavior that, while necessary for survival in war, creates problems in civilian life, Broder told me.

"Veterans talk about a zero to ten anger reaction," she said. "Their anger goes off instantaneously and escalates to ten very, very fast. It is a combination of post-traumatic stress and being hyper-reactive to anything that constitutes a threat."

Such feelings may have led Feliz to put an ax handle in his car.

"Many veterans we see keep weapons at home," Broder said. "They keep them under the bed, in the car. They even bring them into therapy sessions. They sense danger all around. There's no on/off switch."

In 2007, while Feliz spent a second year in jail, the Army hit the switch on his military career. Unable to complete his second enlistment, he received a general discharge under honorable conditions.

With time off for good behavior, Feliz served three years and one month in prison. After his release in 2009, he returned to Lancaster, where he took a job at Tyson Chicken. The following year he enrolled in Thaddeus Stevens College of Technology. He started dating the sister of his brother's wife, too, a Dominican he had known since childhood. In 2011, he returned to the Dominican Republic to meet her family. His life, he felt, was on an upswing.

Feliz spent about two days in Santo Domingo before he flew to San Juan, Puerto Rico, to visit his mother, who had returned there after he joined the Army. As part of their routine procedures, airport customs officers checked his name as they did for all passengers and became aware of his felony conviction. They took his passport and green card and detained him for nine hours before they gave him a summons to report to an immigration judge in Philadelphia.

Since then, Feliz has been fighting to remain in the United States. His Lancaster attorney, Troy Mattes, argued in February of this year before the Immigration Court in Philadelphia that as defined under immigration law, "aggravated felony" differs significantly from how the Texas penal code defines it and therefore does not apply to Feliz. In other words, Feliz's crime, he said, does not meet the definition of a crime of violence as interpreted by the board of immigration appeals and federal courts.

A ruling is expected later this year. If the judge rules against Feliz, he can appeal.

"This guy served in a time of war," Mattes said. "That in itself is a circumstance to be considered by the US government. He did this [crime] ten years ago. He did his time. Give him a second chance."

Feliz has tried to get on with his life. He graduated from college in 2012 and accepted a job with a graphics company. He married in 2013. However, nothing he does feels certain, secure. He does not know his future and where he will live it.

At night, when Feliz does not dream about prison, he sometimes dreams about Iraq. He is in his barracks when Boom! Boom! Mortars explode. He sees himself on guard duty escorting cars into the concrete box.

He has a packet of photos in a plastic bag. Photos of exploded bodies, traces of blood, brains, burned vehicles. An Army buddy, an infantry soldier, took them and gave them to him. They're memories, Feliz said. He doesn't look at them and go crazy. They're just there. In a desk drawer.

His mind wanders. If he is deported, he knows he can adjust to the Dominican Republic. He has been to war and prison. He can do this, too. He has no interest in seeking out screening for post-traumatic stress disorder. He doesn't really care. He is unwilling to fight as hard as his lawyer and his wife. He's almost done fighting. He's thirty-one. He wants to do things other than fight. He wants it to be done.

In Tijuana, Hector Barajas posted a notice on Facebook: "March 10, 2015. With great sadness. Our brother Gonzalo Chaidez, 64 years old deported US Army veteran passed away at 5:30 a.m. at the general hospital in Tijuana."

Barajas won't stay in Mexico. He has applied for US citizenship. If he doesn't get it, he will seek asylum. He'll do something. He considers his daughter. He won't die in Mexico.

Some days, Alex Murillo sits in his Rosarito apartment and thinks back to his childhood in Phoenix. One time he overheard his mother talking about a cousin who had been deported. At the time he thought, That sucks, and then went out and played with his friends. He didn't dwell on it. He certainly never thought it would happen to him. As far as he was concerned, he was an American. Still feels that way. He served in the US Navy. Saluted the flag. Be all you can be. Standing in front of a mirror at boot camp for the first time in his black-on-black night watch uniform. Wow. Look at him. His parents saw him graduate as an honor recruit. He was on his way. God and country. No one can take that feeling from him. His kids won't get kicked out. They are Americans. No one can take that away from him either.

Hans Irizarry does not want to die in the Dominican Republic but he suspects he might. He saves his money and recently bought a kitchen stove. Beats the hell out of the little electrical hotplate he had.

He still gets depressed. A few times he has called a suicide hotline in the States. Once he explained he had been deported. The voice on the other end said he could do nothing for him. Sorry. If you feel like talking again, call us.

Irizarry misses cold weather. The first day of snow. It looks so beautiful. All the snow in the trees. Here in the Dominican, he feels trapped inside someone else's body. His mind is elsewhere but his body is here. He can describe what he's thinking but the people here don't understand. They've not seen it. They can't envision it. He thinks, Fuck, I'm not home, and then everything inside him dies.

He doesn't belong here.

This article was reported in partnership with The Investigative Fund at The Nation Institute, with support from the Puffin Foundation.

Carib Woman, 1818

KHALYM KARI BURKE-THOMAS // APRIL 1, 2015

I am burning in this life / and the next.

For four years I carry
your bones like water
from a well.
          Darling
I am burning in this life
and the next.

Blackness
as the Second Person

MEARA SHARMA INTERVIEWS CLAUDIA RANKINE // NOVEMBER 17, 2014

The National Book Award finalist on chronicling everyday racism,
the violence inherent in language, and the continuum from
Rodney King to Michael Brown.

AUTHOR AND ANTHROPOLOGIST Zora Neale Hurston wrote, "I feel most colored when I am thrown against a sharp white background." In Claudia Rankine's National Book Award-shortlisted *Citizen: An American Lyric*, Hurston's words are applied like a telescope—to insidious, accumulative instances of racial aggression. A book-length poem, much of *Citizen* chronicles, in spare second-person prose, quiet flashes of racism, like the well-educated woman who "didn't know black women could get cancer"; the therapist who screams, "Get away from my house!" not realizing the person at the door is her patient; or the colleague who says, "[H]is dean is making him hire a person of color when there are so many great writers out there." Seized from the everyday and thrust, unadorned, against the page, these moments transcend individual experience, conveying the particular racism of twenty-first-century America, as well as the tunnel of history from which it emerges. "The past is a life sentence," Rankine writes, "a blunt instrument aimed at tomorrow."

In *Citizen*, Rankine also meticulously analyzes the experiences of public figures like Serena Williams, who, in maneuvering her rage against "the so-called wrongness of her body's positioning at the service line," epitomizes the way in which the black body is caught between a state of invisibility and hyper-visibility. Writing in *The New Yorker*, the poet and critic Dan Chiasson described *Citizen* as "an especially vital book for this moment in time." In this magazine, *Tin House* editor Rob Spillman called *Citizen* required reading for "politicians who gerrymander, politicians who restrict voter's rights, politicians who use coded racist language." As with Rankine's 2004 work, *Don't Let Me Be Lonely*, *Citizen* pierces our sociopolitical structure with emotional exactitude, and in turn, demonstrates the inseparability of the two.

Rankine was born in Jamaica, and, at seven, moved to the Bronx, New York, where she attended Catholic schools. At Williams College, under the guidance of the poet Louise Glück, Rankine was shaped by writers such as Adrienne Rich and Robert Hass, whose work, she says, helped her to "understand the ways in which [the] mind has to negotiate the reality of a thing." Currently, she is a professor of English and creative writing at Pomona College.

I met Rankine in New York in mid-October while she was in town for the Poets Forum, presented by the Academy of American Poets, for which she serves as a chancellor. Her demeanor was placid, but it was clear that she was unrelentingly observing the crowds rippling past our sidewalk café table. She laughed easily, spoke slowly, and paused often, as if striving, in real time, to close the gap language produces between intention and comprehension.

—Meara Sharma for *Guernica*

Guernica: When did you start deliberately making note of the everyday moments of racial aggression that comprise much of *Citizen*?

Claudia Rankine: I always took note of them, because I think if you're in the black or brown body, you're negotiating them all the time. It's like women taking note of sexism. It's a kind of incoherency that you are constantly negotiating. But in terms of writing them down, I started working on the book three or four years ago. It was a different project, in which I wanted to show how black people's health was connected to their day-to-day life. I was really interested in the fact that blacks have high blood pressure, heart disease, and diabetes at a higher percentage than the rest of the population. That didn't stay very aggressively in the book, but that's how it started. I began to document these moments as support for this other thing I was thinking about, and then the moments themselves began to take over.

Guernica: In the book, you reference John Henryism, a recently coined physiological condition resulting from prolonged exposure to racial aggression and discrimination. It's interesting that you were initially conceiving of these moments as evidence for the prevalence of real illness.

Claudia Rankine: Yes, I was at Yale and I said to the poet Elizabeth Alexander, "I'm interested in the ways in which black health seems precarious in the United States." She introduced me to the term "John Henryism." And then I went back and researched it and understood that, woah, this thing I am thinking about is actually a condition that's named.

Guernica: Do you think it's useful to have a name for that?

Claudia Rankine: I think having a term for a condition that is prevalent is useful, because then people understand it as something not particular to them. It allows you not to ask the question, "What's wrong with me?" and begin to ask the question, "What's wrong with this place that I'm in?" For instance, if you're a black guy and you got pulled over, and you didn't know that any other black men were being pulled over, you would constantly in the back of your head be thinking, "What did I do?" rather than, "I didn't do anything, these are just the conditions I live under." I think the idea that the systemic problems in a society lead to illness is important to know. We shouldn't be separating out how we live with where we live, and what ails us with the environment we're in.

Guernica: I understand you did quite a lot of interviews with people in your community, friends, and strangers as research for the book. Tell me about that process.

Claudia Rankine: One of the things I wanted the book to do was speak to intimate moments. I asked a lot of friends and people I'd meet, "Can you tell me a story of a micro-aggression that happened to you in a place you didn't expect it to happen?" I wasn't interested in scandal, or outrageous moments. I was interested in the surprise of the intimate, or the surprise of the ordinary. So you're just moving along and suddenly you get this moment that breaks your ability to continue, and yet you continue. I wanted those kinds of moments. And initially people would say, "I don't think I have any." Their initial reaction was to render invisible those moments weaved into a kind of everydayness. And then I'd tell them something that happened to me, and that would trigger something. It was interesting to watch how the emotion of telling these stories built up in the tellers. They often got very upset. You could feel the anger being released. You could feel the irritation, the disgust, happening as the event was retold. So clearly they weren't cool with it.

Guernica: You reference Zora Neale Hurston's line, "I feel most colored when I am thrown against a sharp white background," repeatedly in the book. It resonates with the quality of these moments. You could imagine them occurring quite subtly—as you say, weaved into the everyday. But when pulled out of context, and placed next to one another, they're incredibly affecting.

Claudia Rankine: They really stand as they were told to me. I chose language and decided not to include certain details, but more or less these are the stories that either I experienced or I was told.

And I wanted a feeling of accumulation. I really wanted the moments to add up because they do add up. I wanted to come up with a strategy that would allow these moments to accumulate in the reader's body in a way that they do accumulate in the body. And the idea that when one reacts, one is not reacting to any one of those moments. You're reacting to the accumulation of the moments. I wanted the book, as much as the book could do this, to communicate that feeling. The feeling of saturation. Of being full up. I wanted it to be simulacra.

Guernica: Were you thinking about other books while writing *Citizen?*

Claudia Rankine: A year or two ago I read Lauren Berlant's *Cruel Optimism.* That's a book that gave me a kind of language to think about ideas like "the non-relation in the relation," which is a rephrasing of Berlant, for example. When I read phrases like that in Berlant's work, it gives me a vocabulary to understand incoherency. I feel this moment, I see the moment, and how do I account for it inside my day-to-day reckoning of the world? In *Cruel Optimism,* Berlant talks about things that we're invested in, despite the fact that they are not good for us and place us in a non-sovereign relationship to our own lives. And I thought, on a certain level, that thing that I am invested in that is hurting me would be this country [*laughs*].

I also read *White Girls* by Hilton Als. The ways in which he looks closely at race, intimacy, and the emotional range of an individual when they come up against another individual, in terms of desire, love, dependence. Toward the end of working on *Citizen*, *White Girls* was interesting and useful for me to think about relative to encounters.

Guernica: You've mentioned intimacy a few times. The poems in *Citizen* have a close-to-the-bone quality, but they're also deeply political. How would you articulate the relationship you have between politics and intimacy?

Claudia Rankine: The friends I have, and the people whom I admire, are people who have an understanding of the conditions under which we live, and have a humanist sense of the world. If that's lacking in my understanding of a person's negotiation of the world, I can't be close with that person. I'm not comfortable, for myself and for others [*laughs*]. And yet, one has these people whom you trust, have faith in, whom you believe see what you see, and then you come up against a moment where you feel suddenly tossed out. So I was really interested in those moments. Because we are invested in being together. In having friends. In joining our lives. And yet these are the people who also fail you. And when they fail you in these ways, it signals a larger understanding about who you are as a black person in the world. It's not just a little failure for me. It's something exposed.

Intimacy is important in my work because I don't understand existence without intimacy. All of us are dependent on other people—and in ways we don't know. You cross the street and assume that person isn't crazy, they don't want to mow me down with their car. I don't know that person but I am already in a relationship with them. I am asking them to abide by the traffic laws. If they decided not to, I'd be dead. Even in those anonymous ways, we're in relationships.

Guernica: How do you personally work through those moments of being failed by people close to you?

Claudia Rankine: I mean, I sometimes don't move through them. My tendency is to want to say to the person, "Do you understand why I feel this way?" I usually do say that. And sometimes it doesn't go well. By this I mean we hit an impasse again. Not that I need to hear exactly what I want to hear, but I need to know I am heard. Those moments make for a better friendship. But I can't let it go. For good or bad.

Guernica: Talk to me about your decision to set many of these poems in the second person.

Claudia Rankine: There were a number of things going on. Because some of the situations were mine and some belonged to other people, I didn't want to own them in the first person, because I didn't own them, factually.

But that was the least of it. The real issue was, the second person for me disallowed the reader from knowing immediately how to position themselves. I didn't want to race the individuals. Obviously [the reader] will assume—"She's black, he must be white," etc.—but I wanted those assumptions to be made. Because you know, amid this post-racial thing, sometimes I'll have a student who says, "I don't really think about race. I don't *see* race." And then I'll ask, "Well, how do you read this?" And they say, "Oh, that's a black person, that's a white person." So clearly, you're race-ing these people in order to understand this dynamic. I wanted that positioning to happen for readers.

I also found it funny to think about blackness as the second person. That was just sort of funny. Not the *first* person, but the *second* person, the *other* person [*laughs*].

Guernica: Were you thinking specifically that if you were to set these poems in the "I," a white reader would be able to read this as a kind of memoir?

Claudia Rankine: Exactly. I felt that the first person would have deactivated the scene. Because I think of the described dynamics as a fluid negotiation. I don't think these specific interactions can happen to the black or brown body without the white body. And there are ways in which, if you say, "Oh, this happened to me," then the white body can say, "Well, it happened to her and it has nothing to do with me." But if it says "you," that you is an apparent part of the encounter.

Guernica: You reference Judith Butler's notion that we, as people, suffer from the condition of being addressable, and language navigates this, for better or for worse. How does this idea connect to your inclination toward language?

Claudia Rankine: Each of these failures for me is a failure of communication, via a mode of communication that can be violent or meant to behave violently. Butler provides a way of thinking about how language becomes an instrument of violence. And why we feel it as such. And how our availability, our showing up, our presence, leaves us open to that violence. I think it's a question of language, as it arrives from one body to another. It becomes the thing in between the two bodies.

One of the things that I think about is: How do you make moments that float, transparent? Moments that could just float away. How do you make a body accountable for its language, its positioning? Why not make a body accountable for its language?

Guernica: This connects to a line in *Citizen* that I've been thinking about: "Words work as release—well-oiled doors opening and / closing between intention, gesture." Do words work for you in that capacity?

Claudia Rankine: I think so. I think words are the thing that either triumphs for you, in your desire to communicate something, or fails. I love language because when it succeeds, for me, it doesn't just tell me something. It enacts something. It creates something. And it goes both ways. Sometimes it's violent. Sometimes it hurts you. And sometimes it saves you.

Guernica: Is there something about language's closeness to failure that is appealing, as a writer?

Claudia Rankine: Yes. I love revising things, because you see how you can get the language to get closer to intention. You know there are three ways to say X thing, but one will say it better than the other two. And in saying it better, it gets you closer to something. When you achieve it fully, you create something that's transparent—that people can move into and through their own experiences. As a writer, I don't want people spending time thinking, "What does she mean?" I want, in a way, my text to go away. So that the words on the page become a door to one's own internal investigation. It's just a passage. If the work does its job, it just opens.

Guernica: This idea of transparency and clarity is interesting with regards to genre. In a way, you could imagine this book being presented as a series of journalistic essays. Why does poetry permit the kind of transparency you're talking about?

Claudia Rankine: Because I think poetry has no investment in anything besides openness. It's not arguing a point. It's creating an environment. Whereas if you were writing an op-ed piece or an essay, somebody would be asking, "What's your point?" With poetry you can stay in a moment for as long as you want. Poetry is about metaphor, about a thing standing in for something else. It's the thing that opens out to something else. What that something else is changes for readers. So what's on the page—it falls away.

Guernica: I know you've been working on a project connected to Ferguson. Can you tell me about the experience you had there?

Claudia Rankine: I happened to be in St. Louis a week after the Ferguson protests started. So I went to the neighborhood, just to look around, talk to people, try to understand what they were feeling. I knew what I was feeling. I knew there was a simmering rage but also desired to understand what it meant to be living in the midst of that moment.

It was a very hot day, and there were a lot of people standing around, waiting for something to happen. Things were happening at night, the police force was coming out at night, but during the day they were just sitting in their cars, watching out the windows. And so there was a kind of odd, steamy, hot August waiting happening.

Really, I just kind of looked at the memorial and stood. And then I found myself being approached by people. A man stood next to me, and saw a picture of Michael Brown at the memorial, and said, "He looks like *me*." I didn't want to say yes, because I didn't want to align him with a person who had passed away. So I said nothing. And then he said it again, he said, "He looks like me." So at that point I looked at him and looked at the photo, and he did look like Michael Brown. And I began to think, I wish there was a way to stop him from identifying with somebody who is dead. But the real understanding was that he too could be dead, at any point. He just stood there. He was a teenager. He was still in his pajamas.

And then there was a woman who came up to me with a toddler. I had taken out my iPhone to take a picture of the memorial, so the woman grabbed the toddler's hands and put them up in the air and said to me, "Take his picture." But again, I didn't want to take a picture of a toddler, with his hands up in the air, surrendering to the police that was going to shoot him anyway. So I didn't take the picture. I just put the phone in my bag and then bent down and talked to the child.

Those two interactions—they exhausted me. Because they just had a sense of inevitability. It almost felt Greek. Predetermined, and hopeless. And then you had all these police cars with white policemen and policewomen, just sitting inside the cars, looking out at you. It was like you were in a theater, and they were this encased audience. It made me think of Antigone. And so that's what I'm working on—a rewriting of Antigone, as a way of discussing what it means to decide to engage. The dead body's in the street. What do you do now?

Guernica: In the weeks after the Ferguson protests began, there was a lot of talk about how Ferguson symbolized the "end of post-racialism." Why do you think there's a fixation on the term "post-racial"—and an impulse to legitimize the term by positioning ourselves in relation to it?

Claudia Rankine: Because I don't think people want to look at problems. They want a continuous narrative, an optimistic narrative. A narrative that says there's a present and a future—and what was in the past no longer exists. In the future, we've forgotten it. It's disappointing to find out that the past is the present is the future. Nobody wants that. And yet, that's what it is. Maybe it's a kind of surrealist move, to use language like "post-racial"—thinking that if you create the language for it, it will happen. I wish it worked that way. But that's not our reality.

I was having a conversation with the poet Tracie Morris, who was saying, "You just can't take that stuff on." And I said, "I wish I could not take it on." You know, the news can make me cry. It upsets me. It's not a choice in taking it on or not taking it on.

Guernica: I'm curious to hear a bit more about how you came to poetry.

Claudia Rankine: I went to Williams College, and I studied with the poet Louise Glück, who was a great teacher for me. Many of her collections are book-length projects. She became a model for working a subject over the course of a book, rather than in a single poem.

I then went to Columbia and worked with poets like Henri Cole and Dan Halpern. But before that, I went out to Berkeley and studied with Robert Hass. I was fascinated with the way in which he allows you to sit in the mind of the speaker, and understand the ways in which that mind has to negotiate the reality of a thing.

Guernica: When did you feel as though this was your life's work?

Claudia Rankine: I think when I decided to go to graduate school. You make that decision and you're committing to figuring out how to make your life based on that profession. Poetry is probably the last gift economy. Part of the negotiation is to understand that you're going to do something you really want to do, so you're going to take whatever life comes with that.

Guernica: I was recently talking with a group of friends about the moments in our lives that have awakened something politically in us. One person spoke about how when she was in the first grade, she had a teacher who'd often yell at a black boy in her class. One day the teacher, who was black, shouted at this student: "People like you—they'll put you in jail. And then they'll kill you." It was a moment where the weight of race became clear to her. Can you think of an experience that politicized you, shaped your understanding of the world, in this way?

Claudia Rankine: I know when Rodney King's jury came back and said that despite the video, the police had done nothing wrong, that was a moment for me. I literally burst into tears. I had this weird feeling walking around the streets of New York, that I didn't know who these people were. All of a sudden I felt like an alien. I felt like, holy shit, I am walking around, and all of these people, white people, are okay with my black body being beaten and kicked, even when they're seeing the violence actually happen and don't have to rely on hearsay. That the black body is perceived as dangerous, even when it's on the ground, in a fetal position, with men surrounding it, kicking it. I don't think I understood or felt as vulnerable ever before. Because I think I always sort of believed in the justice system before that, even though I knew the history. I still felt that when you're not leaving it up to hearsay, when you have documentation, people will step up. And it didn't happen. That was really a crisis moment for me. You just feel like, okay, you need to start paying attention. It's the same line, from Rodney King to Michael Brown. It's a continuum.

Guernica: Do you feel as though Michael Brown is different in any way?

Claudia Rankine: Well, what's different is people like Rachel Maddow express outrage. And people on Facebook express outrage, and that's given play, immediately. Did you see the video John Oliver did on Ferguson? One of the things that was fantastic about that was he made all the connections that I was making. And he's a white, British guy. And so for the first time you felt you didn't have to do all the work. There was somebody else with huge access doing all the work, nicely produced, in the form of comedy. That's something different. It's not just happening in your living room, or on the phone with your friends. You're seeing it happen on the news.

Guernica: I wanted to ask you about one other section in *Citizen* that lingered with me: "Though a share of all remembering, a measure of all / memory, is breath and to breathe you have to create a / truce— / a truce with the patience of a stethoscope." I found that so sad, as well as graceful, and I wanted to ask what you were reckoning with while writing it.

Claudia Rankine: Thank you. I think it goes back to this idea of connection, community, and citizenship. You want to belong, you want to be here. In interactions with others you're constantly waiting to see that they recognize that you're a human being. That they can feel your heartbeat and you can feel theirs. And that together you will live—you will live together. The truce is that. You forgive all of these moments because you're constantly waiting for the moment when you will be *seen*. As an equal. As just another person. As another *first* person. There's a letting go that comes with it. I don't know about forgiving, but it's an "I'm still here." And it's not just because I have nowhere else to go. It's because I believe in the possibility. I believe in the possibility of another way of being. Let's make other kinds of mistakes; let's be flawed differently.

Ghost House

INGRID ROJAS CONTRERAS // OCTOBER 15, 2014

The stories of the kidnapped always begin the same way.

THERE WERE STORIES of how the kidnapped were never brought back. You gathered the money, you paid the ransom, you gave the guerrillas what they wanted; but the kidnapped never returned. There were many kids at our school in Bogotá, Colombia, whose family members had been kidnapped. When it happened, the kids didn't come to school and often we forgot they even existed. Then one day they came back with grim faces and bags under their eyes. Nobody asked questions.

Once, it happened in our classroom. The principal provided buses for us to go to the funeral of our classmate's father, who had been disappeared. The casket was empty and that's what the family was going to bury because they had nothing else. Some people buried the orphaned body parts sent back by the guerrillas in the mail as proof of whom they had: a shriveled ear lobe, a hacked, bruised finger, a lock of hair.

My classmate's name was Laura. Everyone was afraid to talk to her, but the rumors were enough to paint a picture: he was driving across Colombia, he was at the wrong place at the wrong time, the family could not come up with the ransom.

At the funeral I did the thing we were taught to do in the third grade the first time a kidnapping happened in our midst: I handed Laura a single rose and said, "*Mi más sentido pésame,*" and bowed. We all knew the same trick. All of us, one after another after another, saying: *My most heartfelt condolences. My most heartfelt condolences. My most heartfelt condolences.* Laura slowly collected a bouquet.

40

The stories of the kidnapped always begin the same way. The person was expected at a certain place at a specific time, and then they were late. The person is missed. The hours grow long.

Except this story is a little different, because in those days, while we were waiting for Papá to come home, the biggest manhunt in history was taking place. There were a lot of things I was afraid of, but Pablo Escobar was number one. That was why I paid attention with every cell in my body when his name came up. That was how I found out that in addition to being called *los Extraditables*, Pablo Escobar and his group were also referred to as *los narcos*, and anything that had to do with Pablo Escobar began like that: *narco* followed by a dash—narco-paramilitary, narco-war, narco-lawyer, narco-congressman, narco-estate, narco-terrorism, narco-money…

On television, they said it was the biggest narco-conspiracy in history, Pablo Escobar had escaped from prison—except what we had thought for one whole year was a prison was in fact a mansion. Every channel on the TV was showing specials of the jail: reporters in front of waterbeds, Jacuzzis, fine carpets, marble tiles, the bar with a discotheque, telescopes, radio equipment, and weapons: grenades, machine guns, and pistols. There was footage also of a pile of quartered body parts the police had found buried underneath the mini-soccer court—no heads; just arms, legs, and torsos. The body parts peeked out from under white sheets.

The reporters said that when the government decided to move Pablo Escobar to a real prison, Pablo Escobar disguised himself as a woman and waited until the hour of the fog. Then Pablo Escobar and his men, enveloped in fog, slipped past the army surrounding the prison, ready to apprehend them, and went out into the mountains—a row of ladies walking into the clouds.

That's how come we didn't notice at first that Papá was late. He was making a short drive from San Juan de Rioseco to Bogotá, a car trip of no more than three hours. At first, we thought there was traffic. Then we thought maybe there had been an avalanche, a common enough event that plagued the roads leading back into the city. We thought of car accidents and hospitals, women in distress, and hitchhikers.

The TV droned in the background: Pablo Escobar this, Pablo Escobar that. Cassandra and I huddled with Mamá on the couch. Night fell.

Mamá's eyes stared in front of her. The drum of rain banged on our roof and windows, and the howling wind crept through the bottom of the front door. Mamá rose to her feet and went about the house moving things from one table to another. Her white gown ballooned about her as she bent and picked things up from the floor. She dropped the dictionary into a cabinet drawer and said, "Your father's car probably broke down on the highway."

My sister Cassandra didn't miss a beat, "Did you call his work?"

Mamá scrubbed her face with her hands. For the first time I noticed the color. Her forehead was white but her cheekbones and overlip glistened a sickly green. I tried to imagine Papá's car breaking down. Maybe there had been a nail in the middle of the road. I imagined Papá on one knee, swiveling the crossbar, undoing the hubcaps, neon orange triangles flashing by the car, reflecting passing headlights. Then I imagined Papá bursting through the front windshield of his car in an accident. I closed my eyes, but the image remained. The tips of my ears tingled.

"Go to sleep," Mamá said. "I'll wake you when your father comes."

"I want to wait, Mamá."

"I'm sure your father is fine. Go and I'll wake you."

Cassandra and I threw ourselves on our beds, the sound of rain tapering over the world of our dreams. I remember trying to remain awake. I passed the time thinking about Papá. After a while, I saw him walk past the bedroom door and went after him. I pursued him down halls with mirrors, and then I realized I was dreaming. I awoke from dreams of waiting for Papá into other dreams of waiting.

Mamá was smoking on the sofa in the living room, the television still on, showing a static image of a weather map.

"Mamá, did Papá come?"

She narrowed her eyes until they closed. She sucked her cigarette lengthily and then seemed to swallow the smoke. It came forked out of her nostrils.

"Mamá," I shook her shoulder.

Her eyes broke open. "What is it?"

"Did Papá come?"

"What time is it?"

"It's seven."

She sat up and put out her cigarette in the ashtray. She rushed to the telephone, picked it up, and then held it in her hand. The telephone buttons lighted fluorescent green in her hand and the dim sound of the dial tone filled the room.

"Mamá, why don't you dial?"

"I'm thinking."

"Mamá, dial! What are you waiting for?"

Mamá's cheeks turned fiery red but she did not cry. She replaced the receiver and repeated, "It will all be okay. Your Papá is okay."

Every few hours the police in Medellín found another Pablo Escobar hideout. It all started because a young cop turned a shower knob. What he wanted to know was whether the apartment where suspicious activity had been reported had running water, but what happened was that the shower wall swung out like a door, revealing a small apartment. Everything was in disarray. Pablo Escobar's coffee, left on the nightstand, was still warm. Pretty soon half the police force in Medellín was going to every suspicious apartment, turning knobs. One cop turned on the stove and almost fell through the floor as it slid away, revealing a staircase. Secret tunnels led from each hideout into a neighboring house, which meant the people of Medellín were all conspiring to keep Pablo Escobar free, but there was no surprise there, because everyone knew Pablo Escobar drove around the slums handing out stacks of money to the poor. Meanwhile, Pablo Escobar's car bombs exploded in public places all over the country, because he wanted the government to back off.

At night Mamá turned into a black widow. She holed up in her bedroom, and stripped the bed. I found her sitting on the mattress, cross-legged and clasping a candle. She was braiding the air with her fingers, mumbling prayers. When I touched her, her body crumbled under my fingers. She bowled over and rocked on her thighs and howled.

It was a pained, low, guttural howl. It washed through my entire body. Everything was terrible. My eyes sprung with tears and my sight doubled: Mamá with four hands covering her face, saying, "What are we going to do, Chula? What in the world are we going to do?"

We howled together on the lap of the scratchy mattress, then Cassandra came running in. "What's wrong? What is it? What happened?"

"The guerrillas have him!" I cried, because deep down I knew.

"Mamá? Give them what they want. What do they want?"

"They don't want anything from *us!*" Mamá pulled her hair. "They want the oil company to pay for his release."

Then Mamá and Cassandra screamed back and forth, Cassandra crying, "Mamá, do something!" and Mamá screaming, "I can't!"

Late at night, there was a sharp pain in my stomach, and my hands trembled as I stuffed them under the pillow. Mamá said that the oil company said they did not negotiate with terrorists, being American, but that they would explore all their options. In my bed I thought of what it could mean and I kicked my feet in sudden anger and my voice stuck in my throat, then tears ran down my cheeks.

We stopped going to school. I stared at the walls and overheard Mamá's conversations on the telephone. Sometimes the voices on the phone, echoing dimly against Mamá's ear, were prim and elegant. There was a policeman, someone from the American embassy, a lawyer. At other times the voices were short and alarming: "We've got that *hijo de puta*, we'll send you his balls in the post."

One morning, Mamá stared at her pale hands clasping the dining table and said, "We are selling everything and we are going away."

"But we can't, Mamá. What if Papá comes home? We have to wait."

"Why don't we drive to San Juan de Rioseco?" Cassandra asked. "That's where he was last seen."

"We can't, Cassandra. They will kill your father if we do that."

"But is the oil company going to pay, Mamá? They have to pay, how else are they going to let Papá go!"

"We are going away and we are selling everything," Mamá said. "Your father will know what is happening and he will meet us. You can each pack a suitcase."

"Mamá, we can't leave," Cassandra said.

"Mamá, he won't find us!" I cried.

"Pack everything you want tonight," Mamá stood and walked calmly to the telephone. "Because tomorrow, everything that is not packed we are selling. We will buy tickets and get out of here. Your father will find us."

Mamá lifted the telephone and Cassandra cried out, "Mamá, I'm *not* going!" but Mamá called everyone she knew and said we were leaving the country and we were getting rid of everything we owned.

In Cassandra's and my bedroom there were two small suitcases, unzipped on our beds. I packed some clothes, but then I went about the house snatching treasures: a small handheld radio, pastel plastic bracelets, a tiny crystal elephant, a wooden spoon, Mamá's black eye shadow, and Papá's red wool sock.

Cassandra picked at the clothes in her closet. She packed her clothes and a chessboard, and then packed the contents of her drawer, crying. I felt very tired of everything and after my suitcase was full I crawled underneath my bed and slept.

I dreamed of Papá. As Cassandra and I waltzed in an empty ballroom, Papá watched us from outside the window. He banged on the glass, but we didn't turn our heads. Papá stood in the garden, saddened, but then I noticed that he wasn't standing in our garden at all, but some field over which the stars shone brightly and black firs rose in the horizon.

The neighbors arrived at dawn. They perused our house with their noses up in the air as if our house were a market. They brought big shopping bags and deep wicker baskets and, keeping close to the wall, they turned our table lamps off and on, blew the dust from Papá's records, rolled up our Indian rugs, rattled the paintings hung on the wall, questioned the authenticity of Mamá's porcelain, and in the kitchen women bickered over the pots and pans.

One woman threw her money at Mamá as she went out the door with a stack of Papá's books—I saw the book spines of *Arabian Nights, Twenty Love Poems and a Song of Despair, The Motorcycle Diaries,* Plato—and then I saw Mamá bend down to pick up the roll of pesos from the floor like she herself had dropped it. The looking-down-their-noses at us was partly because we had fallen from grace, but also because it fitted with their idea of who we had always been, one family in a long line of poor families.

Cassandra and I sat on the living room couch, watching the neighbors hoarding our belongings, depositing them into piles to be guarded by their children. "Don't let anyone take anything from this pile." The children— kids who had once played with us—pretended not to see us. They stared over our heads at the crowd of adults, snapping objects from under each other's noses and hiding things under their arms. A man hooked our umbrella on his arm and pointed at a painting depicting a storm.

"This one would look good in our hall."

"That ugly thing?" his wife asked. She had filled a large glass jar I recognized as our rice container with Mamá's collection of small crystal elephants. "Let's ask about the price, anyway."

Other women were descending the stairs with boxes filled with Cassandra's and my toys, smiling. La Soltera even came from her house next door to see what she could buy. We hated la Soltera. Everybody called her that because she was forty years old and single and still lived with her old mother. She was nothing but a busybody. When she saw us, la Soltera gasped in delight. "*Pobrecitas,*" she said. "So young and already dragged under the mud." She touched my cheek and then she was struck by a thought. She widened her eyes and caressed the couch on which Cassandra and I sat. "Lovely," she said. Then, "Run along, girls. Go sit on the stairs where you can't damage anything." Cassandra pulled me away and made me sit on the stairs and I had to bite my tongue. Cassandra even called Mamá so Mamá could negotiate the price for the couch la Soltera so obviously wanted. I looked on, counting to one hundred, the details of our lives disappearing. At some point I saw la Soltera exiting. When she saw me she bowed exceedingly, then turned on her heels. She seemed to float out the front door, touching the white, pointy tops of her ears. Later a few men came to carry all the furniture away.

When it was quiet again, I said to Cassandra, "I can't believe all our things will be in other people's houses." I looked around at the house, larger than I had imagined with most of our things gone. "It's like we're dead." Cassandra nodded. "I can't believe this is happening."

At five in the afternoon, Mamá sold our car, and as the day darkened, our few remaining belongings made their way out through the front door. Slowly the house became deserted.

On the bottom floor, one of three things that belonged to us was an amulet. It was four aloe leaves strung together, hung above the door. It twirled even though there was no wind. The amulet was supposed to absorb the bad energy that came to our doorstep, but now we knew it was useless.

There was also a small television nobody had wanted. I dragged it from the kitchen and turned it on. The reporters were still talking about Pablo Escobar, but now they were saying that Pablo Escobar had so much money, he probably had altered his appearance. Posters took up the screen for minutes at a time. There were grids of Pablo Escobar faces—with mustache, without it, with head shaved, with nose altered, with the beard of a pilgrim, with the chin thinned out, with the cheeks deflated, with the cheekbones pulled up. I sat by the television, learning the black and white lines of the many faces of Pablo Escobar: the parenthesis by his mouth, the fat nose, the sideways commas of his eyes, opposing each other, as if they were bulls getting ready to charge. Only the sepulchral black, beady eyes repeated themselves down past rows and sideways past columns. Pablo Escobar eyes.

I asked Cassandra, "Can Pablo Escobar change his eyes?"

"Pablo Escobar?" she said. "Pablo Escobar can do *anything*."

The third thing we owned was the telephone. Mamá kept it upstairs in the second floor, and it rang incessantly. She picked it up mid-ring and then she was quiet and breathless as she listened into the receiver.

I pushed all thoughts of Papá away, but the one thing that kept coming back was how Papá kept small portraits of Cassandra and me in his wallet, how he could look at us with just the flick of his wrist. My mind kept returning to the fact that if anybody found his body, they would find our portraits, and then they would know that this dead man had once belonged to someone. Our portraits were behind the clear plastic meant for an ID. They had been taken in the park, with a background of tall trees and clouds. In her portrait, Cassandra appeared without her glasses. We would be able to pass off as twins if it weren't for some minute differences: my eyebrows were messier, Cassandra was lighter-skinned, her forehead was grander, my lips were smaller.

Papá had once said that he showed the pictures to his workers so often, he wouldn't be surprised if they could recognize us if they saw us walking down the street. Papá was always showing our pictures to everyone he met: the elevator man, the guards, the guy at the grocery store. Anyone could have noticed how much he treasured us; the way he faintly ran the tips of his fingers on the faces of the portraits, the way his eyes fell back into memory, the way he enunciated, "*Mis niñas.*"

The hard, possessive hum of *Mis*, the misty aspirated vaporousness of *Ñass*; how the *S* trailed behind like the tail of a long snake.

"I present to you *mis niñas.*"

My loved ones, my pirates, my small queens.

That's what he used to call us.

I sat in the garden and watched the wind push lightly on the gate. At any moment, Papá could turn the corner past the pine trees and finally come home. At last, at long last. I sang the song Mamá had once taught us:

Mambrú se fue a la Guerra.
Que dolor, que dolor, que pena.
Mambrú se fue a la Guerra y no se cuando vendrá.
Do-re-mi. Do-re-fa.
No se cuando vendrá.

Papá would turn the corner into our yard, walk down the stone steps, and look up. Forever changed. The hours shortened and lengthened, sagging and tightening like strings. I stared at the black gate past the garden. The gate swayed with wind, mourning metallically. I gagged from imagining Papá return. The phone rang incessantly and the four aloe leaves twirled.

I discovered that I sympathized with Pablo Escobar's family. They were also trying to get out of the country. The Cali Cartel was trying to kill them. The news followed them as they went from embassy to embassy— American, Spanish, Swiss, and German. The embassies denied asylum, arguing that Pablo Escobar's children were underage and needed a nota-rized letter from their father. A notarized letter meant that Pablo Escobar had to show up at a public notary, give his signature, thumbprint, swear an oath in front of an official, and then so much time would pass between one thing and another that he would eventually be captured and sent off to the Americans, who believed they could imprison him. It seemed cruel, especially after they aired a message from Pablo Escobar's daughter to him: "Papi, I miss you and I send you the biggest kiss of all Colombia!"

When Mamá said we were going to America, bile rose to the back of my throat.

"And Papá? How will he find us?"

"You must trust me, Cassandra. What good are we to him dead?"

I hid in the kitchen and held my head in my hands. The only thing we knew about America had to do with *Singin' in the Rain*, because it was always on reruns on TV. In *Singin' in the Rain*, the rain was sleek on the black-tar street and the police were well mannered and filled with principles. Mamá always got out of tickets by batting her lashes, begging, and slipping po-licemen bills of *veinte-mil*. The Colombian police were easily corrupted. So were the officials at the notaries and the court, whom Mamá always paid so she could be ushered to the head of the line and her applications put at the top of the stack. Often, during the commercial break, Cassandra held her nose in front of the television and spoke like Lina Lamont, the beautiful blond actress cursed with the horrible, nasal voice. She said, "And I cayn't stand'im," and we giggled. She said it over and over until we quiv-ered with laughter and we lay on our backs overcome.

I went down the hall to Cassandra's and my bedroom and I opened the windows. I wanted to say goodbye to somebody, so I searched the empty lot at the back of our house, looking for the cows that had always been there for as long as I could remember. I saw them, standing by each other, chewing grass in the near distance. I bit my lip and mooed at them. There were so many things I wanted to tell them. I was leaving. My father was kidnapped. I would miss them. I named one cow Roberto, after Papá, and I tried to get across the fact that he needed to be a good cow, and honor my father's name. I mooed, trying to tell them everything through the lonely sound. The cows looked up in my direction and threw their heads, but they were only getting ready to lie down on the grass. Maybe they were saying goodbye. I fell on my knees and I did not wipe the tears that came.

At night the walls ran high and bare to the ceiling, and the mirrors throughout the house multiplied the emptiness. The mirror in Mamá's bedroom, facing the bare wide windows, reflected the slate clouds. The windows were open.

I sat in the space where Mamá's bed had been, and when the storm came, instead of getting up to close the window, I watched the surface of the mirror trembling from the wind. If I looked at myself in the mirror, my face shook as if I were in an earthquake.

I looked into the mirror for a long time. For a while, I started to believe I really was in an earthquake. But when I looked away, everything was still. I was still. Great huffs of wind lifted my hair and I listened to the howl of the storm.

The rain reached me and I got up to close the window. But I could not bring myself to close it and I stared at the bruised and bulbous sky. My shirt was wet. The young trees of our garden were blowing in the wind, up-skirted. I reached for the window handle.

"What are you doing?" Mamá asked from the bedroom door.

"Closing the window."

"We have nothing to save from the storm," she said. "There's no reason to close the window. Let the storm come in if it wants.

"We are leaving tomorrow at night," she added.

I turned to Mamá. She was leaning on the doorframe and her eyes were closed against the handle of a broom. My heart was beating fast. I walked past Mamá, swallowing everything, and then tiptoed around the empty house. There were no runners in the hall, no tables, no paintings, but I pretended they were still there. I walked through the house, sidestepping the imagined dotted outlines of our furniture: the paintings, the vases, the lamps, Papá's books. I visited each bedroom and traveled up and down the stairs.

The air around the ghost objects was charged with inviolability. Space held in place compact over ghost tables, chairs, and bed frames. In the dining room, the carpet dipped in creamy light circles where the table legs used to be. That was how I knew where the ghost table was, the sofa chairs, the glass cabinet that had once loomed over us as we ate. I thought of all the objects in relationship to Papá. The chair Papá had sat in. The runners where his feet had walked. The rails he had rested his hands on.

Then, I found the last of Papá's belongings in the house hiding in the dark corner by the refrigerator, overlooked, forgotten, dusty.

It was a scarlet-tinted bottle of whiskey, sequestered in the darkness. I reached for it, and holding it against my breast, I ran and took it to the indoor patio.

Papá's whiskey.

When I uncorked the top I breathed in the scent greedily. The smell was bitter and churned in my throat. I took a small sip, imagining I was Papá. I remembered Papá's wooden-scented breath laughing over his whiskey. It was a gagging feeling, but I continued to take sips until I felt the floor rising up to meet my feet. I couldn't think straight, but there was nothing to think. I left the bottle behind the fridge, and I staggered up to my room crying, crawling to avoid the ghost objects.

I imagined Cassandra couldn't help but feel the ghost objects, like me. When I came into our bedroom, Cassandra was sleeping in the rectangle that used to be her bed. Her chest heaved, and she was snoring quietly; Papá's black wool coat, which Mamá had saved, wrapped around her legs. She looked so peaceful sleeping: her shiny black hair in waves about her head, and her skin with twitching, muscular secrets underneath it. I walked around her ghost bed and I went to lay down in mine.

I spun lying down. I could see the night sky through the window. I stared at the stars shining in the black sky. Like brilliant pearls. I sped forward but they vibrated vertically. They popped and popped.

Only the crescent moon stood in place.

The crescent which Nona said was God's nail. His hand or his foot.

Waiting for sunset, the assigned time of our departure, was torture. So I sat in front of the small TV. There were cartoons for many hours, but then they were interrupted by an image of a man face down on a roof, bleeding his life out. I brought my hands to my mouth, trembling; then the reporter was speaking over the images, saying, "What you will see now is the police preparing to take his body to the medical center for an autopsy." *Him who?* I couldn't breathe, thinking what if it was Papá. Policemen came, and when they turned the body to place it on a stretcher, I saw it wasn't Papá. On the stretcher, Pablo Escobar's hair fell long over his ears, and his shirt was tight over his great stomach.

There was a whole crowd of people on the street, waiting, as the stretcher was lowered from the roof. Everyone was so quiet as the stretcher made its way to the ambulance, people in the crowd just reaching their hands to touch the body and then tracing a cross over themselves. The people touched his hair, his bloodied shirt, his arms.

Then the news cut to live footage in the cemetery of Medellín. Rivers of people chanted *Pablo, Pablo, Pablo!* They pressed against the pallbearers carrying the silver casket, trying to touch it, to carry in their hands the last of Pablo Escobar. The thousand mourners called together: "*Se vive, se siente, Escobar está presente!*"

The camera showed the scene from above as the casket was lowered. Many hands held onto the casket. Someone flipped open the lid, and for a moment the news camera caught Pablo Escobar's face. Red roses framed that pale face, his eyebrows splayed themselves at rest over his swollen eyes, and a thick beard grew out of his chin. He died fat, another man. Then the silver casket clicked shut and it was lowered. A tractor dumped a mountain of fresh dirt over it.

I didn't tell Mamá or Cassandra that Pablo Escobar was dead. When the taxi arrived, I cried incessantly. I rocked, waiting for Papá to show up at the last hour, the last minute, the last second. Now he might be lost to us forever. We were on the highway and the rain streaked our windows. That's when I saw Pablo Escobar out of the rainy car window. He was waiting at a streetlight. He was wearing a hat and a trench coat stained black by rain. I jolted up and pressed my hand to the window and Pablo Escobar stared at me, frozen, and then he spit and turned on his heel, burying himself in the shoulders and umbrellas of pedestrians.

Then I saw Pablo Escobar holding a wet newspaper, crossing himself at the sight of a church, struggling with an umbrella turned inside out, running in the rain with his chin tucked close to his chest and a book under his arm.

I remembered Cassandra said that when Pablo Escobar found out someone had betrayed him, he sliced the person's throat and pulled the tongue out and left it hanging out the slit. I got the pressing desire to touch my tongue then, squeeze it in between my fingers. I wondered what not having a tongue would be like. You would probably forget you didn't have a tongue, and would try to move the red, lean muscle, but there would be nothing to move. Just the empty dark hall of your mouth. You would be alone with your thoughts.

At the airport I puked in the bathroom. When we boarded the airplane it was night, and my chest congested with tears. The air lengthened in long, stretchy strings inside me. I couldn't breathe. There were terms for what we had become: *displaced, refugees, destitute*. I clicked my seatbelt on and from the airplane window I saw the lights of the city shrinking. It was cloudy, and the city of Bogotá disappeared behind the clouds.

From above I saw how red and blue fireworks exploded throughout the city. They opened like thundering umbrellas over the dark. I realized it was people celebrating Pablo Escobar's death.

Behind the clouds, down below, was San Juan de Rioseco.

Behind the clouds, down below, was our deserted house, with the ghost imprints of furniture on the carpet, ghost imprints of memory, and the television left on.

Behind the clouds, down below, were Papá's fingers traveling in the mail. And even though we wouldn't know it right away, Papá's fingers would be left at our doorstep in a cardboard box, waiting, nobody to receive their homecoming.

Data's Work Is Never Done

ANNE BOYER // MARCH 13, 2015

In medicine, the work of care and the work of data converge.

IN THE WAITING ROOMS of cancer clinics, the labor of care meets the labor of data. Wives fill out their husbands' forms. Mothers fill out their children's. Sick women fill out their own. I am sick and a woman so I write my own name. At each appointment I am handed a printout from the general database that I am to amend or approve. The databases would be empty without us. The work of abstracting a person into a patient is women's work—it only appears, at first, to be the work of machines.

Receptionists distribute forms, print the bracelets to be read later by scanners held in the hands of other women. The nursing assistants stand in a doorway from which they never quite emerge. They hold these doors open with their bodies and call out patients' names. These women are the paras in the thresholds, weighing the bodies of patients on digital scales, measuring vital signs in the staging area of a clinic's open crannies. Then they lead the patient—in this case, they lead me—to an examining room and log into the system. They enter the numbers my body generates when offered to machines: how hot or cold I am, the rate at which my heart is beating. Then they ask the question: *Rate your pain on a scale of 1 to 10?* I try to answer, but the correct answer is always "a-numerical." Sensation is the enemy of quantification. There is no machine, yet, to which a nervous system can submit to transform into a sufficiently descriptive measurement.

Illness is chaotic. Medicine hyper-responds to the body's unruly event of illness by transmuting it into data. A patient becomes information not merely via the quantities of whatever emerges from or passes through her discrete body: the bodies and sensations of entire populations are converted into the math of likelihood—of falling ill or staying well, of living or dying, of healing or suffering—upon which treatment is based. The bodies of women and men are both subject to these calculations, but it is the bodies of women, most often, that do the preliminary work of relocating the nebulousness and uncountability of illness into medicine's technologized math.

What is your name and birthdate? A cancer patient's name, stated by herself, is adjunct to the barcode of her wristband, then the adjunct of whatever substances—vials of drawn blood, the chemotherapy drugs to be infused into her—whose location and identity must be confirmed. Though my bracelet has been scanned for my identity, requiring me to repeat my name is medical information's back-up plan: it is the punctum of every transmission of something to or from my body. I might sometimes remember who I am. But repetition is a method of desensitization. To rate your *self* on the scale of 1 to 10? In the intensive medicalized abstraction of cancer, I become a *barely*, my person subsidiary to the body's sensations and to medicine's informatic systems.

The nurses meet me in the examining room after I have replaced my clothes with a gown. They log into the system. Sometimes my blood has been drawn, and I am allowed to look at a printed page of its ingredients. Each week the blood flows with more or less of one kind of cell or substance than it did the week before. Levels of these substances go up or down, determine treatment's future measurement, duration. The nurses ask questions about my experience of my body. They enter the sensations I describe into a computer, clicking on symptoms that have long been given a category and a name and an insurance code.

The word *care* rarely calls to mind a keyboard. The work, often unwaged or poorly paid, of those who perform care (or what is sometimes called "reproductive labor," reproducing oneself and others as living bodies each day, of feeding, cleaning, tending, and so on) is what many understand to be that which is the least technological, the most effective and intuitive. *Care* is so often understood as a mode of feeling, neighboring, as it does, to love. Care seems as removed from quantification as the cared-for person's sensations of weakness or pain seem removed from statistics class. *I care for you* suggests a different mode of abstraction (that of feeling) than the measurement of the cell division rate of a tumor (that of pathological fact). But strange reversals occur during serious illness. Or rather, what appears to be reversal becomes clarification. Our once solid, unpredictable, sensing, spectacularly messy and animal bodies submit—imperfectly, but also intensively—to the abstracting conditions of medicine. Care becomes vivid and material.

The receptionists, nursing assistants, lab technicians, and nurses are not only required to enter the information of my body into the databases, they also have to care for me while doing so. In the hospital, my urine is measured and charted by the same person who charms me with conversation. This is so that painful procedures will become less painful. The workers who check my name twice, scan my medical armband, and perform a two-person dose-accuracy reinforcement procedure as they attach chemotherapy drugs to my chest port are the same workers who touch my arm gently when I appear afraid. The worker who draws blood tells a joke.

The work of care and the work of data exist in a kind of paradoxical simultaneity: what both hold in common is they are done so often by women, and like all that has historically been identified as women's work, it is work that can look invisible. It is often only noted when it is absent: a dirty house attracts more attention than a clean one. The background that appears effortless only appears with great effort: the work of care and the work of data are quiet, daily, persistent, and never done. A patient's file is, like a lived-in home, the site of work that lasts the human eternal.

During my treatment for cancer, all of these workers—the receptionists, paraprofessionals, and nurses—have been women. The doctors, who are sometimes women and sometimes men, meet with me at the point of my body's peak quantification. They log into the system, but they type less or sometimes not at all. As their eyes pass over the screen that displays my body's updated categories and quantities, I think of John Donne's *Devotions Upon Emergent Occasions*: "They have seen me and heard me, arraigned me in these fetters and received the evidence; I have cut up mine own anatomy, dissected myself, and they are gone to read upon me." If it is the women who transmute bodies into data, it is the doctors who assume the form of scanner. They have no particular alchemy. The other workers have extracted and labeled me: I have informatisized my own sensation. It is the doctors who read me—or rather, read what my body has become: a patient made of information, produced by the work of women.

the years

WENDY XU // OCTOBER 15, 2014

where does dark begin settling / my little bones.

Such were the years, a dumb stuffed thing
to say, if truth is we all grow old un-
observed, limbs flail only halfway up
a flight, where does dark begin settling
my little bones. I dream and do love
to have them, blue fish
in a lake, my head more tipped up than down
under damp earth. Some days others like deer
from the shot, peeled back, how nuisance I
find trees dressed in wild
green light. The years come, unstitched
a face, saddled as one would a heavy beast
for walking, likely I became then a member
of heaven, put up, the years come and reaching
their long wet hands.

2

Other Cities

SARA MAJKA // JANUARY 15, 2015

*There were so many places he could have lived, but he lived
in the shack so he could dream of his daughter.*

SEPTEMBER

Some years ago I had my birthday on the same day as my ex-boy-friend did, and we ended up at the same place for breakfast. This was an accident. Me and my mom. Him and his girlfriend. There was a man reading a newspaper by the window, otherwise we were the only people there. My mom and I both got baguette with butter, coffee, orange juice, apricot preserves. The baguette was as pale as uncooked bread.

We went there because it would be quiet and it was. The couple was quiet. I spilled coffee, and the napkins were near the couple. I could have got the napkins, my mom said when I returned. The night before I had asked her about love but she kept reverting to platitudes. Can a romantic love be as strong as what a mother feels for a child? She said yes, but then was unsure. She thought there were all sorts of love and that it could change. I told her Raymond Carver believed in romantic love, but his version had a narrow timeframe.

It was my plan to talk to my friends about love. On the street she asked if I would do it on that day, my birthday. I told her I would hold off for a few more days before we started to talk about love, but that when we did it we were really going to do it.

PARIS

Back then I was remembering my dreams more. I was sleeping late, which meant waking and falling back to sleep several times, and so the dreams were remembered as in waking. When I dreamed about moving to Paris, it was as if I was moving. I had the feeling of it. I had read about Jack Gilbert moving to Europe and it seemed possible. I wrote to a man who was moving to Berlin and told him about the dream. I hadn't heard from him in weeks, but he was leaving, so what did it matter what I could lose. I said I had dreamed of moving to Paris and it was a hopeful feeling, like something opening inside of myself. He was saving his money in a tobacco can, and had told me if it was gone he would know who had it. If you look closely you can find terrific suitcases in thrift stores. Perhaps this involves going to many thrift stores, but you'll find them.

SHACKS

There were so many places he could have lived, but he lived in the shack so he could dream of his daughter. It was the only place it happened. He told me this when I moved into the shack next to him. These were shacks in the dunes, next to the ocean. We swam through until October. Why the shock of the cold could make you sleep I didn't know. But we slept and we dreamt in our shacks, and then often had a drink in the afternoon while we talked. I was dreaming of a lover who had left me, but it had happened a long time ago, and I didn't know why I was dreaming of him. I felt that when we dreamed of others we loved, we were dreaming of parts of ourselves that we had lost. That was why the familiarity and warmth. He felt that when we dreamed of others they were actually in our dreams, as people separate from ourselves. I felt that he was mourning his daughter. That this was the way we worked through loss. But he thought he had his daughter with him because he did in his dream. When I went home and saw the old lover, I knew it wasn't the same person I had been dreaming of, and I missed that other person.

OCTOBER

There was a noise show in my ex-boyfriend's basement. I walked home with a friend afterwards and asked how she was. She was getting back together with an ex but wasn't sure. She didn't think it was a problem then, but it could become one. She thought she wanted to go to Italy, or at least he would need to want to go to Italy. I said, yes, divide the world between those who need Italy and those who do not. This seemed smart to me, so did getting together with ex-boyfriends because it was October. Outside my office the first leaves were turning yellow. Every year the leaves don't turn the way they should for different reasons such as too much rain. I would wish for whatever it takes for them to look like a postcard, but I am confused about the weather this requires.

WHALES

My ex-husband was a great lover of whales. I remember on the whale watch he stood on the deck with binoculars while I sat in the cabin with coffee. There was something so nice to it, the way the sun came in. When he came in the cold came with him and I was irritated. No whales yet, he said, as if it was a football game we were watching. Later I would say to friends that if I had known what I was leaving for I never would have left. But I didn't mean that either; it was just another way to frame a decision I had made with so little thought or evidence. What did I want a man to look like on a whale watch if not the way he looked? What would have satisfied me? Wasn't it enough that he came in from time to time, that someone on the boat knew who I was?

SHACKS

I've never seen anything like those whales, I told the man in the shacks. We wanted to go on a boat, though we had little money. To eat we climbed the jetty to get mussels. We cooked onions in butter over borrowed propane, dumped in a can of beer, and steamed them open. There was worth, for both of us, in doing it this way. We forgot about the boat by the second whiskey. The neighbors thought we were in love and we were, only it wasn't the type you could do anything with. Mornings I washed my clothes in the ocean. Give me those, he said from the shore. He wanted to take everything to the Laundromat. I wanted to make a statement or have something to do with the ocean besides being frightened by its proportion. One day he bought a kite at the t-shirt shop. They were having a sale. All the shops were closing. Don't the seagulls know anything, he said. We went out where the dunes sunk in like a bowl and stayed on the edge. Of course the kite didn't fly. In what world would it have flown?

SHACKS

There was a fifth shack that no one lived in. The owner was sick, and Henry, the man I knew, took care of it. When the owners died, the shacks were torn down because of the fragility of the dunes. Visiting this shack was finding the only place you've ever wanted to live in, right before it disappeared. It was out near the trees, away from the other shacks. It was the only shack you could see fall from. It was a wet fall and the swamp filled in, the ground soft with algae. We rolled our pants to wade through. There were other ways to get there, but this was the way we liked. It was the only shack with two stories. A ladder went to a sleeping loft, and downstairs there were several rockers and a braided rug. Henry bent to sweep flies and sprinkle them outside.

CLAMS

Years before, a woman in town was killed by a lover. The clam warden was a suspect, but he was acquitted because of a variety of things, including DNA evidence. Every week when I clammed he gave me the *New York Times*, as he also delivered papers. His jobs could be seen as a variety of sizes and shapes—looking in our buckets to see if our clams were big enough, and rolling the newspapers and sliding them into tubes—or they could be seen as stories, the stories in the paper and of the townspeople he talked to when he climbed down the jetty to see how clamming was going. It was a lonely and beautiful sight, all of us out on low tide, in boots and packs, slipping past him with our regulation clams.

SHACKS

Word came that the owner of the fifth shack had died and the shack would be torn down. As happened with the others, you could take what you wanted from the shack. There was very little to actually want, but you could be surprised at how much you wanted it, for instance a lamp, if you knew a spot where it could go. Most of the things in our shacks had come from now-lost shacks. There had once been over thirty—you could see the outline of them on clear days. These are the opposite of tombs or a graveyard in that they are taken away when we die. There was a set of glasses that I wanted, and a trunk, and a rug. It was a clear day and there was a plane overhead, and the four of us with Henry to unlock the door. He had explained to me the unfairness of going there early, before the others, saying that systems created openings, but glassware had seemed a reasonable thing to want.

GERMANY

This is all I know about Berlin or Germany and Germans in general. I thought I would list it in case it was helpful and because Germany has remained a part of my life for unknowable reasons. There was a man from Germany I felt I could have married, but he moved away, and I think he has found happiness and that it will last. And I just mailed a lamp to a man who I knew when he was moving to Germany, and I got his lamp, but he came back to the States, and I mailed it back. They eat a lot of sausages there, yes, but it was the ice cream that surprised me. And the cold cuts for breakfast in the hotels. All the castles, etc. Thomas Bernhard is worth reading, and so many authors I love have ties to Germany, lived there, or, like Sebald, moved away from there. This is true of Argentina as well, but I don't feel the same way about Argentina. I love Germany because it has once possessed or is going to possess many of the things that I've cared about, though in fact I have only spent two weeks in Germany and I didn't care for the food. If you move to Germany and you're not happy there it's okay to move back because you will still love Germany, as I've learned that Germany is one of those things.

Or, you'll go to Germany, but come back to a small town in our country and you'll realize there is something or someone you love, and you will stay, though you may not be happy with this town, but in this way the small compromises of life will become larger and more significant to you than Germany. At some point I might send you something, whether it's a lamp or another piece of mail. At times you'll think about Germany, what it was to you, and in that way you might think of me, and I'll think about you, and Germany, and countless other cities I've never lived in.

RAFFLES

There was a party one night and my ex-boyfriend was there and so was his girlfriend. He talked about raffles, his fondness of them, the desire for winning in comparison to chances. He explained the sort of raffle we were doing was called a Chinese raffle. Afterwards I thought it would be better for him to have a field so that I could set fire to it. Not out of vengeance or to do harm, but just for the fact of a field on fire.

BUSES

My ex-boyfriend boarded the bus the next morning and I saw his face as a stranger might. He looked handsome, older. Not knowing I was on the bus, he hadn't prepared his face into one I never quite liked, and this face—a man on the way to work, looking for an empty seat—I found I liked. He didn't see me. For a long time I had wanted to say something to him, and this time on the bus seemed the time I had waited for, but I stared ahead and got off at my stop, near my office.

TRAINS

Several years back I went on a train ride to visit a man I was in love with. I told Henry I had been waiting a long time to make such a gesture, believing there were only two or three chances in life when one can take such a risk. I was with the man for a week and then went back on the train, through Texas, which I remember lasting for many days, while I sat in the observation car, at first feeling close to this gesture and then, as the train went along, feeling further away, though I still kept contact with it, and believed I would for as long as I was on the train.

CITIES

Before I came here I went on another train trip to visit cities I might live in. I picked out two to three potential cities. Perhaps the question isn't why I'm not living in any of these cities, but why there aren't more cities one could live in. For my next train trip I would like to visit minor cities, cities such as Detroit and Pittsburgh that you wouldn't otherwise think to travel to.

SHACKS

A drama had once occurred in one of the shacks, though we knew little about it. One night we were invited for dinner, and walking home we discussed what might have happened. To tell an event from its repercussions is mostly a matter of sense, of sensing the insides of someone, looking not for openings, but for dark spaces clustered too closely together. I felt love that had been complicated. That had been lost, but lost only for one of them, and that it was probably his love for her. Though it's hard to tell. It's not true that it's easier to move on if you're the one who has fallen out of love. Falling out of love made me feel like a woman without any money left. During dinner we had listened to the radio, as someone had been lost at sea. In the morning they would be found, but we didn't know this then, and shared the fear they might not be, as we tried to enjoy this, our last meal together.

LOVE

And if you say it is better to have loved and lost, does this lend itself to more phrases? Is it better to have set sail and lost? Better to have moved to another country and lost? And even then, in these situations, do we not infer love, as if it's the only possible thing to lose?

ISLANDS

I once lived on an island three miles out to sea. We couldn't see the island from the shacks and I was glad for this, as the island had been beautiful, but it was now impossible for me to go there, for I no longer knew the people who lived there. My letters remained unanswered. I tried to find the ferry but I couldn't remember where it was. After this island there was another island. One day I rode their ferry out, standing when we approached my island. I had thought this would satisfy me in some way. We rode the length of it. Saw three houses facing out of deep woods. Thin wooden docks stretching into the water. It was seeing a family home in a dream and knowing there was no way to get there. I stood the whole time, fumbling with a camera. If the other passengers noticed, they didn't say anything. It's monstrous, these things we do to ourselves because we haven't thought something through well enough.

ISLANDS

The other island had once been a leper colony and was now a boy's home. It was a bald island. No trees. Nothing but a hill rising from water. Birds darting everywhere. They gave me many things on this island: videos of the work they were doing, a book, lunch, a tour. We had two hours to wander after, fighting the claustrophobia and panic that these boys endured every day while they cut logs for the fire. In the end we looked for rocks on the shore while waiting for the ferry.

PETRELS

There was a small isthmus on the island, roped off because of nesting pe-
trels. This had been an ongoing situation for many years, I was told on the
tour. The problem was the gulls that darted everywhere, making the sky
ripple like the ocean. They had prevented the petrels from nesting. Some-
thing of the anxiety of birds was explained to me. The government had
sent a man to shoot down the gulls, and poison was also attempted, but you
can imagine the problem of the bloody birds. Finally the man camped in
a tent and at night played the sounds of gulls in distress and occasionally
shot off fireworks.

FORTUNES

Not long ago I spent the day with an ex-lover and another man, a man
whom I had never gone out with but had feelings for. Because it was a visit
to a different town, there were several restaurants and cups of tea involved,
which meant there were many fortunes. If this continues on I'll have it all
figured out, I told the ex-lover, as he made me another cup of tea. And yet
by the end of the day I had lost all the fortunes, and would only find them
later, scattered in different pockets.

SCULPTURES

He was an artist, which also meant parking lots with sculptures that moved
in the wind. These too felt as if they could tell me something, but what they
were saying was less clear.

LOVERS

All this aloneness has taken some time to get used to, and time, too, to get
over these lovers we have lost. It's a wonder there's ever time to find new
ones.

WHALES

Henry used to leave in the morning with a thermos of coffee and another
of soup and a bottle of wine. He would take a notebook and his camera
and would walk the fire roads to see the whales. I never learned where
these roads were, though I could have asked. It seemed useful for him to
have a world separate from mine. He found a place to watch the whales

and described it to me. A canal that cut near the lighthouse and was so deep that the whales came up close. They would lie near him, some of them turning on their sides, touching the water with their fins.

MUSHROOMS

There was a woman from town who came to the dunes to look for sea-shells and scavenge for mushrooms. They said she ate mostly from what she found—cranberries, clams, the mushrooms—but that since her mother had grown sick, she had to travel to be with her and was often gone. You can reach a point where you think you won't fall in love again, not because the options aren't there, but because the inconstancy is no longer something your heart desires. I had thought she might teach me to mushroom, but only passed her once, in town, in the dark, when she was coming back from taking care of her mother.

GOATS

I once knew a man who kept goats with other friends. He had thought to make money selling goat's milk, but the goats came down with some sort of disease. The man thought perhaps syphilis. Others thought he couldn't take care of the goats and tried to take them away. The man said he was able to keep the goats, but perhaps these people were right after all. After a time the goats got their heads stuck in a chain-link fence and died that way.

TRAVEL

Sometimes it seems the places I've lived the longest, and the things that I've worked for, have disappeared in a way I wouldn't have guessed. And the places I've lived for a short time, places where not even my furniture came with me, or places where I've never lived, have remained with me, perhaps because I needed nothing from what I found this way. That our natural state is motion, is bodies in transit. Or movement fascinates me in the way it erases so much, and what stays with us—one person that we loved, a house, the way the ocean looked—apart from all that change, all that time filled up, sometimes seems a way in which it might be possible to exist.

PLANS

Anytime I have, even for a moment, done something right, I'll immediately try to repeat it, and it will become the wrong thing, made useless by repetition. It's only the surprise of the moment, which isn't something we can contain or plan for, and yet life requires some sort of planning, something beyond the instant.

OTHER CITIES

I've sometimes said that after my next affair, I'll move to another city rather than stay in the same city with this person. When you lose someone, and they stay in the same city, they can feel like a phantom, something you see that doesn't actually exist. In this other city, seeing them will be impossible. It's creating a city in their absence, and, in this way, the other city will always be better.

DECEMBER

Before I left we went walking in the dunes. It was an exploration of what we would mean to each other later. Sometimes it takes years to find this out—what we won't be able to let go of, what will cause us pain as we understand what we've done wrong. We wanted a quicker way, so we went walking in the dunes in the snow, which was like being lost in the desert for many years. We got stuck in the cranberry bogs. Both of us caught our ankles in ice, telling the other to go forth, to get help. Our knit things blowing in the wind. What did we find out? Very little. That we loved each other, that we thought getting stuck in ankle-deep ice to be a funny thing, the way you couldn't tell if it was ice or snow until you stepped down, and how funny it was that the bogs seemed to go much further than what we had remembered when we had come, the month before, to pick cranberries for a sauce.

The Rise and Fall of Public Housing in NYC

RICHARD PRICE // OCTOBER 1, 2014

A subjective overview.

"Tear down the old, build up the new. Down with rotten antiquated rat holes. Down with hovels, down with disease, down with firetraps, let in the sun, let in the sky, a new day is dawning, a new life, a new America."

—Mayor Fiorello La Guardia, touting slum clearance and the construction of public housing projects in New York City, 1936

IN 1935, the first public housing complex in New York, prosaically christened First Houses, (landmarked since 1974) on the Lower East Side of Manhattan, offered 122 apartments featuring oak wood floors and brass fixtures. The rent, adjusted to each family's monthly income, ranged from five to seven dollars. The recently formed New York City Housing Authority—the agency charged with the design, construction, and administration of this and future housing developments across the city—stopped accepting applications when their number went north of three thousand.

As of 2012, according to figures compiled by Mark Jacobson for *New York Magazine*, the NYCHA oversaw 334 projects, 2602 buildings, nearly 180,000 apartments, and 400,000 to 600,000 tenants (the wide range a result of the impossibility of tallying the number of off-lease tenants). In Jacobson's words, "If Nychaland was a city unto itself, it would be the 21st most populous in the U.S., bigger than Boston or Seattle, twice the size of Cincinnati."

And in defiance of their current hell-hole reputation, the waiting list for apartments stood, in that year, at 160,000 families.

In the beginning it seemed like a good idea.

When the NYCHA was established in 1934, at roughly the midpoint of the Depression, a great number of working-class people were still living in housing that had been described, fifty years earlier, as dangerously decrepit, including a swath of the Lower East Side known as the "Lung Blocks," notorious for their transcendently high rates of tuberculosis, diphtheria, and cholera.

From the beginning "the projects," as they came to be known, were never envisioned as havens for the truly hopeless and disenfranchised.
The idea was to provide a living environment designed to improve the quality of life of people who had already exhibited, in their applications and interviews, a desire to improve.
One needed to be steadily employed. Family savings and previous rent habits were taken into consideration. Social background. There were income floors and ceilings.
No prospective tenant would carry the slum like an infectious disease inside these towers.
By the late 1940s the NYCHA had both raised the minimum income requirements and established a twenty-one-point non-desirability template for eviction, including single motherhood, poor housekeeping, an irregular work history, and "lack of furniture."
And by the late 1940s the projects seemed to be working for some. In 1947, 2770 families were evicted for making over $3,000, that year's income ceiling.
From 1935 until the end of World War II, public housing, idealistic in concept, paternalistically overseen, and architecturally innovative, could be considered to have been in its youth.
And then Johnnie came marching home…

In 1947, with Robert Moses riding the bulldozer, the NYCHA announced the construction of fifteen new developments that would accommodate sixty thousand new tenants.
One of these was the Parkside Houses, formerly eleven acres of granite outcropping in the north Bronx. The blasting commenced in '48.
Three years later, in the spring of 1951, the first tenants, the Originals,

began to move in. I would enter as a two-year-old and live there until college took me upstate in 1967.

For many in this postwar wave of newcomers, the move to the new projects was just as much about seeking decent affordable housing as it was about finding any housing at all.

In the years immediately after the war, returning GIs married in record-breaking numbers only to discover that the city's available housing stock was borderline nonexistent, forcing many of them to live in crapulous overpriced living quarters that they could barely afford or, in the case of my own mother and father, to move in with their parents or in-laws, their home on earth reduced to a childhood bedroom, cramped common space, unasked-for personality clashes, and an unbearable lack of privacy. And then came the first baby…

And so, when Parkside finally opened in '51, those whose applications had been accepted grabbed the kid and took off running as if they were escaping from behind the Iron Curtain.

For these working-class children raised in tenements and aging apartment buildings, Parkside, with its relatively roomy two-bedroom affordables, its landscaped gardens and playgrounds and communal benches, wasn't only a new beginning, it was a *first* beginning, and mingled with the tang of fresh paint was an air of optimism, of gratitude.

They were on their way.

They could finally *breathe.*

They could finally *concentrate.*

This was the beginning of public housing's golden age. And it would last for roughly fifteen years.

Similarly résuméd couples in their mid- to late twenties found each other effortlessly, quickly forming tightly knit cliques. The men were postal workers, chauffeurs, garment factory foremen, institutional cafeteria managers, cabbies, truck drivers, subway motormen, and the odd luncheonette or bar owner. The wives/mothers did what wives/mothers did back then. Housewifing, maybe taking on a little part-time work to cut the drudgery if their own mothers could cover the kid. Or kids.

Keeping up with the Joneses was a piece of cake.

Bragging rights were hard to come by.

None of the men seemed interested in taking advantage of the GI Bill to further their prewar education.

On the other hand, they all had jobs.

Everyone read the *Daily News* and the *Daily Mirror,* and occasionally the *New York Post* (vaguely Red), but rarely the *New York Times*, which, unlike the tabs, was too unwieldy for public transportation.

They were patriots but not particularly political.

In their downtime, many of the Originals, both men and women, took to the benches in front of the buildings, Greek-chorusing about this and that, the talk easily reaching their friends directly overhead, hanging out of apartment windows in order to join in the conversation. The buildings were only seven stories high, there was no reason to shout.

Everyone smoked like chimneys.

Summers were spent together in the flyspecked bungalow colonies of the Catskills, women and kids living there seven days a week, the men coming up on Friday nights.

The men had roving card games, poker, pinochle.

The women played gin rummy, mahjong, coming to each other's apartments in quilted housecoats and curlers, clutching vinyl-covered packs of Newports and Winstons.

Many a kid, myself included, fell asleep to the clack of ivory tiles or the riffle of cards, nodded off to a non-stop soundtrack of laughter, blue language, and hacking coughs coming from the game in the dinette, our bedrooms comfortingly wreathed in cigarette smoke. And those kids, born in primarily two waves—from 1948-'50, brought in as infants and toddlers, and the second wave, my younger brother's micro-generation, projects-born in '53-'54.

There were some families that had three or rarely four children, but most couples called it a day at two. Like our parents, we formed tight-knit squads united by birth year and building proximity, roaming the projects from early childhood to high school. And if we didn't quite cover all eleven acres in our travels (the geographical comfort zone for us being fairly medieval), we at least covered our quadrant.

Except when it came to the Playground—everyone went to the Playground.

Half kiddie-friendly, with cement sprinkler ponds and monkey bars, half gladiator pit, composed of handball and basketball courts—but it was all about those basketball courts because for the boys basketball was the test and everyone had to take it; twelve-year-olds and up, playing like their lives were on the line, adolescent gunners banging under the netless hoops with knotted temples and raging faces, shouting matches and physical throwdowns breaking out constantly. But the fights were always one on one and the weapon of choice was a closed fist; nothing more.

Most of Parkside's darkness in those first fifteen years occurred indoors—morbid or raging marriages (heard through open windows) rarely ending in divorce, spousal black eyes, corporal punishment for the kids—in 1956, my six-year-old half-a-friend from apartment 4-C routinely being made to touch a hot iron every time he "misbehaved"—spare-the-rod beatings on the first and second floors that left the word "spanking" in the dust, and other manifestations of general domestic viciousness.

Alcoholism.

Drug abuse was unheard of until it wasn't.

A vacating tenant in the mid-'50s leaving his set of works behind a loose bathroom tile, the maintenance man's discovery sending shockwaves through the building.

There were two adolescent ODs, in the early '60s, one kid found on the roof of a building overlooking the Playground, the other in a shooting gallery back in the old neighborhood that his parents had hoped to leave behind when they moved to Parkside.

Followed by my own 26-year-old cousin, visiting one afternoon to help me decorate the living room for a sixth-grade dance party, then going off to the bottom of the Bronx to succumb to a hotshot that same night.

There were no muggings or robberies. The crimes tended toward the more sensational; lurid one-offs that had nothing to do with the immediate environment.

A double homicide, the teenaged perp (destined to spend the rest of his short life in a state-run criminal psychiatric facility) having crawled through a random ground-floor bedroom window then stabbed to death a mother and daughter in their sleep.

A Holocaust-survivor suicide.

A ten-year-old friend wrongly thinking that it would be funny to put Clorox in his grandmother's soda and watch her drink it…

〜〜

Racial balance in public housing got off to a rocky start. In 1940, the massive Queensbridge Houses, which was and still is the largest public housing complex in America, opened with FDR in attendance. But among its 3,959 families, only fifty-two were black.

By 1953, however, the numbers had considerably evened out; in all NYCHA developments of the city, the breakdown was 58.7 percent white, 33.7 percent black, and 7.4 percent Puerto Rican. By 1959, reflecting the shifting demographic of the city, black and Puerto Rican residents made up 57 percent. If America had ever come close to approaching the fata morgana of a true melting pot, it was in these projects, in those years. But the numbers were misleading.

Although the NYCHA tended to pay heed to the racial makeup of the neighborhoods in which the new developments were being built in order to assign the new black and white tenants in corresponding proportion, the administration was more concerned with a prospective family's ability to meet the income floor than with any de facto segregation.

But those income floors varied from projects to projects, with the result that some housing developments came to be known informally as "low income" or "middle income," or, more crudely, good and bad, and to the extent that straight-up historical and contemporary racism tended to comparatively hobble the earning power of African-Americans and Hispanics, those "low-income" projects tended to be darker.

Parkside was "middle income," whiter than some of the other developments but more mixed than others. The tenants were by nature racially, ethnically, and religiously clannish, but no more than most and not to a great extent. The proximity of families, four to a floor, twenty-eight to a building, made intolerance intolerable. You let it all go or you lost your mind.

Civility reigned. Occasionally, genuine friendships formed.

Among the white Originals, the non-white, primarily black Originals who had moved in at the same time were regarded as "Hardworking" and "Strict (in a good way) with their kids."

An effort was made—on both sides—but conditioned acculturation was a tough nut to crack, and strained liberal-sounding commentary was everywhere; convoluted flattery, thoughtless patronization.

Did you ever notice how Viola's boys never leave that apartment without she's got them looking neat as a pin?

I was telling my own monsters, I wish they had manners like those Powell boys.

I came into the building late last night, I saw this big colored guy, by the elevator, I almost had a heart attack. Turns out it was Henry Davis and he was a perfect gentlemen.

I was going to ask my son to go over to the Carters and invite Andre to join the Cub Scout den, I mean, why not—but then I thought it would only make the kid uncomfortable.

It was the generally accepted wisdom that after a colorblind childhood, the kids at a certain age would naturally gravitate to their own. Sometimes the parents helped this along, and when they did their actions cut like knives.

After her sixth-grade graduation in 1959, Dolores, a mixed-race eleven-year-old girl, since early childhood tight with a group of white girls in the building, first experienced being disinvited to one birthday party—no explanation given—and then another. A dance party. A group trip to Rye Playland, to Orchard Beach, to Freedomland and Palisades Park. No room in the car, you can come next time. In a few weeks the kid was bewilderingly friendless. Her mother, Terry, though, understood what was going on right away. Now that all the girls were starting to hit puberty the other mothers were afraid of young black boys coming around, drawn to their crowd by Dolores. Terry's sport over the next year became daring those other mothers to meet her eye in the hallways or the elevator. Embarrassed, they never did.

In the gladiator pit, however, racial delicacy, racial hypocrisy, was nonexistent, had never existed to begin with because, well, it was a gladiator pit. But pickup teams were never divided along racial lines and the everyday verbal put-downs between the whites and the non-whites curiously lacked teeth.

Your people, Marcus, they're so fucking cheap they rinse out the scumbag.

Who you calling cheap, Shenkman, nobody cheaper than a cheap Jew. You know in football why Jews like to play defense? They want to get the quarterback.

Are you kidding me? I knew a nigger from Edenwald once…

You don't call nobody nigger.

You people call yourselves nigger all the time.

What did I say about that?

You people are fuckin' hypocrites then.

How about I start calling you a spic, Del Pino.

How 'bout I fuckin' kick your ass.

Who's the hypocrite now?

Del Pino's father said the car needs a lube job, Mario said no problem, lifted the hood, and dove right in.

Shenkman's mother…

Don't fuckin' talk about my mother.

Shenkman's father…

Least I got one.

Shit, Marcus got three.

I would kick your banana-boat ass except I don't want to get grease on my sneakers.

Well shit, at least my *people…*

Well shit, at least my *people…*

Well shit, at least my *people…*

And then back to the game, back to the same elevators, same hallways, same TV shows, TV dinners, public schools and homerooms.
And so it went, this bruising semi-tolerance, people going along to get along, for the most part, all through the '50s and into the mid-'60s. And then it began to change.

Public housing had never been thought of as permanent housing. It was conceived as *springboard* housing, the idea being that a working-class family would utilize their years in residence to raise children free of the mean streets and free enough from financial necessity to allow them to take their education all the way, after which they would have no need to ever return except to visit their parents—if, in fact, the parents still lived there. In the best of all hoped-for worlds, the parents would move up and out too.

And that, starting in the early to mid-'60s, is what began to happen, as a small number of Originals who had accumulated, through a decade's worth of job promotions and increased wages, did what they were supposed to do—leave—many moving to more upscale variations of a housing project; the privately owned Lefrak City, which had just opened in Queens, or low-rise garden apartment complexes in Westchester, New Jersey, or Long Island.

And as many of the remaining Originals saw the Parkside demographic inexorably shift out of their favor they began to slow-motion panic and white flight was on.

For a few more years the racial balance held, most of the Originals unable to afford to move out.

In those years the relationships between the newer tenants and the Originals tended to be warier than before, the interactions briefer, or altogether absent.

These were the "new" people, unknown entities, many from the intransigent racially and/or ethnically segregated poorer neighborhoods of the city, people for whom moving to Parkside fifteen or more years after 1951 was considered an improvement from where they were before. And the song of the benches began to veer off key.

Don't ever mention this to anyone, but the new family in 7-D? I think they beat their kids. The little boy always looks so terrified.

I don't know what high looks like, personally? But if you ask me, half the time I see that one in 4-B she looks high.

Who was that man who rang 5-C's bell last night? Does her husband have a brother?

That one's got a real attitude.

I told my kids, from now on never get in the elevator if there's more than one of them inside.

That one's got a real attitude.

I'm sorry, I've never been a prejudiced person, but…

78   *That one's got a real attitude.*

In 1968, the NYCHA began accepting tenants from welfare hotels. In 1968, the white population of all NYCHA housing projects was down 29 percent.

Yet still, into the late '60s, Parkside more or less maintained a solid racial balance, a combination of no other affordable alternatives and a core of old-timers who still enjoyed their life there and saw no reason to move.

But then, beginning roughly in 1970, Co-op City, a 15,000-unit high-rise complex built on former swampland and over the bones of a defunct amusement park a few miles from the Westchester border, began offering apartments and townhouses for sale. A two-bedroom went for $3,000. Capitalizing on the white fear of a black planet, the sales brochures even included a coded promise to prospective buyers: "No subsidized apartments"—AKA, no welfare people.

In our building alone, twenty-one out of the twenty-eight families, primarily Originals, both white and black, put down their deposit and left—including my own.

This mass exodus was repeated building by building across the Bronx, leaving behind those who financially couldn't or wouldn't go, and creating nearly overnight a public housing occupancy vacuum that was quickly filled by those who considered moving to "the projects" an upgrade.

And by the early 1970s it could be said that public housing had turned a corner—increasingly segregated, and increasingly economically strapped. But it was in no way dying.

As elsewhere in the NYCHA kingdom, many Parkside families continued to embrace the springboard concept, taking advantage of their relatively better living situations and eventually leaving for even better living situations. Men and women went to work. Another generation of parents continued to occupy those Greek-chorus benches, their children continued to finish school and move on.

But then the projects, as all of New York and urban America, began to pay the piper.

"[Housing projects are] monstrous depressing places—rundown, overcrowded, crime-ridden."
—President Richard Nixon, declaring a moratorium on new construction of public housing projects across the nation, 1973

Parkside in the late '70s was a community in which economic security was tenuous at best; the market crashes and rising unemployment of that decade combined with institutional racism, political indifference, and an unspoken acknowledgement in the NYCHA that it was now in the business of running a welfare state, was the true beginning of the end. The '80s were worse, that decade bringing with it the twin plagues of AIDS and crack, and an entire generation was lost to addiction, incarceration, and violent death. By the late '80s, rather than leaving the houses, generations began to stack up in the same apartment, each one faring economically worse than the last.

From its inception in the 1930s, despite its social-engineering ideals, the NYCHA, like any city agency, had always been a bloated bureaucracy packed with political appointees, yet it still managed to get the job done and maintain a decent standard of life for its tenants. But when the overarching economic-social crisis began to hit home in the '70s, '80s, '90s, and into the present, the NYCHA seemed not only inept and useless, but increasingly abusive and callous to its tenants, chaotic and penurious in its services, alternately crying poverty and mismanaging the federal funds it had.

And then in 2012 came the revelation that it had been hoarding one billion dollars in federal funds, the money just sitting there as maintenance services became borderline nil, as apartments ran to mold, as gunfire made playgrounds free-fire zones, as the lack of promised security cameras in elevators, lobbies, and hallways turned every violent assault into a mystery and a manhunt, including, in 2014, the stabbing of a six- and seven-year-old, one fatally, in an elevator, the killer making it back out into the street like a phantom.

But still and still, despite all the grim statistics, NYCHA bureaucratic sociopathy, and the endless nightmare headlines, life goes on.

In most housing projects these days, a hard-times hidden economy thrives, what Mark Jacobson and others call the gray market, consisting of improvised and in some cases ingenious ways of making ends meet—apartments doubling as daycare centers, some licensed, some not; takeaway lunches sold out the door or lowered from the window; a legion of bootleg car mechanics whose garage is the street; come-to-your-house handymen, plumbers, carpenters, computer programmers, and repairmen; just-text-me drivers for hire; CD and DVD duplicators leaving for the commercial strips of Fordham Road, Harlem, and elsewhere; wholesale candy hustlers, kids mostly, heading out to Grand Central Station, Penn Station, and tourist-centric Times Square, introducing themselves as grassroots fundraisers in order to sell ten-cent chocolate bars for two dollars a pop, a 2,000 percent markup. Many tenants, out of necessity, have evolved into community activists, media-savvy bridges between the NYCHA, the NYPD, and City Hall.

In a way, through all this, from its beginnings in 1951 through the various social pandemics of the last four decades, Parkside has reasonably prevailed, a relatively quiet place to live with a low crime rate. Some say it's due to the fact that the houses became, within the NYCHA placement system, a destination for the elderly. And elderly it is. A good number of the Originals shunned the exodus and continued to live there until the end of their lives. And many of the first wave of newcomers from the late 1960s and early '70s, those whose presence triggered the flight to Co-op City and other destinations, remained to become old-timers. And like all old-timers they complain about how the good old days are gone, then brag about their Parkside-raised middle-aged children now living in the same suburban enclaves that the Originals left for forty years earlier (although no one thinks of moving to Co-op City any more, perceived these days as just another ghettoized housing project). A lot of those graying children want their Parkside parents to finally move out—they're too old, the houses too dangerous, they'll help out financially, they'll support them, they'll get them an apartment out in Jersey or Yonkers, or Freeport near their kids and grandkids, or they simply invite them to move in, then make jokes about the free babysitting. From what I've been told, despite their grousing, very few of these old-time newcomers—having struggled to make a stand in Parkside through all those years—take them up on their offer.

The author has drawn from the following sources: WNYC's "New York City Housing Timeline" and "The Land That Time and Money Forgot," by Mark Jacobson, New York Magazine *(September 9, 2012).*

Luz

LAURA BYLENOK // NOVEMBER 3, 2014

If, in the church, there was blood / her blood was colorless

Warp (v): To thrust (one's hand) forth; to lay (hands) on; to cast (one's head) down; to strike (a stroke). Obsolete.

Her blood was water:
there was water all over the floor

when I found her I ran
hands through her damp hair

ran to the street ran my eyes
up to the muscled sky, a thigh flexed

squatting over us, God—as a nurse
with her fingers already on the bone

snapped *ándale*, get over here
and help me lift the body

to disinfect the wound. Before
she died her blood laid its hands

on the steps and on the rain barrel,
on the tile in the garden. *Te riego*

I heard her tell the lime tree
flowering in the yard.

Before that before she fell before
she died she swelled:

her ankles and her fingers grew
like pale tubers, thrust

from the soil too soon.
She salted everything she ate

until her rings bit into her skin
and her skin grew over them.

In the church I saw her
sanding the feet of Jesus

from a crucifix to collect the sawdust
in her handkerchief, and so she salted

her tea and her tortillas
with, she said, a holy salt,

a tasteless salt from her pocket
pinched and sprinkled

on cakes and on eggs and in milk
until she swelled so much she prayed

for us to bury her but let her keep
her rings, her wedding ring.

When she fell in the garden
watering the plants

she prayed and fell
against the garden wall with her hands

full of soil and salt
like seeds.

We disinfected water to disinfect
the wound: the blush

of iodine droplets in a bowl
clarified to nothing

more than prayer: *te ruego*
to the water, to the nurse,

and on her lips I heard her
say *te riego*.

In the church I always saw her,
absentminded, touch her own hands

as if to touch something under the skin.
At the funeral

her hands were laced
in gloves to hide the stitching

where a finger was
sliced off to take a wedding ring.

If, in the church, there was blood
her blood was colorless

on the white lace and on her skin
there was no mark

to recognize by blood
our hands can hold water

or gold or seeds, our hands can hold
our hands hold earth.

Pull Back to Reveal

HENRY PECK INTERVIEWS BEN WIZNER // OCTOBER 1, 2014

The privacy advocate and legal advisor to Edward Snowden on today's surveillance empire.

BETWEEN 2011 AND 2013, a gargantuan structure took shape in the Utah desert. Covering one million square feet and costing over a billion dollars, the facility is the largest data center of the National Security Agency to date. Designed to hold what the *Washington Post* called "oceans of bulk data," it's a tangible manifestation of an American empire based in virtual space, a modern-day watchtower for electronic surveillance.

The scope of US surveillance had been far less conspicuous than the NSA's architecture (which itself is off limits to the public) until the release in 2013 of top-secret NSA documents by the computer analyst Edward Snowden. These revelations were particularly significant for Ben Wizner, director of the American Civil Liberties Union's Speech, Privacy & Technology Project. Wizner had for years been bringing cases challenging the legality of surveillance programs, only to see them dismissed due to lack of "standing"—plaintiffs were unable to prove they were subjected to secret surveillance activities. The unmasking of NSA programs has placed Wizner upon decidedly firmer ground. Shortly after the world learned of Snowden, Wizner became his legal advisor.

The National Security Agency's budget reportedly topped $10 billion in 2013, and the scale and pervasiveness of its programs have shaken the American public and ignited a national debate about surveillance. As Wizner maintains, the NSA has "lost the trust of many people, and more than that, this whole idea that trust is enough to regulate these very powerful institutions has been weakened and undermined." Beyond government programs, the technology industry has access to unprecedented amounts of personal data that it may commodify or be forced to deliver by the powers that be. Says Wizner, "No secret police ever had dossiers on us that compare with what social media companies have."

The hazards of such extensive surveillance have been identified in the misuse of cached personal information, but also in the chilling effect surveillance has on civil society. In a 2013 survey, PEN, the world's oldest international literary and human rights organization, found that NSA surveillance drives US writers to self-censor, and that individuals are increasingly less likely to make career or political choices that might garner unwanted attention. In July 2014, Human Rights Watch released a report on the damaging impact of surveillance on journalism, law, and American democracy, finding that surveillance undermines media freedom and the right to counsel, and ultimately hinders the public's ability to hold the government to account.

Ben Wizner and I met recently at the ACLU's offices in New York's Financial District. Against the drone of helicopters embarking and landing at the heliport on Pier 6, we discussed the ripple effects of US surveillance, the politics of fear, and what it might take for the security state to restore its democratic legitimacy.

—Henry Peck for *Guernica*

Guernica: How do the Snowden revelations figure into the idea of modern surveillance as a kind of empire?

Ben Wizner: I think there's a way to misread the Snowden revelations as being a story about the NSA, or even a story about the United States. And while they primarily have been a story about the NSA and the United States, the story within that story is the proliferation of surveillance technology, the plunging costs of data storage, the decreasing effectiveness of democratic controls, and a resulting world in which not just great powers but all powers will have the ability to record and store all human lives. So in that version of the narrative, the United States is both the driver and the shape of things to come. The message is to all people everywhere, about how these technologies will be used to monitor and control our lives—by democratic governments, by despotic governments, by corporations, by powerful entities that collect and aggregate the details of our lives.

Guernica: There are some laws that account for surveillance methods, and some practices that appear beyond the grounds of the law. Does the law support the empire, or does the empire supplant the law?

Ben Wizner: It's very difficult to describe the way the law interacts with the empire, and the security state. On the one hand, I think there is a real insistence that the empire and the country are governed by the rule of law. And that insistence is sincere, on the part of most of its proponents. On the other hand, it creates a whole language and jurisprudence to disguise what's really at stake. Let me give you one example of that. Since the Bush administration embraced a criminal torture policy, and essentially made torture systematic and not exceptional, in the US military, in secret CIA black sites, even to some American citizens on American soil, like Jose Padilla, not a single victim of that regime has been allowed a day in court. Even those who are indisputably innocent and victims of mistaken identity have not been allowed to go in and vindicate their rights and try to hold anyone accountable. Every single one of those cases was dismissed on some kind of justiciability ground. Most commonly the government would argue, and the court would accept, that the subject matter was a state secret, that whether the law was violated or not, unfortunately there was no way to adjudicate those claims without exposing the state's most important secrets and harming the national security of the country.

Now this was a pure legal fiction. I say that because secrecy was not really what was at stake. It would have been possible to litigate these claims on public evidence; many of the victims whose cases we tried to bring in US courts received compensation from European countries for their second-ary roles in the same events. But there's a discomfort and aversion to call-ing it what it is, which is impunity. We have no tradition in this country of holding our intelligence community officials legally responsible for law-breaking. That is because, I believe, it's their job to break the law—there has been a political decision since World War II that we're going to have secret spy agencies, and that we are going to task them with going abroad and breaking the law, and that to try to pull that back into a system of laws would be perverse and would cause the entire thing to collapse. That's not a conversation that the security state wants to have, because there's no limiting principle to it. But that's the outcome that has to be achieved, and then we work backwards to a set of anodyne-sounding legal principles that reach the same outcome, whether it's state secrecy, whether it's standing to bring a case if it's about surveillance, whether it's a doctrine of immunity that says that this kind of official can't be held accountable.

Guernica: But is this exceptional to the US?

Ben Wizner: There are no countries that I'm aware of that place legal restrictions on their ability to do surveillance abroad. So the difference is that the United States has much more capability. It has the infrastructure of the Internet that runs through it, so it has the opportunity to do more surveillance, and it actually has some positive law that authorizes surveillance, where most countries don't even put anything in writing. Again, that's not to say that that's the state of law as it should exist—it shouldn't. It is just to say that most countries in the world don't give themselves the license to wage war anywhere in the world, but they do give themselves license to wage surveillance, wherever they can if they're able to—they just don't have the capability.

Guernica: You mentioned positive law that authorizes surveillance, and includes some checks and balances. Is the Foreign Intelligence Surveillance Court (FISA Court) an effective check?

Ben Wizner: Remember the FISA Court was essentially the outcome of the last great surveillance debate that we had in this country during the 1970s. One thing that that debate had in common with this one is that it began with a dramatic act of law-breaking. There would have been no surveillance debate had not a bunch of advocates broken into an FBI office in Media, Pennsylvania, stolen all the files, and mailed them to the *Washington Post*, which led to a series of disclosures, hearings, and then ultimately this FISA regime. I think that it had its successes, but the real scandal with the FISA Court is the way that its mission was secretly transformed in the last decade. It was created to be a court that authorized warrants for secret surveillance. Many courts play that role.

What happened with the FISA Court in the last several years is it started being more than that. It started writing thirty-, sixty-, ninety-page opinions that analyze the legality and constitutionality of surveillance programs. Any court that hears only from one side should not be in the business of doing that. Having the government come in and say, "We believe that the Fourth Amendment permits us to do X, Y, and Z, and here's a whole new surveillance program that we want to run," and the court has no opportunity to hear any opposing views from academics, from human rights activists, from others. So one of the reforms that's being discussed right now would create a structure for at least a quasi-adversarial system within the courts. So that you don't have a court adjudicating constitutional questions with one side.

I think the other way in which that court has been criticized is that it's been called a rubber stamp. If you look at the statistics for the number of warrants approved and the number sought, it's something well over 99 percent. People who work in the system say those numbers are misleading, that there are many times when the court looks at an application and says, "This is not adequate, go back." I will say that however permissive the FISA Court was, it was too restrictive for Dick Cheney, David Addington, John Yoo, George Bush. They saw it as a hindrance to what they wanted to do, in 2001, 2002, 2003. And they created a whole program that circumvented that court.

So, it does play some role. Having any institution where the government has to go and justify the surveillance that it's doing is going to be important. It creates some obligation and some obstacle. What we worry about now is that some of the new statutes from 2008, for example, allow that court to authorize programmatic surveillance rather than individual surveillance, allow that court to issue the kinds of orders that we saw from the Snowden revelations, that say things like, "Verizon shall turn over all of its records on all of its customers every day, and we'll store them for five years." That, although they have to go to a court to do it, reduces the role of the court to ministerial rather than judicial.

Guernica: The idea of empire tends to suggest power connected to wealth, whereas the surveillance empire seems to wield more of a psychological power.

Ben Wizner: Yes, unless you're talking about other kinds of empires. If Silicon Valley is the seat of an empire, then you talk about the surveillance economy. The prevailing Internet business model is one in which we agree to be spied on by corporations in exchange for use of free services. If we've learned anything in the last year, it's that you cannot draw a firm line between corporate surveillance and government surveillance. If the NSA lost all of its ability to collect and intercept information, but could still get that information through legal process from Google and Facebook, they wouldn't lose that much. No secret police ever had dossiers on us that compare with what social media companies have.

Guernica: Several technology giants expressed outrage after the Snowden revelations showed how their systems were being accessed by the NSA. How has the tech industry entered the surveillance empire—wittingly or not?

Ben Wizner: I think one of the great contributions that Snowden has made is to make some very powerful tech companies adverse to governments. When these companies and government work hand in glove, in secret, that is a major threat to liberty. But these tech companies, which are amassing some of the biggest fortunes in the history of the world, are among the few entities that have the power and the clout and the standing to really take on the security state. And again, I want them to be adverse to each other. I want the tech companies to see it as part of their responsibility to protect users from government. But I want the government to be a more active regulator of tech companies and to protect us as consumers from the depredations of these companies. I'd like to see the Federal Trade Commission be a more aggressive regulator against some of these companies, just as I'd like to see these companies stand between us and the NSA and the GCHQ.

I do think that we've already seen a lot of evidence in the last year that the companies are more willing to stand up to the security state. Now of course there are some people, including on the left, who think that civil libertarians are picking the wrong battle. That over the next several decades, it's the Internet Goliaths and not the security state that are going to be a larger threat to democracy—by destroying and hollowing out the middle class, creating such disparities that free societies won't be able to sustain themselves. I think that's a provocation, a very interesting argument, and something we need to worry about and think about as technology companies essentially destroy professions one by one. But I'm comfortable with the position civil liberties organizations are taking that the surveillance by the state is at least a more immediate threat to free societies.

Guernica: It seems many people give their information willingly without thinking that it will be abused. But what about fear as a tool of the surveillance empire, or the construction of fear to further its aims?

Ben Wizner: We talked a lot about fear in the aftermath of 9/11. Immediately after 9/11 you had anthrax, you had snipers—there was a very strange atmosphere in the United States. But that's not the way America feels in 2014. I don't think most Americans are worried about militants from the Islamic State coming over from Syria and the Sunni Triangle and waging war in Peoria. I really don't.

I think it operates much more as a political discourse in Washington, and the fear is the fear of being portrayed in a certain way, not the fear of terrorists attacking. And it's a very odd kind of discourse that's been created, where expressions of fear by politicians allow them to portray themselves as strong, and professions of courage by politicians put them in the weak, pre-9/11 box. What I mean by that is those who say that 9/11 changed everything, that we're facing a new kind of threat, that terrorism poses an existential threat to our societies, that the threat is so severe that we need to throw away or bend our old legal institutions, we have to come up with new systems for detention, we have to allow interrogations that have always been considered illegal, we need to fire missiles around the world with rules that are too loose, we need to do that because they are coming to get us—those are the people who call themselves tough on terror. Those are the hard-nosed warriors.

On the flip side, those political leaders who say that this is a criminal threat, these people are criminals, they're not warriors, our institutions are strong, we have been able to face up to these kinds of threats in the past without shredding our Constitution, we can do it again now, we have to enforce our laws, even if that means holding our own leaders accountable for breaking them—those people are dismissed as foolish and naïve and having a pre-9/11 mindset, when exactly the opposite is true.

Guernica: Do you think Americans should be more afraid of terrorism?

Ben Wizner: No, I think the opposite. I think it's imperative that we be able to contextualize the threat of terrorism. You do actually hear this talk in some forward-thinking military circles. The word they use is "resilience." Politicians are afraid to talk this way for the reasons I described earlier, but people in the military understand it. Resilience is the idea that terrorism is a threat that will never be eradicated but will not destroy us, so we need to respond to it rationally and proportionately. If there are a few hundred people in the world who are doing us harm, should we be spending twenty million dollars for each one of them, when there are other threats that are more immediate and more serious, like climate change?

There is a lot of progressive thinking about this within the security state, especially in the military, but I think also in the intelligence agencies. There are studies being written about climate, for example, and how it's a national security threat to the United States, how it will affect the Southern Hemisphere, and how that will affect us in lots of ways.

Guernica: I'm wondering also about how invoking "national security" contributes to the production of fear. Keith Alexander's pronouncement that the Snowden revelations caused "irreversible and significant damage to our country" was not at all precise, but heightened the sense of severity in security terms. There's secrecy here—not disclosing how the revelations are damaging, or what the consequences are, but assuring you they are real.

Ben Wizner: Right, although I think they've had a much harder time doing that in the past year. And I think that the Snowden revelations have been quite corrosive to their authority and credibility. The video that you've seen on a loop, and that did more damage to the security state than anything else, is the director of national intelligence, James Clapper, saying under oath in congressional testimony that the NSA does not collect any records on millions of Americans. That was a lie. It wasn't a lie to Congress, as it's been described, because the people in Congress asking the question knew that it was a lie—it was a lie to the rest of us. And there have been many more lies that have been revealed in the last year.

I say it's corrosive because the authority of the security state rests so much on trust. "Trust us, we don't need courts to adjudicate this because we have a good system of rules in here. People who violate our rules will be punished, don't worry. We don't need the full Congress to know everything because we've told a few members of Congress—the ones, of course, who are closest to us and are more enablers than overseers." I think that the security state in the last year has been thrown wildly off balance, has lost control of the narrative. It had been accustomed to saying words like "terrorism" and "national security" talismanically, and to having the rest of us fall into line, and that has not happened. And not just because stories keep coming out and they don't know what's coming out next, but also because they have lost the trust of many people, and more than that, this whole idea that trust is enough to regulate these very powerful institutions has been weakened and undermined.

Guernica: So what does this mean for the security state, if trust is a building block of it?

Ben Wizner: Time will tell. This is not a victory lap—I see the security state as a very, very worthy adversary. It still has enormous resources and a lot of advantages, and many decades of experience in nimbly responding to moments of crisis and renewed energetic oversight. But then again the goal has never been to dismantle it, at least for us. The goal has been, in some sense, to restore its democratic legitimacy. And to restore its democratic legitimacy is to end the programs that can't survive public scrutiny, and to put the others on sounder legal footing after open public debate. And this is what Snowden has said if you listen to him. I mean, he certainly has his own ideas for what he'd like the outcome to be, but mainly he has been a proceduralist. He talks about bringing the people back to the table. You're reminded of what the president's first defense was in June of 2013—he said these activities have been approved by all three branches of government. But again, that was the problem. Not a very strong defense. If now that the public has been brought in these programs are being ended, it shows that they didn't have support or legitimacy, and too much was concealed. So I don't think of the question as: What will the outcome be? There will be no outcome. The question is: How will these forces play out against each other?

Guernica: As you said, your goal has never been to dismantle this entity. How do you determine how much surveillance is necessary to keep America safe?

Ben Wizner: You might compare this issue to nuclear proliferation. We're talking about technologies that can be dangerous, that will get progressively easier to construct, and that we will need, eventually, to come to terms with globally on how to control them. We're at a stage right now, which is 1949, in that there are a couple of countries that are capable of dominating the field here. But in a much faster way than with nuclear proliferation, these technologies are going to be available to every country in a short time. So we're all going to have to decide.

Right now America's position has been, "We have a big enough head start here that we don't want any kind of global regulation of these authorities." If you think about something like Stuxnet, and the hubris that goes into unleashing that kind of new tool on the world, it depends on the belief that it can't be done to us or that our defense will always be stronger. Add onto that that the very nature of surveillance, and especially mass surveillance, relies on the manufacture of vulnerabilities in a system that we all rely on. And so, in order for the NSA or the GCHQ to be able to suck up vast amounts of Internet traffic, they have to either create or discover and maintain vulnerabilities that can be found by other bad actors.

Guernica: This is especially pressing as we see more overlap between civilian and military control of cybersecurity than in other civilian infrastructure.

Ben Wizner: Right, but even the military is divided here. And there are sizable parts of the military that are devoted to cyber defense, and that would put the dial in a slightly different place. We're talking about the balance of offense and defense here. And some of the real cyber experts from within the government will be the first to say that it's more important that we protect ourselves, say, from China, than we be able to attack China, because our system is worth more. If you had an army of 100,000 people and its job was to attack and defend, you wouldn't send 99,000 of them to Iraq, and protect the country with 1,000. There's a way in which the addiction to these mass surveillance tools has weakened a global infrastructure, and I think that that tension—the fact that there is a tension and sometimes conflict between surveillance and security when it comes to surveillance and cyber defense—is something that the general public has not grasped. If they were told that Edward Snowden cared more about cybersecurity than Keith Alexander, they would think that that was some kind of sick joke. It happens to be true.

Guernica: Former Secretary of Defense Leon Panetta said in 2012 that the Internet "is a battlefield of the future." In this space, military targets are largely indistinguishable from civilian actors. Can the Internet be made a truly secure space?

Ben Wizner: The irony is that if any entity in the world is capable of really securing the Internet, it's the NSA. Every year they hire the best and the brightest engineers, mathematicians, people who are not evil at all, who are really dedicated public servants, interested in hard problems, and if more of them were put on defense than offense, they could make the Internet and our communications systems vastly more secure from the kinds of cyber threats that we hear about all the time. There would be a cost. The cost would be that it would make surveillance more difficult and more expensive. But the Fourth, Fifth, Sixth, Seventh, and Eighth Amendments to the US Constitution were enacted to make the job of law enforcement more difficult, not easier. It's a feature, and not a bug, to create inefficiencies in the government's ability to exercise power and conduct surveillance. And I think that that's part of what's been lost over the last decade or more, which is the notion that if something would arguably make us more secure, that's the end of the argument and not just the beginning, not just a factor.

Guernica: Your nuclear proliferation analogy suggests deterrence, which is playing out in a different way in the chilling effect surveillance is having on journalism, civil society, and public expression.

Ben Wizner: That will happen more as time goes on, as a function of the kind of mission creep that is inevitable with these systems. The NSA sitting on this mountain of data, mountain of human lives, is not going to be the immediate threat to most citizens. But when that information passes to law enforcement agencies, and eventually to local law enforcement agencies that have access to it from handheld devices, when the Big Brother manifests itself through the Little Brother—then I think people will wake up to what a different society we've created.

One of the examples that I like to use is that of our friend Professor Petraeus, who in my mind did nothing that should have required him to lose his job. One woman sent a nasty, anonymous email to a second woman, and before we knew it the FBI was looking through thousands of David Petraeus's private emails. He didn't even have to be suspected of anything, he wasn't the target of an investigation, but because this information is collected, never deleted, and law enforcement can get to it, it creates these databases of ruin, this sort of massive surveillance time machine.

What's protecting us from the worst uses of that right now are rules. How robust will those rules be in the face of another terrorist attack, especially when it's shown conclusively that the dots that could have been connected were in this database? If you collect all the dots, they'll always connect in hindsight. That's what Snowden was talking about when he said that you can have a "turnkey tyranny" situation. But even if you don't believe that our whole democratic system will be switched off right away, it's hard not to expect that the lockbox that safeguards all this private information will be unlocked. And then, I think, the result will be a profound kind of chill—if we know that the entities with the capability to record everything are making it available to people who have more immediate control over our lives.

Guernica: There are many possible ramifications to this, like the disclosure of healthcare records.

Ben Wizner: Some people have experienced a corporate version of this already with their credit scores. The ways in which the information about them is being collected are invisible, but the results are very concrete, and the system of due process is woefully inadequate. Try to get a mistake fixed on a credit score and you find yourself in Kafka world. But government will be doing the same kinds of things. It is in some sense already—there are preferred lines at airports that are the result of algorithms and information that is collected. You know, we may have secret citizen scores someday that tell agents of the state what level of scrutiny to apply to us in various security interactions. Surveillance isn't just about privacy—what do they know—it's about power and process and fairness.

Guernica: You've been working on cases against the intelligence community for a long time. How has this work evolved in the past year since the Snowden revelations?

Ben Wizner: The general atmosphere has changed a lot in the past year. People see courts and Congress as these isolated institutions that do what they're going to do, and it's really not true. They're very sensitive to the public and the zeitgeist. If you read judicial opinions in the years after 9/11, they all began with descriptions of the 9/11 attacks. As they were denying an innocent torture victim his day in court, we were treated to a description of how terrorists attacked the Twin Towers and killed thousands of Americans. If you read decisions by judges in the last year, you will notice the profound skepticism that they now have toward government claims. They are less deferential as a result of this new, remarkable debate that is going on. That is not to say that the intelligence community was revealed to have a glass jaw. There are still massive budgets, massive authority, huge capabilities—the NSA will survive and thrive after the democratic reforms from courts and from Congress. But there is a different atmosphere. The security state has to make its case now, rather than just relying on residual fear.

Guernica: What qualities are needed to confront the surveillance empire?

Ben Wizner: I do genuinely admire courage. Courage creates possibilities that people did not know were there before. Glenn Greenwald's dismissiveness toward the security state—while it hasn't made him a lot of friends in the mainstream media, it has created much more space for them to do their jobs. I don't think we would have seen the *New York Times* and the *Washington Post* report these stories as aggressively if you hadn't had someone with Greenwald's courage out in front.

We will see in the next months and years whether Snowden has had a similar effect on people who hold security clearances within the system. There are many millions of them, we can't and shouldn't expect most of them to do what he did, and it's unfair to demand that of anyone else. But a few principled and conscientious people who are willing to risk their own security and freedom can make a major difference. If they do this, I hope that they will choose the model that he did, which is to work through journalism rather than taking it on themselves entirely to decide what the public should know and not know. I think Snowden was wise beyond his years to realize that a model that corrected for his own biases would be better for the country, better for the system. Even if he doesn't always agree with what journalists publish or don't publish, it's a better model to not have it all on his shoulders—even if the legal consequences are all on his shoulders.

Outlaw's Territory

REBECCA BENGAL // SEPTEMBER 2, 2014

*Disregarding Hunter S. Thompson's advice, Danny Lyon set off to
"record and glorify the life of the American bikerider."*

THE DUST AND THE GREASE and the leather and the tattoos
and the cigarettes; the dents in the otherwise gleaming chrome;
the smudges of dirt; the gnawed bread; the jugs of cheap wine;
the pool cues, the coffee cups, the bottles of Hamm's and High Life; the
mudspatter, the bitten fingernails, the windblown hair, the asphalt road.

The front porches and the picket fences and the children and the fields and
the flags with their troubled allegiances. American, Confederate, white
crosses. The wildflowers.

The aura of the deliberate projection of the self, the careful roll of the
t-shirt sleeve, the backswept hair, the sideburns, the dyed, upswept hair
(on the women), the hairspray, the pomade, the jeans, the lace-up boots,
the emblem of the club, the belt, the Wayfarers and the cat eyes and the
caps, the scarves, the embroidered patches, the vests, the lone earring, the
blackened teeth, the chain. The coffin.

Rare was the person who was warned by Hunter S. Thompson that they
were taking too great a risk, yet Danny Lyon, in his early twenties and
just beginning his second major project, riding his Triumph alongside the
motorcycle gang the Chicago Outlaws in the mid-sixties, managed to elicit
some cautionary words from the Doctor. "I think you should get the hell
out of that club unless it's absolutely necessary for photo action," wrote
Thompson in a letter to the young photographer. But Lyon, fresh off sev-
eral years photographing the front lines of civil rights protests in cities
like Birmingham, Alabama—his images of police attacking demonstra-
tors found a disturbingly familiar echo in some of last month's pictures of

the protests in Ferguson, Missouri, prompting discussion in the *New York Times*—was already establishing himself as someone who not only wasn't about to leave, but was going to get in as deep as they'd let him. "Absolutely necessary for photo action?" His resulting book of black-and-white photographs and oral history interviews, *The Bikeriders*, republished in April 2014 by Aperture, is a resonate reply: Hell, yes, it was.

Both Thompson and Lyon were practitioners of what was then beginning to be called the "New Journalism," or participatory journalism, or personal documentary; they didn't presume to have a reportorial non-bias or hold their subjects at an anthropological distance, but instead threw themselves in the thick. For Thompson, who published *Hell's Angels: A Strange and Terrible Saga* in 1966, this had damaging consequences: he suffered a vicious beating at the hands and boots of the Angels. Lyon encountered several ex-Angels in the Chicago Outlaws, but when Thompson's letter arrived, he was already in too deep to extricate himself from their world, which by then had also become, in some ways, his own.

They ride against a backdrop of moody Midwestern skies in the shadow of Chicago, ditching their American cars (made just an afternoon's ride away in Detroit) for Harleys (made ninety miles up the road in Milwaukee). "You just scream through there, all this groovy feeling…" they say, racing down the drag strip. With *The Bikeriders*, Danny Lyon set out, he writes, to "record and glorify the life of the American bikerider." He worked from the inside out, not simply because he needed to truly see the bikerider, but because he needed to *be* the bikerider.

Like James Agee and Walker Evans with *Let Us Now Praise Famous Men* a quarter century before him, and Mike Brodie with his rails-riding photographs in *A Period of Juvenile Prosperity* four decades after him, Lyon wanted to experience firsthand the romance of what he was depicting, at the races, out in open country, back home. His bikeriders are handsome and jagged, or hard-lived and maybe a little crazy-looking, with dangerous, fiery grins curling from their mouths. They wear a studied tough, they crush on their heroes, Marlon Brando, James Dean, on the cover of a magazine, scrapbooking their pictures like starstruck teenagers. They absorb them and transform themselves, becoming the founding fathers of a lawless fantasy, which is of course the American dream itself.

While Thompson's *Hell's Angels* may have presaged his subject matter, if Lyon has a real predecessor in form and in spirit, it's Agee and Evans, whose seminal *Let Us Now Praise Famous Men* documents the lives of three Alabama sharecropper families. It was Agee, the writer, even more than Evans, the photographer, whom Lyon admired. (At one point in his career, he made a photographic pilgrimage to Agee's hometown of Knoxville, Tennessee.) Remember that it was Agee who lived and slept among the families, while Evans took a room in town. Lyon was clearly as besotted by his subjects as Agee was his dirt-poor farmers; with his camera he captures them startlingly up close and intimate, and each frame is fully loaded with the materials of their world. Sometimes you are right inside, on the back of the bike; sometimes you're peeking out an open window, but so close you can overhear the conversations as the riders gear up to head out on the road. And the conversations! They're not reminiscent of Agee at all, really, but more of Studs Terkel: the text of *The Bikeriders* is composed of gritty and working-class oral histories, casual and seemingly offhand, rife with rhythm and repetition, straight from the horse's mouth. You can hear the accents in their written speech. You get wrapped up in the strange stories they tell.

Here, for instance, is Cal, one of the central figures in the book, and one of the few riders with whom Lyon kept in touch later: "You know, like I'd get salty. In other words, I told 'em how it is. And so this guy, man, they called him Jesus 'cause he looked just like Jesus Christ. The fucker had long hair, way down there, man. And it was combed straight and beautiful hair, man, you know, for a dude. Anyhow, he acted like God, too. That's another thing. Every time we'd go on a run he'd find the highest place and he'd pray. You hip to it? The dude was a hypnotist, too, man. He used mass hypnosis. A whole group. Are you hip to this now? The dude was an artist and here he was a Hell's Angel."

Though tinged with danger, and hinting at the racial prejudice that was prevalent in the scene, Lyon's photographs are essentially romantic and glory-making, the transcribed monologues and interviews revealing some of the unsettling sides of the Outlaws' world, the things Hunter Thompson warned of. When Thompson got jumped by the Angels while writing his own book, it was in response to a remark he'd made, about the way he perceived some of them were treating their women: "Only a punk beats his wife," he'd said. The Chicago Outlaws were no more noble. Here's

Kathy, one of the most frequent speakers in the written section, and one of the main female subjects of the photographs, telling her and bikerider Benny's how-we-met story. She'd agreed to meet a girlfriend at a bar, and showed up in a pair of white Levis, which, when she tried to leave, became a kind of canvas for the dark side of the Outlaws. "So I walks out the door real nice, bein' grabbed about five times so that when I got outside, I could see on my slacks were just hand prints all over me." In her interviews, she's open about her marital troubles with Benny, who beats her black and blue, and like so many victims of abuse, she jumps from the offensive to the borderline defensive: "I've never seen 'em, really, take anybody that wasn't willin'. I never have. Except in Dayton. But our guys didn't do that."

Lyon doesn't apologize, or examine; he simply lets Kathy speak. He also doesn't comment in the book on the racism, though hints of it are evident in the pictures: the white crosses, the Confederate flags, the absence of any nonwhite person. This was a large leap from his previous project, working with the Student Nonviolent Coordinating Committee, photographing the civil rights movement in the American South of the early sixties. "Pictures have no mortality to them," Lyon said to *BOMB* magazine in 2012. "The moment they're made, they go into the future. I deal with that and I love it."

Looking at *The Bikeriders* now is to do so with the knowledge of what was to come after: *Easy Rider*'s Dennis Hopper and Peter Fonda riding headlong into a prejudiced South; the real-life tragedy of the Hells Angels' violence at Altamont, captured on film by the Maysles brothers and Charlotte Zwerin; and for the photographer himself. As Lyon told *Photo District News* earlier this year, "In my America, people were all different, they were handsome, and everything around them was beautiful. And most of all, they were free." Revisiting these photographs, we come to understand them as the pivotal stage in what would become Danny Lyon's life's work; the beginning of a career whose main subject is outsiders and marginal figures—whether protesters (his recent Occupy movement series) or prisoners (his *Conversations With the Dead* on death row and the Texas prison system)—and whose primary political agenda is life, liberty, pursuit.

They Seem to Be Immortal

ZACH ST. GEORGE // APRIL 15, 2015

The expansive, ongoing fight to save the sequoias.

IN THE FALL OF 1891, Samuel David Dill wrote a letter to his boss. "I saw Mr. Moore he says he will go right to work and cut the specimen and have it hauled out," he wrote. "He will have to get a saw made to order about 23 feet long." In the accompanying photo the tree hangs at a fifty-degree angle, felled but still falling. The land around it is mostly cleared already, just a couple other giants remaining in the coppiced wood. Two men, employees of the lumber barons Austin D. Moore and Hiram T. Smith, stand beside the stump, watching eight days of hard work come crashing down.

Dill was a collector for the American Museum of Natural History in New York. The Mark Twain Tree, as that giant sequoia was known, "was of magnificent proportions, one of the most perfect trees in the grove," wrote George H. Sherwood in a 1902 piece for the museum, "symmetrical, fully 300 feet tall, and entirely free of limbs for nearly 200 feet." Moore and Smith donated the tree, and the museum covered the cost of labor and transport. Once they'd felled the sequoia, lumberjacks cut a four-foot-thick section of its trunk, then split it into pieces. They loaded the pieces onto wagons to get them down from the Sierra Nevadas, then put them on train cars for the journey cross-country.

Another segment of the tree was eventually sent to the Natural History Museum in London, where it sits like an altarpiece at the top of a flight of stairs at one end of the main hall. The reassembled section is an almost perfect circle more than sixteen feet across, measured inside the foot-thick bark. Visitors stand far back, trying to get a full view, or move in close to peer over the railing at its close-packed rings. The tree is annotated in small white letters matching dates and events to the years of its life—1850: Darwin publishes *The Origin of Species*; 1500: Leonardo da Vinci invents flying machine; 1000: Leif Ericsson reaches North America; 600: Start of Islam; 557: Our sequoia is a seedling. The tree was 1,341 years old when it was felled, which, as Dr. Karen Wonders has noted in a piece on logging big trees, makes it a contemporary of the Byzantine Emperor Justinian.

The ancient trees always seem to inspire this measuring of their lives against ours. Though the comparison brings no real clarity to either the life of the tree or that of Justinian, we are impressed. We are staggered by the sequoias' age as well as by their size. Cumulonimbus greenery billows from red-orange bole, tall as three blue whales laid fluke to prow; there is nothing as big as a sequoia and never was, and few things as old. In a world full of brevity and smallness, size and age are valuable. But it's hard to say what they are worth.

Encountering the trees in the mid-1800s, early Euro-American settlers' first impulse was to cut them down. As Richard J. Hartesveldt wrote in a chapter on logging in the National Park Service's *The Giant Sequoia of the Sierra Nevada*, "The thought that a single sequoia log contained more board footage than a whole acre of northern pine held, for a Lake States logger, a pocket-jingling interest." Board feet are easily put into dollars; they're of a more human scale. The intangible is outweighed by the tangible, the past and the future outweighed by the now. If that were the end of the story, we would find it familiar: it is the story of our bigger past, when there was more space for wild things, when there were Rocky Mountain grasshoppers and bison and passenger pigeons, when the Colorado was unbound and grizzly bears still wandered California.

From the beginning, though, many people recognized the trees' intangible values, and fought to stop the destruction. The Scottish naturalist John Muir was foremost among them. After he died in 1914, a draft of an essay titled "Save the Redwoods" was found in his papers ("redwoods" serving for both the sequoias and their coastal cousins). Several sequoia groves were by then under federal or state protection, but many more were still in danger. In the piece, he pleaded for their protection, tallying what had been lost since his first visits to the Sierra Nevadas decades earlier, and what he expected still to be lost.

Although 100 years later the sequoias are safe from the ax, they are still not safe in a bigger sense. A long focus on simply guarding the trees only sets them up for a more devastating destruction. For decades, settlers and then grove managers stopped the low-burning fires that for millennia had regularly swept through the groves. Scientists now know that the fires were crucial to the vitality of the groves: they cleared brush without harming the fire-resistant sequoias, fertilized the soil, and killed fungi and other pathogens. Most importantly, the heat opened up the cones in the sequoias' boughs, scattering the new clearings with their seed. Without regular fires, the sequoias' shade-tolerant rivals grew up, creating fuel ladders into the canopy, and starving out sequoia seedlings. Many groves remain clotted, in a sort of suspended animation, vulnerable to catastrophic fires, their seedlings withering. This story, too, is familiar: it is the story of best intentions mislaid; of the cat that was meant to eat the rat, but ate only songbirds. Surveying the empty nests, it is hard to appreciate the original gesture.

Lately, the sequoias' situation is even more tenuous. California's current drought gives one vision of the future Sierra Nevada—warmer and drier. Already the trees are showing signs of stress. They're self-pruning, shedding needles to conserve water. They're not in danger yet, but scientists worry that if drought comes more frequently and for longer, as they predict it will, the trees will eventually die. This story is perhaps the most familiar of all: it is the story of our constantly shrinking future, where Glacier National Park has no glaciers and Joshua Tree National Park no Joshua trees. We gird ourselves for it, wondering how it will be when the Joshua trees wither and the glaciers melt, when it is hotter and drier and the sequoias die; in every case, it is hard not to wonder whether we will be forgiven.

While one ending is averted, another story begins. California's largest timber company has begun planting sequoia seedlings in new groves scattered across its holdings, many of them hundreds of miles north of the sequoias' natural range, where the climate is cooler and wetter, and hopefully the trees will be able to survive far into the future. The company calls it a "genetic conservation program." There are reasons to be cynical about the company's motivations, reasons also to suspect that trying to save the trees is as much an act of hubris as was cutting them down. But there are also reasons to think—to hope—that the seedlings will grow big and old, that this effort to save them and all the rest aren't really in vain. A seedling is nothing but a possibility, and perhaps this story will turn out the same as all the rest. But that ending will be for another time.

Sequoiadendron giganteum, the species, is not in danger of extinction. Even in Muir's day, seed collectors scoured the groves, hauling away bags of cones. Today giant sequoias grow from Scotland to Turkey to Australia. The species is safe, but it's the safety of pandas in zoos. What's special about the sequoias is not so much the individual trees as their collective effect. The groves are often compared, aptly, to cathedrals—open, echoing, high-ceilinged spaces, weighted with a sense of the eternal.

A crew of ecologists and foresters from the US Geological Survey hike through Sequoia National Park, pushing a path through the snow of winter's first storm. They're shaded by sugar pines, firs, and cedars, all of them dwarfed by the red-boned sequoias. This grove, the Giant Forest, is sparse and clean, resembling in the most important ways its condition before the arrival of Euro-Americans. Foresters here in Sequoia and Kings Canyon National Parks have been intentionally lighting fires since the 1960s, but controlled burning is difficult, expensive, and often misunderstood by a public generally less concerned with the overall health of the forest and more with the individual, iconic trees.

The sequoias here are now self-pruning as a defense against California's ongoing drought. Two members of the field crew stop to examine the crown of each of the big trees, gauging what fraction has browned, entering the figures in a palm-sized computer. With the data, the foresters hope to establish a baseline, which could be used for comparison if the trees lose their needles again.

"You see this really bad one?" one of them says, pointing as the crown of an old sequoia comes into view around a bend.

"Wow," says Nate Stephenson, the group's leader. Along with two members of his field crew, for whom this is a routine hike, Stephenson is joined by another forester and two office administrators. More snow is coming, and this could be the last chance for a field trip. "Wow!" he says again. The tree's bark is rust-red, furrowed up and down, pocked with woodpecker holes and scars from fire. At its blackened base, the tree opens to reveal

a deep hollow. The crack tapers closed, as though the tree is zippered to-
gether from the top. Its bark is layered like shale, grown over in places with
yellow-green lichen. In other places bare wood is exposed, charred black
and the texture of cracked dry mud. Into it someone has carved a five-
pointed star. The snow beneath the tree is carpeted with golden-brown
needles, each a cluster of cricked fingers with overlapping scales like birds'
legs. Stephenson peers at its crown, two hundred feet up, flecks of deep
green amid the golden-brown. Maybe it was girdled during the last fire,
leaving it vulnerable, he says. "It's probably going to die."

Whether you take the dead needles as a dire warning or not depends on
your point of view. By the scale of Stephenson's experience, the dying
needles are unprecedented, at the very least. He's worked in the park since
the late 1970s. "Some of them have reached the point where they're pretty
darn stressed, and I've never seen that in my entire career," he says. "I've
looked back in the old written records, and talked to the old-timers, they've
never seen it." Stephenson says that nearly everything else about the park
has remained much the same since well before his arrival; the dying nee-
dles are something new.

This impression of steadiness, though, disappears when you take a longer
view. Measured against the life of a sequoia, the last 150 years have brought
chaotic change to the groves. Now, even as the groves' human minders
work to remedy the errors of their predecessors, climate change threat-
ens the long-term survival of the native groves. To put it another way, for
thousands of years, predicting the groves' condition from one century to
the next would have been easy. To predict their condition even fifty years
from now is impossible.

By the longer view, such periods of turmoil are regular, and the species
appears not stolid, but migratory. Fossils of a species very similar to the
sequoias can be found across Europe and North America, and as far
away as Australia and New Zealand. Some of them are 200 million years
old. Modern sequoias probably crossed the Sierras just as the mountains
were rising, eventually receding to their narrow plot of its western slopes.
Looking at the trees from this longer perspective, many, Muir among them,
have called the sequoias the last few of a once-great race, doomed to ex-
tinction long before the arrival of Euro-Americans.

Stephenson says the sequoia forest here is only a couple generations old.

By analyzing the pollen in layers of sediment, scientists are able to tell that, starting around 10,000 years ago, a warmer climate killed the sequoias off everywhere except at the edges of streams, pushing them close to extinction. Around 4,500 years ago, the climate became cooler and wetter, allowing the trees to expand to their current range. The trees can live at least 3,200 years, so the oldest ones alive today are the offspring of those that first recolonized this area, he says. This grove, measured in this way, is almost new.

Although the most vulnerable among them may die, most of these sequoias will probably survive the current drought, Stephenson says. Even assuming that intervals of drought in the region do grow more frequent and longer, we don't yet know what the trees are capable of weathering. In the short term, it's conceivable—probable even—that grove managers will decide to water their groves. Managers have already floated the idea. That might be sufficient for a few generations, but it's a stopgap. Probably the best long-term solution would be to expand the trees' range, something unlikely to be accomplished without human intervention, since many of the sequoia groves are currently barely reproducing. Assuming their present range becomes hotter and drier, it would make sense to expand their range into some place likely to be cooler and wetter—by our current best guess, somewhere north. Over the millennia, sequoias have thrived far north of their present range. In a certain sense, planting them in Northern California would be a reintroduction.

But even assuming that the sequoias will require human intervention for long-term survival, and that migration to a cooler, wetter climate is the best course of action, brings us to a puzzle: the sequoias will probably be okay during our lifetimes, and those of our kids and grandkids. For which generation are we trying to save them? Are we really culpable for their current situation, or were they doomed to extinction millennia before our arrival on the scene? Are we thinking on the trees' scale or our own?

"Monarchs of monarchs," Muir called the sequoias in *Harper's* magazine, trees of "godlike grandeur" and "giant loveliness." He marveled at their size, recalling a dance floor he'd seen made from a single tree's stump, and at their endurance. "I never saw a Big Tree that had died a natural death,"

he wrote. "Barring accidents, they seem to be immortal." The world that an old sequoia occupied as a seedling is lost, the people who lived there alive to us only through the artifacts and words and names they left behind. The tree alone remains, living now much as it did then. A sequoia sprouting today is similarly solitary, heading far into the future without us. Muir was right, in that way—theirs seems a different kind of mortality.

The Dutch economist Kees van der Heijden wrote in a 1997 paper, "Scenarios, Strategies and the Strategy Process," that most of what we know about the future is due to inertia—an object in motion tends to stay in motion, an object at rest tends to stay at rest. A tree today will likely be a tree tomorrow, a forest today will likely be a forest tomorrow. But our world is full of unbalanced forces—fire and landslides and men with crosscut saws. Inertia is quickly lost or gained. A few days further into the future, and a tree might as easily be fence stakes or matchsticks. The trees really live just the same as we do, day by day.

So the future is uncertain—obvious enough. But that also means that the trees can never truly be saved in any permanent way. Saving the trees in Muir's day only delayed their doom. Restoring fire and attempting to bring the groves back to their pre-Euro-American condition also won't be a permanent solution, if drought grows longer and more frequent. But it makes more sense to look at the sequence in reverse: saving the trees from the ax made saving them now possible, as saving them now will make it possible for them to be saved again by future generations.

We celebrate Muir for helping found the Sierra Club, for his advocacy of the national park system, for tirelessly trying to save natural spaces. The future cannot be imagined, of course, but he tried, and in imagining people who, like him, would appreciate wild things, who would value the big and old along with the quick and small, he in some way succeeded. He imagined *us*.

In another photo, twenty-five men and two boys are arranged in rows across the cut face of the Mark Twain Tree, standing on hammered-in pegs. They look like hunters beside their kill. The men wear vests and ties, hats and kerchiefs, and hold double-bit axes and rifles. With crossed arms, hands on hips, thumbs hooked into pockets, they are unsmiling, unconcerned, even defiant. More than anything, these men and the mill owners who hired them look shortsighted, craven in their failure to understand or care what the trees meant or would come to mean. They felled the immortals and thought of a future very near to them. But prescience is rare. They have become nearly as unreal to us as we were to them. They are anonymous, and in their anonymity, we do not blame them.

Glenn Lunak has a neatly trimmed gray mustache and a flannel tucked into his forest-green pants, and speaks with a slight Midwestern accent. He is the holotype of a forester. Lunak, the tree improvement manager for Sierra Pacific Industries, is driving high in the hills above Chico, in Northern California. Sierra Pacific is a third-generation, family-owned timber company. It's the biggest timber company in California, and is one of the largest private landowners in the United States.

Over the next eighty or 100 years, in patches of about eighteen acres, Sierra Pacific will clear-cut more than half its holdings, or nearly a million acres. To call it tree farming "takes the romance out of it," Lunak says, but that's essentially what it is. By clear-cutting, replanting with a mix of native species, and periodically thinning to maximize growth rates, the foresters are able to harvest exponentially more board feet per acre than they could using the traditional "hunt and peck" method of periodically finding and harvesting just the most attractive trees in a natural forest, then allowing it to grow back in. Each clear-cut and replanted plot is thinned about fifteen or twenty years in, and then the remainder of the trees are harvested when they're between eighty and 100 years old.

Environmentalists were outraged when the company announced the plan in the early 2000s. Clear-cutting destroys habitat for wildlife and causes runoff, they argued (and still argue), and Sierra Pacific uses herbicide to prevent the growth of weeds that would compete with its trees for water when it replants. It typically plants a mix of five species of pine and fir, which environmentalists describe as a monoculture compared to the hundreds of species of hardwoods, shrubs, grasses, and flowers that might populate a natural forest. "Conversion," as Sierra Pacific calls it, looks bad, too, especially viewed from somewhere far off, like a helicopter or a satellite. The clear-cuts look like mange, everything good stripped off and hauled away.

Looking at a clear-cut, what is maybe most difficult is to imagine it as a forest. Nothing about the debris and exposed dirt suggests it. But, adopting Sierra Pacific's longer perspective, it can be viewed as a freshly plowed field. Using data on the growth rates of its different crop species, combined with soil conditions, precipitation, elevation, and other information, the company is able to estimate how many board feet it will grow per acre over time. Although individual acres may be destroyed by disease or wind or fire, over thousands of acres and millions of trees, the company can be confident in what it is passing on for its next generation to harvest.

As the tree improvement manager, Lunak's job is to find and breed the best-adapted individuals of each of the species the company grows, gradually creating straighter, healthier, faster-growing trees. From beginning to end, the process of choosing good breed stock, breeding, and replanting a better-adapted tree can take ten or fifteen years, he says. The company has been involved in tree breeding since the 1980s, in partnership with the Forest Service and other industry members. Lunak says, a few decades in, it's already possible to judge his success. The full measure of his work won't be apparent, though, until the trees are harvested and can be compared over their full lifespan. As with a clear-cut viewed too soon after the harvest or from too far away, the true nature of what is being passed on won't be clear for many years.

Lunak drives from pavement to red dirt roads behind a locked gate, stopping once to wait while a worker in gray camo pants moves his bulldozer from the middle of the road. A beagle sits among the pedals at his feet, watching Lunak go by. He passes a clearing growing in with neat rows of Christmas-tree-sized seedlings, then into dense evergreen forest, blackberry vines creeping from the margins.

Back in 1980, Lunak says, when he was the replanting manager for this district, the state nursery had some giant sequoia seedlings. "I think I bought 500 giant sequoia seedlings, planted them just to see how well they would do," he says. "It's been years since I've driven back here." He pulls into a clearing and hops out. Lunak looks around, taking in two decades of change. Though this is a conversion plot, clear-cut and replanted, the woods look almost natural, a mix of pines and firs and cedars, plus the sequoias. The trees are seventy, eighty feet tall, many of them with trunks more than two feet wide. "This is pretty cool," he says. "This is way cool!" He laughs. He wanders into the woods, snapping over dead lower branches. He stops at a sequoia growing on a slope. The tree's bark is lighter than that of the old sequoias, the corrugations in its bark more regular. Its canopy tapers neatly in a perfect Christmas-tree form, a spearhead reaching to the sky. "It's only thirty-four years old," he says. "I guess they're growing pretty good, by God!"

"Maybe we'll call it the Glenn Lunak Retirement Grove," says John Hawkins, who manages replanting in the area, and they laugh.

"I'm gonna come out here next year after you thin it," Lunak says to Hawkins. "It's going to be so cool, it'll be like a park." What was unreal is made real, board feet made into something more.

In his 1986 book *Under Whose Shade*, Wesley Henderson wrote that on his high school graduation day, father Nelson Henderson, a second-generation farmer in Manitoba's Swan River Valley, said to him, "The true meaning of life, Wesley, is to plant trees under whose shade you do not expect to sit." On the way into the grove, Lunak had quoted Henderson—"and I take that to heart," he'd said. Now, as he drives out, Lunak is quiet. The woods on either side are tall. Sunlight flickers through the shade.

Lunak stops next on a dirt road traversing a hillside. He and his companions lean against the truck, eating sandwiches for lunch. From up the road comes the sound of an engine, someone on a four-wheeler. Hawkins steps around the truck and holds up his hand. The driver stops. He pulls off his helmet, and they recognize him as a company biologist—he's been out in the woods trying to trap fishers, but all he got was gray foxes.

"So, there's giant sequoias here," he says. "Did you guys plant them?" The foresters laugh, tell him yes.

"Huh, pretty cool," he says. He puts his helmet back on and drives away. On the uphill side of the road is a natural forest, thinned but never fully cleared. Below is "Mountain Hollow Unit," a conversion plot, recently clear-cut and replanted. A large tanoak stands alone in the middle of the plot, oddly reminiscent of the picture of the Mark Twain Tree. It was spared to provide a little habitat for wildlife and to soften the visual impact of the clear-cut. The clear-cut around it is stubbled with Ponderosa pine, incense cedar, Douglas fir, and species Sierra Pacific didn't want but that grew anyway, bull thistle and Manzanita and nutmeg. Scattered among them are several hundred sequoia seedlings. It could be that if, in 100 years, Glenn Lunak is remembered, he will be remembered not so much for his work improving the genetics of Sierra Pacific's breed stock, but for his plan to save the sequoias. This is the cathedral.

Lunak's boss first came up with the idea at a conference on giant sequoias, but Lunak is in charge of planning and implementing the program. In 2010, the company started collecting cones from sequoia groves. Lunak says it aims to collect seeds from groves each year, waiting for storms to knock down fresh cones. A nursery sprouts and grows the seedlings, 20,000 or so from each grove. In many areas across the company's holdings, previous owners planted sequoias as an experiment or out of curiosity, as Lunak did in the 1980s. These trees have allowed him to evaluate areas where the new groves can be expected to do well. The trees grow naturally only between about 4,000 and 7,000 feet of elevation, and always mixed with sugar pine. Roughly hewing to those criteria, Sierra Pacific plants the seedlings in a mix with native species, between 20 to 40 percent of the total, creating more than a dozen new groves per original grove, each bearing the full genetic diversity of its parent community. "What is the climate going to be doing fifty, 100, 200, 500 years from now?" Lunak says. "By replicating these grove representatives in numerous growing environments, we know some won't do well, but by growing across this range of environments, we feel we will be successful in preserving the genetics of these groves over the long term." Eventually, if all goes to plan, there will be more than 1,600 of these groves spread across the northern Sierra Nevada and southern Cascades, covering some 32,000 acres, compared to the roughly 47,000 acres of natural sequoia groves. As the company thins and harvests other trees, it will favor the sequoias, Lunak says, leaving them to grow fat and old.

As part of its agreement to collect cones on federal and state-managed groves, the company has pledged not to sell the sequoias it grows from those cones as timber, though there are indirect ways it could recoup its investment. Once they're big enough, the groves could be entered into California's carbon credit market, and someday they could maybe even be sold to the public as conservation easements, or parks. They could also be used as breed stock. Several years ago, Lunak conducted a study of the scattered sequoias that previous owners had planted across the company's holdings, comparing them to nearby Ponderosa pines of similar age. In all but the most marginal ground, sequoias outperformed the pines in both diameter and height. Dr. Bill Libby, a geneticist specializing in sequoias, told me he thinks that under the right conditions, sequoias could have timber quality comparable to coast redwood, and could grow faster than any other species.

Dan Tomascheski, a vice president at Sierra Pacific, said that since they started the program in 2010, it's cost roughly $150,000, not including the time that Lunak has spent on it. It's not much money for a company whose founder is worth $3.6 billion, according to Forbes (company earnings aren't available, as it is privately held). Both Tomascheski and Lunak insist the program is purely altruistic. People outside the company who helped with the planning told me, though, that Sierra Pacific intends to make its money back, one way or another, although they believe the program is generally well-intentioned. That a broad range of grove managers has agreed to allow Sierra Pacific to collect cones is also telling.

Of course, a single company can do bad as well as good; more than one environmentalist I spoke with about the program called it greenwashing, a public relations move, and it might be that. "I used 'disingenuous,' because I work directly with Sierra Pacific Industries folks in forest collaboratives," John Buckley told me when I asked him over the phone how he would characterize Sierra Pacific Industries. "I think there's a difference between calling someone a hypocrite and calling them disingenuous." Buckley is a member of the Sierra Club and founder of the Central Sierra Environmental Resource Center, a Tuolumne County environmental nonprofit. Sierra Pacific's supposed concern about climate change and its effect on giant sequoias is, at the very least, he said, at odds with what he's seen from the company over the years. "They've consistently derided and denigrated those who have put forward the need to reduce greenhouse gas emissions," he said. Buckley was a wildland firefighter and Forest Service employee before he started the nonprofit twenty-five years ago. He said he disagrees deeply with Sierra Pacific's clear-cutting practices, although he called it a "competent and professional tree-farming company."

Lunak walks down the slope and stops in front of a sequoia. Its trunk is lavender, two inches wide at the base, its boughs four feet wide and four high. "Three years' growth and look at that sucker," Lunak says. But it doesn't look like much, not yet. It's still only a possibility. If and when these saplings grow to trees, 1,000, 2,000, 3,000 years from now, will people know their story? Will they recognize that they were deliberately planted? What language will those people speak? What world will they live in? And the trees themselves—will they take on the characteristics of natural groves, with snow covering them every winter and regular fires burning through to keep them healthy? Perhaps the grove in Sequoia National Park will be gone then, gone like the glaciers of Glacier National Park and the bears of the Californian flag. I ask Lunak and the others what they think this place will look like in 500 years. In a progress report the company released soon after my visit, Lunak wrote that in 160 years—or roughly the time required to grow, harvest, and replant the surrounding pine and firs twice—the sequoias could be between 170 and 240 feet tall, and between eight and ten feet in diameter. After the third rotation, at roughly 240 years, he wrote, the biggest of them would have swelled to nearly twelve feet across. But this day, looking out over the seedlings, he seems unsure how to answer. "Well, I can imagine that one at thirty-four years old," Lunak says—the exact age of the trees we'd visited just an hour before. "Trunk diameter will be between twenty-four and thirty inches." It is difficult even to speculate. Wherever these seedlings go, they go alone.

Muir's house in Martinez is a blocky white Victorian, with thick columns and red trim and turquoise under the eaves. The land, just a handful of acres remaining from what was once a sprawling orchard, is scattered with olives and palm, pomegranate, rows of apple and pear and peach and grapes, all surrounded by a high fence. The parking lot and Park Service building at the east edge butts up against one of Martinez's main roads. A graffiti-covered rail bridge and a highway pass along the southern edge. From the bell tower you can see both a large solar grid and a refinery to the north. Across the street is a yellow and teal Valero station. Tourists wander the grounds, snapping photos. The house is now a national monument.

In 1876, John Muir wrote an article on sequoias for the *Sacramento Daily Union*. "Judging from its present condition and its ancient history, as far as I have been able to decipher it," he wrote, "our sequoia will live and flourish gloriously until A.D. 15,000 at least—probably for longer—that is, if it be allowed to remain in the hands of Nature." AD 15,000 is the same as eternity, millions of uncertain days. Nothing of it can be known, not of the people nor of the trees. Looking forward, though, it seems unlikely that simply allowing the trees to remain in the hands of nature will be enough.

Much before then, the success or failure of our efforts to save the original cathedral groves will be clear, and also the success or failure of Sierra Pacific's program. Perhaps in 500 years only the new groves will remain. Perhaps people will walk among them, traveling from around the world for a glimpse of immortality. Just as likely, the trees will have fallen to wind, flood, lightning, or any of the other myriad accidents that can kill a living thing. Maybe they'll have been cut down for shingles. Maybe the program will have even somehow made things worse. Maybe the sequoias of Scotland and Australia and Turkey will have slipped their bounds and come to appear natural, or maybe climate change in California won't mean what it did. Sierra Pacific may well be saving the sequoias, but this is probably not the last time they'll need saving.

Muir's tree is to the west of the house. He brought the sequoia seedling back from a trip to the Sierra Nevadas in the early 1880s. The tree is stunted, only a little taller than the sequoias Glenn Lunak planted in the 1980s. It tapers rapidly to a spindly crown, and its trunk bears long, weepy indentations, as though it's collapsing inward. The tree is dying of a fungus, and probably has been since Muir planted it. Bill Libby, the geneticist, told me that every sequoia below 750 feet of elevation gets it. Planting them this low, Libby said, is "practically a death sentence."

Chances are that Muir noticed the tree wasn't thriving, said Keith Park, the arborist who looks after the tree—he may even have guessed before he planted it that it wouldn't do well. "It's limped along for many decades, and may limp along for many decades more," he told me when I talked to him on the phone. Still, the canker rot is ultimately fatal. Park said he wanted to preserve the tree for posterity, to keep alive this connection to John Muir. He took cuttings from the tree, and a cloning company has managed to grow some seedlings. They should be big enough to plant next year, although he's not sure yet where they'll go, he said. Maybe back to the mountains. To flourish gloriously, to AD 15,000.

exodon paradoxus (bucktooth tetra)

DANA RANGA, TRANSLATED FROM THE GERMAN BY
MONIKA CASSEL // MAY 1, 2015

joypolice, even when there's hunger and fear, we grab hold

Commitmentpolice, a large family, among us also lots of Cains and Abels, everyone is a policeman, joypolice, even when there's hunger and fear, we grab hold, loudlypolice, we conduct a raid on love and, at night, the rain, everyone is a policeman, even hunger and fear, poorsinnerpolice, shivering decorates us, I hunt you and you hunt me, overandoveragainpolice, you die first, afterwards we are the dead

3

Inflections Forever New

ARIEL LEWITON INTERVIEWS MAGGIE NELSON // MARCH 16, 2015

*The poet and cultural critic on gender fluidity, the politics of motherhood,
and the expansive potential of the queer movement.*

"**A** PARADOX IS MORE than the coexistence of opposing
propositions or impulses," Maggie Nelson writes at the conclu-
sion of her 2011 book of criticism, *The Art of Cruelty*, an explo-
ration of the ethics of aestheticizing violence. "It signals the possibility—
and sometimes the arrival—of a third term." French semiotician Roland
Barthes took up such a third term, and Nelson describes his concept of the
Neutral this way: as "that which throws a wrench into any system…that
demands, often with menacing pressure, that one enter conflicts, produce
meaning, take sides, choose between binary oppositions…that are not of
one's making, and for which one has no appetite."

Nelson has no appetite for binary oppositions; she is hungry for paradox.
In her prolific early career (four books of poetry, five books of nonfic-
tion) she has continually occupied the interstices of complex, contradic-
tory language and ideas. Writing fluently across registers—from the lyric
to the procedural, from the scholarly to the vernacular—Nelson folds per-
sonal and often confessional narratives into probing critical and theoretical
inquiries.

While *The Art of Cruelty* brought Nelson mainstream recognition, she has
been a much-admired figure in literary circles since her 2009 book *Bluets*,
which navigates the deeply personal pain of heartbreak through a philo-
sophical, cultural, and historical investigation of the color blue.

In her latest work, *The Argonauts* (forthcoming from Graywolf in May
2015), Nelson leans on another Barthes formulation as extended metaphor
and point of return. Caught in the early throes of a love affair, Nelson

utters *I love you* to her partner Harry during sex, the words "tumbling out of [her] mouth in an incantation." A few days later, "feral with vulnerability," she presents her new lover with a Barthes passage that references the Argonauts of Greek mythology, who had to replace every part of their ship, the *Argo*, over the course of their difficult voyage. Just as they continued to call their ship *Argo* even after its total reconstitution, the phrase *I love you* is imbued with "inflections which will be forever new" each time it is spoken. "I thought the passage was romantic," Nelson writes. "You read it as a possible retraction. In retrospect, I guess it was both."

Ideas of nomination and physical change are particularly apt here given the nature of Nelson's partnership with Harry, which serves as an emotional center and structural scaffolding for the text. Several years into their relationship, Nelson becomes pregnant as fluidly gendered Harry undergoes top surgery and begins injecting testosterone. With bodies in flux, who are they to themselves and each other? "In other words we were aging," Nelson writes, in a line that reads both earnest and tongue-in-cheek.

The Argonauts is a book about representation. Language is a limited tool, Nelson admits, but it's the one she wields, and therefore it must serve. "Words change depending on who speaks them," she writes. "One must become alert to the multitude of possible uses, possible contexts, the wings with which each word can fly." It is also a book about family. For Nelson, this means her biological family (including a fraught relationship with her mother), the new family she forges with Harry and their children, and the philosophers, artists, and theorists she refers to as "my queer intellectual family, my feminist family."

In person (or Skype's approximation), Nelson is warm and funny. During our conversation last month, I expressed disgust for the film version of *Fifty Shades of Grey*, which I'd seen a week earlier. Nelson was sympathetic. "At first I was like, whatever delivers the kink far and wide, great!" she said. "But it doesn't seem like true perversity—it seems like normative ideologies stuffed into perverse outfits or something." In the film, the (anti)heroine falls in love with a sadistic billionaire. "Some gnarly capitalist?" Nelson said, rolling her eyes. "That to me is super not hot! *Super* not hot!"

As we spoke about queer family-making, identity politics, and the shifting sands of gender, Nelson was simultaneously incisive and eager to interrogate her own logic. "I don't always know," she said at one point. "I don't always get it right. So that's a form of self-inquiry I feel like I have to perpetually perform."

Maggie Nelson's self-inquiry may be a performance, but it is not a solipsistic one. "I feel grateful for the kind of ongoingness of conversations I'm able to have," she told me, "in public, and with friends, and also in my own home."

—Ariel Lewiton for *Guernica*

Guernica: Both *The Argonauts* and your 2009 book, *Bluets*, are comprised of fragments, and integrate personal narrative with theory, history, and criticism. But it seems to me that the way you're working through all of those elements is quite different in this new book.

Maggie Nelson: I do think of it as different from *Bluets*. I think of the unit of this book as anecdote, whereas in *Bluets* I thought of it as propositions. In *Bluets*, I was in pain, and it felt like banging my head against logic, or philosophy. That's why it has the Pascal quote, "And were it true, we do not think all philosophy is worth one hour of pain." But this book was really like family. Not just my family, but all the people I'm thinking through: Audre Lorde, Eve Sedgwick, all the people who are like my queer intellectual family, my feminist family. So I'm thinking *with* them.

I've lived a life in feminist and queer theory—teaching it, coming up with it—so it felt like the first time I was reckoning directly with that in print. It felt to me like this wasn't going to be a very personal book, it was just going to be reckoning with these thoughts and ideas. There was *some* personal stuff in there, but you know how things go—you show it to people and they go, "Cool, but tell me more about *your* life." So I wrote more and more content that was "personal" and then I ended up structuring the book in a chronological fashion, from 2007 to 2013. So then its narrative arc became about housing this theory within a select period of time.

Guernica: So writing about your nuclear family was almost an afterthought?

Maggie Nelson: Yeah, it's a lot easier to write about people when you're not living with them! Harry is a pretty private person, and I guess

I never really thought I would write a book about him or our life together. I think he had contradictory feelings, like he simultaneously wanted a book about us and also didn't. But the conflict that presented, hating what representation does to you, eventually became what the book is about. Representation is not good enough. And yet, it's sometimes what we have to give as love. And that's a problem. But staying silent because it's a problem is not my game.

Guernica: Recently there have been a few articles in the *New York Times* that deal with genderqueer subjects, and the *Times* style guide does not allow the use of pronouns preferred by the trans or genderqueer community [like the singular their, *xe, ze, hir*]. So out of respect to their subjects, the writers of those pieces managed—impressively, I think—to write long-form features without using any pronouns at all. And the *Times* has come under fire for its policy. After reading your book, I realized that in the *Times* profile of Harry from 2008, the editors insisted that he choose a male or female pronoun. So he is "Ms. Dodge" throughout. How much is our ability to articulate constrained by the language systems that we have to use?

Maggie Nelson: The language has constraints, but in some ways, the connotation is where all the action is as much as the denotation. The denotation would be like, "What pronoun are you going to use?" But when I talk about context in the book, every genderqueer or trans person who uses a pronoun might feel it differently. Some people's *she* or *he*, if it's a trans *she* or *he*, is very solid, and they don't want to be outed otherwise. For other people that's not the case; it has more irony, and it's always understood as queer.

I was trying to conjure an environment in which people could think about context, a space in which you're given a relationship, but you're not being handed the language, like, "Here's the language by which I'd like to talk about this relationship." The book is not pedagogical except as an experience.

Guernica: In an early anecdote from the book, you're talking to a friend about how you don't know what pronoun to use for Harry. Many parts of the book dealing with Harry and your relationship are in the second person—a direct address—but there are points later on where you use "he." I'm curious about what that means to him, or to you.

Maggie Nelson: One of the reasons for the chronological structure of the book is that sometimes people can't imagine being on the inside of something without a pronoun to use, but I wanted to depict that you can be in relationship to something without having it be nailed down. It can be, "I don't know what to call it but I'm already *in* it." The chronology there was very intentional.

I can't speak for Harry, but I will say that I think everybody knows what it's like to have strategic identifications throughout a day. Everybody code-switches, some people more than others. Everyone knows what it's like to spend a day passing in certain environments. It's really more about how we negotiate with others the things that may or may not be visible about ourselves. So it's not just that I can't speak for Harry because I don't know things about him, but also because these are not stable entities.

Guernica: *The Argonauts* charts a period in your personal life when bodies are changing dramatically. You're pregnant at the same time that Harry is undergoing top surgery and injecting testosterone. In terms of your pregnancy, you describe feeling "a radical intimacy with—and radical alienation from—one's body." I'm interested in hearing more about this.

Maggie Nelson: Well I say this line: "In other words we were aging," to sum up the passage about those changes. I'm not sure how to put this, but I didn't want things like gender transition to be, like, the money shot in talking about bodily change. The truth is that we are all changing all the time to each other. Anybody who's been in a relationship for more than a year, more than five years, knows this.

I remember that lovely passage in Joan Didion's *The Year of Magical Thinking*, after the death of her husband, John, where she realizes that when he looked at her, he saw all of her faces back to when she was young, not just the old face. There's that layering of selves that we can have with someone else across a long relationship.

I go to the baths, the Korean spa. I love looking at the maps of people's bodies. The women have so many mastectomy scars and ectopic pregnancy scars and stretch marks, and all these things are amazing and wondrous to me. I guess I find it stranger not to attend to flux than to attend to it. But in a relationship it's also scary—you don't know where you're going to end up when you go through change.

Guernica: You ask, "Is there something inherently queer about pregnancy itself?" And there's this moment during your pregnancy, following an ultrasound, when you realize you're carrying a differently gendered body inside of your own, a body who will become your son, Iggy. It seems really obvious, but I was fascinated by that idea—I'd never thought about it in that way before.

Maggie Nelson: Well, most of the bio men on earth were born to women, so it's pretty ordinary! But I think because I had come from a matriarchy—my father died when I was young, and I only have a sister and a stepsister—when I told my mom and my sister that I was having a boy, they were both like, "That does not compute within our family relation!" It was like, "Girls only here!" Now that all seems very strange to me.

But it's one of those amazing things of life that feminists have been dealing with for a long time. You may be Audre Lorde and a lesbian separatist… and then you have a son. I feel excited in that I think boys born to feminists have a leg up. At least, the ones I've met seem like they do. There's something really vital about that exchange. I think I'd only imagined, beforehand, handing down a feminism to a young girl. But I'm newly excited by the challenge.

Guernica: The book is partly about your nuclear family. You spoke earlier about how it's also in conversation with a different kind of family—the feminists, queer theorists, artists, and philosophers whom you refer to, after poet Dana Ward, as "the many-gendered mothers of my heart." In a book that has so much to do with the fluidity of gender, that deals with the way that parenting can be untethered from gender roles, I found myself pausing at the word *mother.* Even if we move away from the idea of a mother being specifically female, the word still carries a distinct set of connotations. You wouldn't say "the many gendered *parents* of my heart." What does motherhood mean to you personally, now that you're a mom? And from a theoretical standpoint, can we talk about motherhood, or mothering, in ways that are not gendered?

Maggie Nelson: I don't want to just take the easy way out and plead paradox, but I guess that's what it is to me. Not to be too doctrinaire, but we live in the patriarchy! And therefore anything explicitly associated with the female gender, including motherhood, needs to be defensively claimed, because it's either devalued or sentimentally idealized, but not supported.

I so thoroughly believe that female human beings have worth that I don't feel the need to argue it, but I think that there's a part of me that very specifically wants to make space for those ideas to be centralized, if only for the moment.

I know that a lot of feminist fears about the trans movement have been, "Wait, we never got to the part where we focus on women! We tried for a minute, but we don't want to lose the category all of a sudden. We haven't *heard* yet from the females with children called mothers, we haven't heard yet from all these groups!"

On the one hand I'm very sympathetic to that, but the category of Women or Mothers, any of these categories are on shifting sands and always have been. Denise Riley, whom I quote in the book, says, "On such shifting sands feminism must stand and sway." And I think it's that standing and swaying that's really integral. Yes, I'm writing about motherhood, but I bristle a little bit, especially living with someone whose parenting falls between the cracks of what the culture is ready to recognize as mothering or fathering, but who most certainly is an excellent parent.

When I bristle at talking about something that's called motherhood, I have to figure out within myself what I'm bristling at or from. Internalized matrophobia? Internalized sexism? Or for good solid queer reasons, on the other hand? I don't always know. I don't always get it right. So that's a form of self-inquiry I feel like I have to perpetually perform. The book tries to perform that by putting forth a lot of different propositions about these questions. The idea is to exist in a space where you're taking the time to hear a birth story or taking the time to think about sodomitical maternity, but you're also getting the space to think about acts of ordinary devotion or care without always tethering them back to being called "mothering" by people who are female, cis or bio-gendered human beings who bore children. It's a balance.

Guernica: A lot of the theorists you draw from, and the other thinkers you're engaging with, are of an older generation. They're not your contemporaries.

Maggie Nelson: Put very nicely! [*laughs*] Unfortunately, it's probably more a sign that I dropped out of keeping up with academic theoreticians in 1994. Someone who read the book recently said, "I love how you're not afraid to date yourself with the theorists that you mention." That was a slightly less kind way of putting the question.

Guernica: Fair enough. Well, are there contemporary theorists, academic or otherwise, with whom you feel your beliefs resonate or are in conversation?

Maggie Nelson: I teach at an art school, and art is more my milieu than academics. Academic writing has a kind of one-upmanship quality about argumentation and it's not my favorite mode to read. But I'll read anything interesting that comes my way. There are people I really like: Sara Ahmed, Paul Preciado [formerly Beatriz Preciado], Gayle Salamon, Saidiya Hartman, Fred Moten. But I don't think that the conversation has fundamentally changed from the questions people were asking in the '70s.

There's this famous Sojourner Truth speech, "Ain't I a Woman," that she gave to this white women's caucus [in 1851] saying, You're talking about women, but ain't I a woman too? I've plowed fields, I've been whipped, and yet your notion of womanhood does not seem to include me. But ain't I a woman?! Like I said before, the shifting and swaying of these foundational categories, they're very old. They've been complicated in numerous ways, and the trans women conversation and complication is also not new, although there's a lot more attention being paid now. Before they were talked about more in petri dishes, and now we're talking about them in bigger environments.

I think kids growing up now, hopefully, will have more choices. It always annoys me when people ask me, "What do your kids think about your relationship or Harry's gender identity?" And I'm like, "Well, now I know what *you* think!" Our kids just aren't living in the same generation, and if they're not introduced to those things as a problem, they won't internalize them as a problem. Which isn't to say they won't meet bigotry in their lives. But I think Harry's and my goal as parents is to have them meet that bigotry with a kind of astonishment. Like, "Wow, what an idiot you are that you don't know what a genderqueer person is!"

I love teaching. My students tell me things I don't know about what's hip and current. Last week I was teaching feminism and queer theory, and my students were telling me what it meant to be on the asexual spectrum. Identifying as asexual or on the asexual spectrum is big for a lot of the students at my school. I was asking them a bunch of questions, and we were studying Foucault that day. So what I had to give them, in turn, was to say: "Let's try to understand that when we say we have a thing called a sexuality, and then we name it, and then we make a spectrum... let's just get under that and talk about what *is* a sexuality, and how did it come about that we think we have one, and what do we gain and lose?"

And one of my students said something really beautiful. She said, "I think that labeling yourself has its bad parts, but it's also a way not to feel broken." And I thought, that is kind of the perfect way of saying it.

Guernica: When it comes to how we form alliances, and how we work for justice, we can't accomplish very much by shedding all identities and standing alone. When does it become strategic to adopt a particular kind of identity?

Maggie Nelson: Absolutely. One of the best books I read recently is called *Golden Gulag* [by Ruth Wilson Gilmore], about the California prison system. It's kind of a profile about this group called Mothers Reclaiming Our Children, Mothers ROC. Those mothers may not always be identifying as mothers every moment of their life, but, just like Mothers of the Disappeared in Argentina, there have been many maternally-based nodes of resistance. I'm not going to berate people for organizing under these principles. I think they're incredibly effective and useful. I don't have a knee-jerk anti-identitarian bone, while at the same time I'm completely interested in what lies beyond identity politics.

And labels can be fun! Some people are like, "As a card-carrying bear, where I also have a little bit of fairy in me..." People have fun collaging these; there's a fun people have with their identifications. The irony of them can be lost if you're just wholeheartedly anti-identitarian.

Guernica: Your work highlights various systems of oppression, including capitalism. In *The Argonauts*, you draw explicit parallels between gender, sexuality, and commodification, whether it's quoting Beatriz Preciado on the "pharmacopornographic era," or Judith Butler on "taking on a gender as a kind of consumerism." You talk about the frustration among queer activists who sought to dismantle these oppressive systems, only to be faced with, as you write, "the assimilationist, unthinkingly neoliberal bent of the mainstream GLBTQ+ movement, which has spent fine coin begging entrance into two historically repressive structures: marriage and the military."

Maggie Nelson: One rough paraphrase of queer thought might go: Queer, pervy sex is so non-normative and so exciting, and these relations *have* to fray patriarchy and capitalism just because they're not accepted by it. But the people who felt like that have been so demoralized to see this clamoring for assimilation.

I live near Pasadena and there's an Apple store here. Right outside the store are people from HRC [Human Rights Campaign], the mainstream gay and lesbian rights organization. As soon as you go into the Apple store they're like, "Do you have time for gay rights!?" And of course, if you stop, it's just about marriage. I always feel like I'm in this vortex: *The Apple Store—Do you have time for gay rights?—It's all about marriage!—The Apple Store!*

I think the crushing sense of normativity—that gay rights means this, in front of the Apple store—can be so hard to take! People have been joking, saying, "Oh, we're in a really transy moment," calling it "transdy" [a portmanteau of *trans* and *trendy*], because of shows like *Transparent,* and the *New York Times* finally getting with the program. Yet it's always the same. Is it exciting to have a codified identity, which then gets a codified set of rights and recognitions and visibility? Are we supposed to take it from there, within the same system? Or are we trying to upset the table before we want a place at it?

Of course, the problem is that no one lives a pure life—there's no tool without blood on it. Harry and I got married. My smart friend Jack Halberstam, who's a queer theorist, would say to us, "No unjust system *ever* changed by joining it! That's an ironclad rule." And I totally believe that's true. On the other hand, we have these two kids to look after, and we're not going to turn down things that are going to get us into emergency rooms or other situations—especially because Harry's a genderqueer person. There's just no telling what can come down the pike, in terms of how you're recognized as a parent or partner.

But whenever you get involved with talking about rights, you're talking about being a citizen. You're talking about being a citizen in capitalism; you're talking about what rights are granted to what identities, under what laws, and all that is a big mix. Marriage is, among many other things, a formality to channel capital through a family. And that's why the big DOMA lawsuit was about paying too many taxes! "I wouldn't have had to pay all these taxes if Theodora had been Theo"—that was the big tagline. It's all about protecting assets.

I'm thrilled that the DOMA decision went the way it went. None of us stand pure outside the system; that would be preposterous. But you have to be mindful. You may get X, Y, and Z changes, but then you go, Oh shit! Everything's still really unjust, and the planet's still warming, and there are still radically poor people outnumbering the rich by 100,000 to one! So you have to think it through, which doesn't mean standing apart from what's on offer or what can be fought for, or appreciating with gratitude those rights that are fought for very hard by heroic people. It just means having a robust critique of those structures and systems in place at the same time.

We're all human beings with bodily needs living within a system. We don't need to prove that we're not a part of the fabric of the culture in order to want to change it.

Guernica: Do you feel like your thoughts about gender and identity changed over the course of writing *The Argonauts*, or changed within the context of your relationship with Harry or with your children?

Maggie Nelson: I think writing kind of burns out the flaming question. Sometimes it might feel like when you're living with certain paradoxes and they're unarticulated, you feel pressure to choose. I feel more comfortable living in the paradoxes that I've named and laid out, whereas when I started they might have felt like real agitations. At least I see them more clearly after having sketched them for myself and made a place to stand in relationship to them that felt okay enough to last through the course of a book.

Guernica: Your book title, *The Argonauts*, derives from a passage by Roland Barthes about how every time you name something or articulate something, you can imbue that thing with an entirely different meaning, even if you're still calling it by the same name.

Maggie Nelson: Of the many reasons the book is called what it is, it's drawing attention to that naming. Naming the boat the *Argo*, naming the people on the *Argo* the Argonauts. In the parable that Barthes tells about it, all of the parts of the *Argo* can be changed so every part of the ship is no longer the original ship. And yet it's still called the *Argo*, much like our bodies and selves are replacing all the time.

This is back to where we started, talking about writing. Some people who've read the book say, "Wow, you're really down on language," and I think, "If I were really down on language, I wouldn't be trying to do this in language! I'd be doing something else!" I love language. It doesn't bother me that its effects are partial. To me that is very sanity-producing. It would be weird if the effects of language were more than partial, if your whole life existed within your texts. That would be much scarier to me than language being an inadequate tool to represent.

In terms of being changed, I feel grateful for the kind of ongoingness of the conversations I'm able to have, in public, and with friends, and also in my own home.

A lot of the debates in the media—in the *New York Times*, and there was recently a long story in *The New Yorker*—they're often put forward as old-school feminist who depends on category of Woman, up against new moment of trans feminism or trans women demanding access to women's-only spaces, and they're setting these extreme positions up against each other.

One thing I love about being with Harry is that we go back and forth, like sometimes *he's* the old-school lesbian feminist arguing to me, and sometimes *I'm* the old-school feminist. Yet I feel like Harry and I are always at the same table, and most of my friends who disagree vociferously about nearly everything are all still at the same table. It doesn't have to be these straw-man setups that the press loves, where people take each other down in a movement because they just can't see each other's point of view. That's not how people live their lives, and it's not how a robust, queer feminism is going to go forward into the future.

Guernica: So what seems like the next frontier for a robust, queer feminism? How does it move forward?

Maggie Nelson: In the book I talk about Eve Sedgwick and how on one hand she wanted queer to be so big of an umbrella that it basically encompassed everything from radical ecology to Latino immigration, activism, with a total loss of focus on gender and sexuality. And then on the other hand she said, if it ever loses that link, then it's lost! Talk about paradox! For pragmatic reasons, for lessening of violence and for allowing people to live better lives, I think that the march forward for GLBTQ+ rights is a worthwhile one. But for me, hopefully the frontier is alliance-making across all these issues, whereby people can get over whatever prejudices they're holding in order to keep their eyes on making livable lives for people in all states of vulnerability, no matter what their gender, sexuality, race, class, origin, whatever.

I think that alliance-building is happening. You have people like Dean Spade who are working really hard to reformulate issues, to say prison reform is a queer issue. And not just for the sake of queer prisoners, but as an umbrella looking at vulnerable populations and where they're clustered, and how prison reform might address that. I think that kind of alliance-building is totally crucial going into the future.

What do *you* think?

Guernica: Intersectionality, man!

Maggie Nelson: Exactly. That's the name of the game.

Stormbringer

JENNIFER HAIGH // FEBRUARY 16, 2015

In this way Tracy had an edge over the rest of us, despite his girl's name.
His history was a mystery—his family, his temperament, his early failures,
and shames.

MY PARENTS ARE PRACTICAL people, conventional in their thinking. They raised me with the usual ideas about good and evil. One was easily attainable if you obeyed the Commandments, flossed daily, and followed the Golden Rule. The other stemmed from exotic temptations the average person didn't have to worry about.

I met Tracy Pasco in the spring of 1980—in my Pennsylvania hometown, a time of relative optimism and ease. The local industry, coal mining, would in a few years falter and eventually fail completely, and hundreds of families would pick up and leave. At the time no one saw this coming, though we should have: the Mineworkers' dealings with management had grown increasingly shrill. But the union's blind stubbornness was seen, for a long time, as toughness; and my father's job at the mine—he was a shift boss—seemed perfectly secure. Bakerton in 1980 was still a working-class town, neither rich nor poor; its junior high small enough that the arrival of a new pupil, late in the school year, qualified as an event. My class's initial fascination with Tracy was due less to his own qualities than to our intense boredom with each other; by the eighth grade we were all familiar as cousins. Children are ruthless in their recall, particularly when the memory involves some bodily humiliation. Lord help the classmate who threw up in the gymnasium, who wet his pants in kindergarten. His disgrace will follow him all his days. In this way Tracy had an edge over the rest of us, despite his girl's name. His history was a mystery—his family, his temperament, his early failures, and shames.

I'd have called him an ordinary-looking boy—curly hair, freckles, a crooked eyetooth. But females are the real judges of male attractiveness, and my sister, who was not prone to such rhapsodies, once described his eyes as *crystal blue*. Nina was just a year older but miles ahead of me socially. From an early age I recognized her general superiority: the better student, popular in school, chipper, and helpful around the house. She was even good at sports, the one area where I might have dominated. My parents must have regretted not quitting while they were ahead.

That Nina and her high school friends were aware of Tracy Pasco was, to me, a stunning discovery. The girls in my own class tracked him like a pack of hunting dogs. I was too young for a girlfriend, but not for girls. The eighth grade had several pretty ones I studied with more or less equal interest. The Pantheon, I called them: Beth Leggett, Melissa Wyman, Robin Godfrey, Tara Sneed. Their giggling curiosity about Tracy frankly dismayed me, though I hoped to use it to my advantage.

In those days our teachers seated us, unimaginatively, in alphabetical order—Pasco, Patterson—and I saw my opportunity. When Tracy came to class without a pencil or loose-leaf notebook paper, I was quick to offer him mine. Later, when Beth Leggett cornered me in the hallway, I revealed the following facts: Tracy came from an army base in Texas, where his father had been stationed, and was an only child—at the time, a rarity in our town. His mother was dead, his father raised in a farmhouse on Number Nine Road, not far from my own house, where he and Tracy now lived. These few biographical details were all I had to offer, and I'd planned to withhold them as long as possible, doling them out strategically to sustain multiple conversations with multiple girls. Instead I told Beth everything the moment she asked.

"Dead?" she repeated in a whisper. "Nathan, are you sure?" She was strawberry-blond and precociously shapely, with breasts—I might have called them "bosoms"—like a grown woman. I was glad for any excuse to talk to her, even about another boy.

"He wouldn't make that up," I said.

"Well, what did she die of?"

"How should I know?"

Beth glanced over my shoulder. I sensed her interest flagging.

"I'll find out," I said—though how exactly I would do this wasn't clear. Tracy was a quiet boy. Though he looked like an athlete—taller than average, and well-muscled—he hadn't signed up for Boys' Intramurals. In class he sketched or doodled constantly. Other boys drew the same things—cars, boats, dinosaurs, airplanes—but without Tracy's skill.

Once he was caught in the act. Our English teacher that year was a woman named Ginny Seaver—a new hire, fresh out of the state university. I didn't realize at the time just how young she was. She owned a yellow Ford Mustang, the only one in town. Occasionally I saw her driving to school, the windows down, the radio playing the same music I listened to: Electric Light Orchestra, Led Zeppelin, The Who. All these years later, her face is a blank to me. I remember only her hair, worn in the style of a popular TV actress who'd kindly posed in a red swimsuit in order to be displayed on my bedroom wall, animating my puberty. Miss Seaver may have looked nothing like her, beyond the hairdo; but in my erotic imagination they were one and the same.

In class she paced the aisles as she lectured, filling the air with a flowery perfume. One morning she halted beside my desk to look over Tracy's shoulder. "Tracy! Art isn't until fifth period." Even while scolding her tone was gentle, teasing. I noticed everything about her: her bare white arms, the red imprint left by her watchband, a long blond hair clinging to her skirt.

Quickly Tracy closed his notebook. The tips of his ears, I saw, were flaming red.

"Let me see," Miss Seaver said. Grudgingly he opened the notebook. She leaned down and studied it intently. I watched her in a kind of trance, noting the square outline of her bra through the back of her blouse.

"This is very good," she said softly, sounding surprised. "Come see me after class."

"She wanted to look at my drawings," Tracy explained later, as we walked down the hall after the final bell.

I was queasy with jealousy. "What for?"

"What's an Art Fair?"

I explained that it was held every spring at the high school, to showcase the best work by high school students. In rare cases a junior high kid was included. My sister Nina, annoyingly, had been one such prodigy.

Tracy smiled halfway, hiding his crooked tooth. "She was sitting at her desk. I got a good look down her blouse. She has little titties." He opened the notebook under his arm. "I think I got them right."

He flipped to a page at the back of the book. If I close my eyes I can still see it: a pencil sketch of a naked woman, faceless, her arms bound behind her, her body lashed around the middle to a tree. When I recall it now, it's the position that shocks me, though at the time I was mesmerized by the anatomical features: the nipples rendered in meticulous detail, the dark shading between the legs. From what little I'd seen of female nudity (in a neighbor's basement, his dad's collection of old *Playboys*), Tracy's sketch was alarmingly accurate. I stared mutely, overcome by waves of feeling: anger, fascination, jealousy, and shame.

"She didn't see this one. I flipped right past it. I pretended like the pages were stuck together. That was a close call," Tracy said, a note of exhilaration in his voice.

We never talked about the drawing again, but I thought about it a great deal. My own nascent sexual impulses—furtive, anxious—were a rich source of embarrassment. It was unnerving to get a look at someone else's.

Without any great effort on either part, we became friends. For boys that age, it's a simple matter: place them a few times in each other's path, and barring some outsized display of aggression from one or both, they will get along well enough. Our friendship was based on proximity. We lived on the same side of town and fell into a habit of walking together to and from school. One benefit of this arrangement was that girls often walked behind us, close enough to hear our conversation, when there was any, and chime in.

I've tried to remember what we talked about. TV, mainly. (I recall one show we particularly liked, a mid-season replacement, that featured home videos of misbehaving family pets.) More often than they'd have guessed, we discussed our teachers. Like most boys our age, we adopted a smart-aleck stance toward the adults in our lives—their clothing and manner-isms, the idiotic things they said. For me—for most of us, I suspect—it was a hollow pose. That parents and teachers generally liked me had given me, always, a feeling of security and well-being, something I would understand only years later, after I had squandered their regard.

The Art Fair was held in the last week of school, a Tuesday. My family went together, piled into our minivan: my parents up front, behind them Nina and our grandmother. I had the rear-facing seat all to myself. It was, altogether, a familiar scene. For years I'd been dragged to Nina's choral concerts and ballet recitals, her science fairs and spelling bees.

The high school cafeteria had been divided with rows of tall screens. Pinned to them were charcoals and watercolors, etchings and photographs. There were table displays of ceramic pottery, figurines in papier mâché. My sister's drawing hung in the first row, a pen-and-ink sketch of Gram (who'd been brought along, I cynically believed, as living evidence of Nina's artistic talent). Two women teachers stood studying the portrait. When our family approached, with Gram up front, they commented on the likeness.

"Nina, this is just marvelous," one said. Then, lowering her voice, "It should have won a ribbon, in my opinion. An honorable mention, at least."

Nina blushed prettily. She didn't expect to win anything, she insisted. She was only a freshman; she had plenty of time.

Even her humility irked me. "Can we go now?" I asked, but my parents were already ten paces ahead, studying a woodblock print of a sailboat that, in my view, a toddler might have made. The Art Fair, clearly, was going to take all night. I lingered far behind, looking for girls; but the only ones I saw were in high school and thus too terrifying to talk to. Still, they were more interesting than calligraphy or macramé.

I stopped to study a pencil drawing of an airplane. A bright red ribbon was pinned beside it. The picture was unsigned, but clearly labeled: *Tracy Pasco, Grade 8*. On the surrounding wall were other sketches, by juniors and seniors mostly. The only eighth grader in the entire show had won second place! Later, on the drive home, I crowed as though it were my own personal triumph. Even Nina hadn't won a ribbon at that age.

I congratulated Tracy the next morning as we were walking to school. "Second place, that's unbelievable. The first place drawing was by a senior. A *senior,*" I repeated for emphasis. "Yours was better, though."

It was raining, I remember. My mom had made me wear a slicker, but Tracy's shirt was getting wet. By the time we got to school it would be plastered to his back.

He stared at me as though I'd lost my mind.

"My 747 was in the Art Fair?" His face reddened. "She asked me if I wanted to be in it. I didn't know what it was, so I told her no."

It took me a moment to understand that he meant Miss Seaver. "Maybe she wanted to surprise you."

"How did she get my picture?"

"Mrs. Neugebauer"—the art teacher—"must have given it to her." I stared at him, mystified. Honestly, why did it matter? Tracy had won a contest he hadn't even entered. There was no greater victory in life.

I remember him flushed and tongue-tied. I remember being a little afraid, because he looked ready to pop me one.

"I told her no," he said.

"I was never all that good," Nina says now—still, after everything, modest to the core. "Certain people just have it, this way of seeing. I didn't. I was diligent. And, you know, over-praised."

She fumbles for the remote control, which is not actually remote—it's attached to the bed by a thick electrical cord—and finds the button to raise her feet. The art supplies I brought last time—a thick pad and pastels, still in their shrink-wrapped box—lie on the wheeled table beside the bed. A nurse or Nina herself must move them three times a day, so Nina can eat her meals.

"I hit a point where I just stopped improving. Other people kept getting better, but I was as good as I was ever going to get. Does this thing even work?" She stabs repeatedly at the call button.

"Practice will take you a long way. Not the whole way. That was a painful thing to learn."

"Not so hard, maybe." I take the remote from her hand and gently press the call button. This time there is a faint beep in the distance, at the nurse's station down the hall.

School ended just after Memorial Day, thanks to a mild winter. In other years we'd made up snow days halfway through June. The final day of the term was celebrated with Field Day, an annual tradition: a picnic lunch, an outdoor talent show, all manner of highly structured fun on the lawn behind the school. When I think of it now, I'm struck by the great pains taken for our happiness and amusement, the poor teachers charged with policing our preteen horseplay—for them, a long and tedious day. Naturally we were ungrateful, the boys especially. Year after year we griped about the morning's indignities—dodge ball, sack races, an endless series of inane games even girls could play. We clamored for a full day of base-ball. It seemed the height of injustice that our bats and gloves were with-held until noon.

"Sorry, guys," said Miss Seaver, teasing us a little. She was dressed for the occasion—thrillingly, to me—in jeans and a t-shirt, wooden clogs on her feet. "Everybody plays."

In homeroom we were assigned teams for tug-of-war and the three-legged race. We were an odd number, because Tracy's desk was empty. Miss Seaver seemed perplexed, frowning as she marked him absent. Nobody ever missed Field Day.

"Where is he?" Beth Leggett whispered to me.

"How should I know?" I'd left for school at the usual time and waited at the foot of his driveway, but Tracy had not appeared. "Home sick, I guess."

My recollections of the day are generically pleasant—drawn, likely, from several Field Days and averaged into a single one. At three o'clock we were summoned into the shadowy building, to our respective homerooms, for the final dismissal. Like every year, it was a moment of high drama.

Sunburned, breathless, joyously grass-stained, we waited for the bell. When it came we charged for the door, the whole throng of us bursting out of the school building into the sunlight. I remember a delirious sense of freedom, the muscular thrill of summer vacation upon me at last. Then, abruptly, a sharp confusion: a bunch of kids had congregated near the fence, staring at something in the faculty parking lot.

"What happened?" I asked—nonsensically, as though the scene required some interpretation.

A teacher's car—I recognized it as Miss Seaver's yellow Mustang—had been vandalized. Spray-painted across the driver's side panel, in tall jagged capitals, was a word I'd heard only in whispers. I had never said it aloud, myself.

We stood gaping as Mr. Kovacs, one of our few male teachers, pushed his way through the crowd. Later I wondered who had summoned him, and how. How I myself would have articulated it: *Somebody trashed Miss Seaver's car.* That, of course, didn't begin to cover it. The word was the thing. Somebody had written that word.

"What's all the commotion?" he said.

In my memory, there was a sudden silence as Miss Seaver came up behind him. Someone, apparently, had summoned her too.

"Ginny, don't look," said Mr. Kovacs, but of course she'd already seen it. Red-faced, her eyes filling, she turned away and walked back toward the school. You have to admire that. She was just twenty-three, a girl really. And yet some teacherly decorum (or maybe just her wooden clogs) kept her from running, which she must surely have wanted to do.

Ginny, don't look. It startled me, then, to hear a teacher addressed by her first name. In the context of the day's other, greater astonishments, it's hard to believe I found this shocking, but I did.

"The police are coming," Mr. Kovacs told us. "They'll be here any minute, so get moving. We can't have the whole eighth grade standing in their way."

❥❥❥

"You missed everything," I said, breathless.

I was standing on Tracy's front porch, a first. Normally I waited at the foot of the gravel driveway. That afternoon I couldn't wait.

He looked unsurprised to see me. He pushed open the screen door and took a couple steps back—meaning, I guessed, that I was invited in.

The house was dark inside, the walls covered in scarred wood paneling. I barely noticed, caught up in the anticipation of what I was about to say. He led me into the kitchen, where something crunched beneath my feet. Tracy or someone had been eating peanuts. The floor was littered with their shells.

We sat at the kitchen table, gray Formica. Beneath my elbow was a crusty stain, mustard maybe. "You'll never guess what happened."

The condition of the house shocked me, though I tried to hide it. The stovetop was ominously blackened, as though it had seen a fire or two; the burners covered in yellowed tinfoil that looked worse than the stove. Near the refrigerator was an actual hole in the linoleum, the size of a man's shoe.

"I bet I will," Tracy said.

I stared at him a long moment, the realization dawning.

"Imagine her driving home in that thing," Tracy said, and against my will I pictured it: Miss Seaver at the wheel of the yellow Mustang, the word *CUNT* big as life on the driver's side door. "What a riot."

A tiny smile pulled at his lips.

I can still recall the odor of the place. At that age I enjoyed the smell of other people's houses, the exotic contrast with my own, which smelled of cleaning products and my mother's cooking. Tracy's house had a smell like nothing I'd encountered, cigarettes and wet dog and other things I couldn't identify.

Outside a car idled loudly.

"You should go," said Tracy. "That's my dad."

I followed him to the screen door. In the gravel driveway was the battered pickup truck I'd often seen there. Behind the wheel sat a skinny guy with an extravagant mustache, his face deeply tanned. He was younger than my own father and appeared to be dead asleep, though he'd been driving just a minute ago. This was as close as I would ever get to Tracy's dad.

"Is he sleeping?" I whispered.

"Who cares," Tracy said, opening the door.

"About the car. I won't tell anyone." I made the promise automatically—child enough, still, that not-telling was a point of honor. Only later did I realize he hadn't asked me not to.

"I know," he said.

That summer I distanced myself from Tracy. It was easy to do, without the daily walk to school. Once or twice, riding past his house in my parents' van, I saw him pushing a lawnmower. I waved, and he waved back, and that was the extent of our communication.

I didn't tell. More strikingly, I hadn't even asked why he'd done it. I suppose I knew the reason, or thought I did: he did it because he hated her. *Why* he hated her was an entirely different question, one my young self would have been hesitant—embarrassed, somehow—to ask.

I never saw Miss Seaver again. Nobody did; she moved away from Bakerton and was not heard from. Now, probably, she is Mrs. Somebody, her maiden name retired like a star ballplayer's number. Even today, with the whole world plugged into computer networks, women's identities are more fluid than men's. Slippery creatures, shape-shifters. If they wish to be, they are very easily lost.

She never drove that car again. The town cop, a man named Andy Carnicella, escorted her home that terrible afternoon. The yellow Mustang was repainted dark green and sold quickly—this according to Tara Sneed, whose father owned the used car lot in town.

〜

In high school everything shifted. Fortunes rose, fortunes fell. I joined the track team and did respectably in the long-distance, a sport that demanded no special talent beyond an unusual tolerance for boredom. Beth Leggett continued her reign as prettiest girl, but Tracy Pasco was no longer of interest to her or anyone else. His eyes might have been crystal blue, but whatever handsomeness he'd possessed had been, in a single summer, dramatically ruined, in the form of truly disfiguring acne. At that age most of us had pimples, but Tracy's were the worst I'd seen. From a distance—the only way I ever saw him—his face looked almost purple, and in spite of everything I felt sorry for him. Through a conspiracy of malevolent hormones, he had lost the attention of the Pantheon, which was surely worse than never having had it.

He ran with a rough crowd. At school they were largely invisible. I saw them mainly on the school bus, long-haired punks who monopolized the rear seats, silently spitting tobacco into cones of notebook paper. Dressed, always, in concert t-shirts: Iron Maiden, Black Sabbath, bands I rejected unequivocally. It seems a foolish distinction now, but their taste in music was, at the time, enough to make Tracy and his friends irrelevant.

I would have put him out of my mind entirely, if not for my sister. One afternoon during my junior year, I'd boarded the team bus—we were about to leave for an after-school track meet—and glanced out the window to see Tracy and Nina walking together through the deserted school corridor. (Bakerton High's only notable architectural feature was a bank of large windows along the west side of the building.) This was so utterly impossible that I blamed my vision, the blinding glare of the afternoon sun.

Then, a week later, I saw them again.

"I like him," Nina said when I grilled her about it. "He's a very talented artist. Not that you would care about that."

She was right; I didn't. "He's a creep. I'd stay away if I were you."

"Since when do you care who I talk to?" She looked genuinely puzzled. "Anyway, I thought you guys were friends."

"He's not my friend," I said.

"I never even knew him," Nina claims now. "Certainly we never dated."

I question her memory, but not her honesty. She truly believes everything she says. Their one date, to a Sadie Hawkins dance, ended badly, with Tracy driving his dad's truck into a telephone pole. Tracy was unhurt, but Nina came home bruised and bleeding. She was forbidden ever to get into a car with him again, and dutiful daughter that she was, she readily agreed.

After high school I went on to the state university. Like a number of our classmates, Tracy joined the Navy—with the mines no longer hiring, there was nothing left in town for them to do. I didn't see him for many years, though he crossed my mind occasionally—uneasily, like a shameful secret from my past.

My performance at the state university was, I will admit, less than stellar. After many false starts, I settled on a business major and left, with no diploma, after five years. Due to a series of misadventures I won't go into, I found myself living, at age thirty-four, above my parents' garage, in the in-law apartment Gram had inhabited until she died. I paid utilities but no actual rent, an arrangement my parents agreed to when I promised to make double payments on my student loan. A job of any kind was by then a rare commodity in town, and I felt lucky to be driving a truck for Anheuser-Busch, delivering kegs and cases to the local bars.

Late one summer afternoon, I'd just finished my last delivery—the Commercial Hotel—when a guy at the bar called my name.

"Hey. Patterson."

It took me a moment to place him. His hairline had receded, and what was left had been buzzed short. His skin had cleared up and he looked very fit, nearly muscle-bound, as though he spent considerable time in the gym. If not for the crooked eyetooth I might not have recognized him. He looked older than I did, or was, or felt.

"Tracy," I said. "How've you been?"

He took cigarettes from his pocket and mouthed one from the pack. "I'm surprised to see you back here."

"I live here. You know, for now."

"Let me buy you a beer. My dad died." Tracy lit up, waving out the match as though it annoyed him. "I came to clear out the house."

"I'm sorry."

"It was a couple months ago," he said, as though this negated any possibility of grief.

We drank, and Tracy told me about his life. In the service he'd trained as an electrician, a trade he still practiced sporadically. With his Navy pension—he had fifteen years—he could afford to work only when he felt like it. That he'd never married did not surprise me. He owned a little house in western Montana—a shack, he called it—on twenty acres. He'd driven east, I-90 to I-80, over two weeks' time, stopping here and there in towns along the way: Gillette, Wyoming; Sioux Falls, South Dakota. I'm almost certain he mentioned those places by name. To me they sounded magical, a part of the world I had never seen.

Glad for someone to drink with, I lingered longer than I should have. We were on our third or fourth beer when the two women came into the bar, a blond and a redhead. Tracy's eyes followed them avidly. "Holy shit, is that Beth Leggett?"

"Beth Vance now, but yeah."

"I almost didn't recognize her." Tracy studied her openly. She was still beautiful, though after three kids no longer quite so shapely. "She got married?"

"And divorced," I said.

A moment later Beth spotted us. "Nathan!" She charged across the bar in our direction, smiling brightly. Her enthusiasm was puzzling, given that I saw her every Friday afternoon at Saxon Savings, where she'd worked since high school.

"Back in a minute," Tracy mumbled. "I need to make a phone call."

Beth approached looking crestfallen. "Where did your friend go?"

She hadn't recognized Tracy; she'd simply been drawn to him. In that moment I understood the basic facts: Tracy was handsome and Beth was single. It was junior high all over again.

"He had to make a phone call."

She glanced uncertainly at her red-haired friend, waiting at the other end of the bar. "We're going to have dinner, but maybe we can all have a drink afterward?"

"Sure," I said.

I watched her follow the other woman into the dining room. A moment later Tracy reappeared.

"I can't believe that's her," he said.

"In the flesh. She wants to have a drink with us later." I drained my glass. "The Pantheon. That's what I used to call them, Beth and Tara and Melissa. Wyman, remember? She's married now. She was home at Christmas for a visit."

"How'd she look?"

"Good," I said.

"How's your sister?"

I felt a sudden chill.

"She's fine." There was much more to say, but I wasn't about to say it. At art school Nina had excelled globally, until she hadn't. Her recent history was a family matter, something we didn't discuss with strangers. My parents, when asked about her, still bragged shamelessly, their pride in her a habit they couldn't break.

Tracy smiled, hiding his crooked tooth. "I always thought you scared her off me."

I should have excused myself then, and almost did. The lie—*I have an early morning tomorrow*—was ready on my lips.

Instead a remarkable thing happened. Tracy touched his index finger to his nostril.

"Wanna get high?" he said.

At this point in the story an explanation is in order. My drug use, at that time, was the defining feature of my life. It wasn't the only reason for my lackluster academic career, my spotty work history, my strained relations with my parents; but it was the dominant one. Somehow Tracy had divined this, or maybe he hadn't. Maybe he'd have asked the same question of anyone he drank with, as I would have in those days. A couple of drinks always made me crave.

Wanna get high?

Today, some years sober, I can admit that those three words roused me—still do—like a defibrillator, an intoxicating jolt to the heart.

I followed Tracy into the parking lot, to a Dodge Ram pickup with Montana plates. We rode in silence out Number Twelve Road, the rusting skeleton of the old Twelve barely visible in the twilight. Without asking I took one of his cigarettes.

"I thought you didn't smoke," Tracy said.

At Garman Lake he pulled off the road and parked. From the glove box he took a compact disc—Deep Purple, *Stormbringer.* His musical taste, apparently, hadn't evolved since high school.

"The bitch got fat," he said.

It took me a moment to understand what he was talking about. I didn't see how such a thing was possible, and yet for a horrible moment I thought he meant Nina.

"Beth Leggett. I always knew she would." He cut two slender lines with a credit card and took a powerful snort. "I used to think about how I'd do her. A tire iron, I thought, but now she's too fat to feel it. A sledgehammer, maybe." He bent over the CD case and inhaled mightily. "I'd save the tire iron for Melissa Wyman. A tire iron right upside the head."

I lit a fresh cigarette with the last one, aware of my hand shaking. A fire whistle blew in the distance. I leaned over the CD case and inhaled.

"Come on, Patterson! Tell me you never thought about it."

"I never did," I said.

I live in Virginia now, the DC suburbs. After rehab I went back to school—not college but something more in line with my abilities—and in the space of a year learned to write computer code, got hired at a software company, and married a woman, also sober, who is the love of my life. Though my relationship with my parents remains tense, I go back to Bakerton every month or two, to visit Nina. She is able, mainly, to live on her own, in the garage apartment I used to inhabit. If she's feeling well, we might spend a pleasant evening at her kitchen table drinking peppermint tea and reminiscing about the past.

She has no memory of the night she came home bruised and bleeding. A car accident, she said, and everyone believed her, because back then Nina always told the truth.

Her breakdown had nothing to do with Tracy Pasco, nothing much even to do with her failure as an artist. Her symptoms came on gradually her final year in art school, the usual age of onset, though it took a couple of years to identify their cause. She is lucky, as schizophrenics go, in that her delusions are largely controlled by medication, though the drugs have left her foggy, lethargic, and obese. Her memory, as I have said, is unreliable, and the weight gain is demoralizing. Periodically she becomes so disgusted that she stops taking her medication, with predictable results.

She is my earliest friend, keeper of my secrets—witness to my early failures and shames, and a few of the recent ones. She is no symbol of lost promise, no symbol of anything, and yet seeing her reminds me of a particular time in our lives when potential seemed to be everywhere: in every art class a budding Picasso, a young Katharine Hepburn in every cringe-inducing school play. These prodigies—Nina was one of them—are unfairly blessed and cursed. The lucky ones will disappear into ordinary lives, doting mothers and proud fathers, coaches and teachers paid to nurture the next generation's false hope. This is no middle-class affectation; Bakerton—once solidly working-class and now unworking, a town industry has abandoned—runs on the same illusion. It is a generous fiction like the Tooth Fairy or Santa Claus, an elaborate ruse in which whole communities are complicit, fueled by wishfulness and misguided love.

I won't tell, I said, and for a long time I didn't.

Sober now, I follow the news reports. I will never know if Tracy has done the things he's accused of. (The nurse in Gillette, strangled with her stockings; the kindergarten teacher in Sioux Falls, beaten with a blunt object. A tire iron, the authorities believe, though the weapon was never found.) Tracy has never been convicted of anything. A grand jury refused even to indict him. He is a free man.

Gillette, Wyoming. Sioux Falls, South Dakota. He mentioned those places by name, as though he wanted me to know.

The night at Garman Lake ended uneventfully. Tracy drove me back to my apartment above the garage, where I lay awake for many hours with a pounding heart. The next morning—bleary, exhausted—I drove straight to Wellways, nearly three hundred miles. This time I stayed the full thirty days—and, in Group, finally broke my promise to Tracy.

I told.

His drawing of Miss Seaver, his attack on her yellow Mustang: out of shame or fear or some reflexive, senseless loyalty, I'd carried these secrets for more than twenty years. Confessing was a profound relief, a crucial step in my recovery; but it was essentially a selfish act. Had I come clean back in 1980, to a parent or teacher, Tracy might have been rescued, given the help he needed (though in Bakerton, then or now, it's hard to imagine that happening, as several in Group pointed out). At minimum he'd have been identified; he'd have a record somewhere. Someone—the omnipotent authorities, the people who protect us—would be watching him. Or so I would like to believe.

What he did or didn't do to Nina. Another truth I will never know.

Garman Lake has become, for me, a haunted place. I realize this is irratio-
nal. Beth Leggett, Melissa Wyman, Robin Godfrey, Tara Sneed: each of
these women is still very much alive.

Tracy Pasco lives two thousand miles away, in a secluded shack in western
Montana. In my dreams I see him driving, stopping here and there in
towns along the way.

The End of Borrowed Time

MASHA GESSEN // EXCLUSIVE

I have reached that age when the women of my family began measuring their lives in months rather than whole years.

"**M**AYBE I SHOULD just become a man," I thought, riding my bike, about midway across the George Washington Bridge. Then, in the shorthand way of memory, I flashed back to sitting on the porch of my father's house in Newton, Massachusetts, in August 1992, a day or two after my mother died. A friend had driven down from Vermont to sit with me. She was another young Jewish dyke whose mother had died of breast cancer, so we didn't have to say much: we just sat. Afterward, we lost touch, and when I next heard from this friend a dozen years later, he was a man. He told me that transitioning had been a relief in part because he had gotten rid of the parts of the body that had killed his mother and could kill him. This friend looked really good as a guy. I imagined I might too. Then I thought about my kids, my friends, sex, and even the TV series *Transparent,* all of which reminded me that transitioning would require more of a commitment than just wanting to put a good spin on surgical menopause. By the time I got to the Manhattan side of the bridge, I was back where I had started: I took pleasure in my androgyny, but I was also extremely attached to what the women in my family, when they were alive, used to call the "woman parts"—and I had just scheduled surgery to remove them.

Keeping my "woman parts" had for some time been a matter of principle and a point of pride with me. I learned nearly a dozen years ago that I carry a mutation in the BRCA1 gene, the mutation that correlates with a vastly increased risk of breast and ovarian cancer. This was back in the prehistoric age of genetic testing, before 23andMe and Angelina Jolie made my mutation famous. The doctors and genetic counselors told me to have my ovaries surgically removed and gently suggested I consider a preventive mastectomy as well. I did a lot of research and concluded that they were wrong: I should have my breasts removed, to reduce my chances of developing breast cancer from near-certain to almost-none, but I should keep my ovaries to ensure overall good physical, mental, and sexual health, which I felt outweighed the risk of my developing ovarian cancer. That risk is estimated at roughly 50 percent by the age of seventy, for those with the mutation, and with every year I've kept my ovaries the likelihood of getting sick has grown.

I did my due diligence and then some in researching my options. I interviewed oncologists, surgeons, survivors, the lexically suspect "previvors," and even a behavioral economist in order to describe, define, calculate, and feel my risk. I had both of my breasts removed in 2005, and I kept my ovaries.

I have written a series of articles and a book about medical genetics, drawing in part on my own experience. Over the years, a couple of people have complimented me on my brave decision to buck medical wisdom and keep my ovaries, and dozens of people have criticized, even berated me for it. I've had people stand up at readings to tell me what to do with my woman parts; I've had doctors whom I called as a reporter start offering me unsolicited, and invasive, medical advice. All of this served to make me even more attached to my ovaries.

Their reasoning was straightforward. Ovarian cancer is virtually impossible to diagnose before it advances so far as to become incurable. It is barely even treatable. It is almost universally deadly. But removing your ovaries and fallopian tubes reduces the risk of developing the cancer drastically (it doesn't eliminate it completely—sometimes the cancer starts in the peritoneum anyway). My counterarguments were solid. The ovaries produce hormones essential for the functioning of a woman's entire body. Without them, you are likely to develop high blood pressure, heart disease, osteoporosis, depression, cognitive problems, and sexual dysfunction, such as loss of libido and of the ability to enjoy sex (I am specifying the sorts of sexual dysfunction I mean because doctors of both genders often refer to vaginal dryness as the only worrisome sex-related side effect of removing the ovaries). The doctors recommending preventive surgery, I argued, were concerned with preventing ovarian cancer but not with keeping me healthy overall. Their perspective was further skewed by the relative simplicity of the surgery—the ovaries can be removed on an outpatient basis. By forgoing their seemingly easy solution, I was choosing long-term health.

I was also doing something I had learned as an AIDS activist and journalist in the '80s: I was educating and empowering myself. I found a side door to a study of screening methods for ovarian cancer: I've paid to have my blood drawn and analyzed for a set of markers every eight months for a number of years, and the researchers have told me, unofficially, that they think I am still healthy.

And I have been betting against time. Cancer medicine is advancing by leaps and bounds. I figured that if I held out long enough, there would be a cure or at least an effective treatment for ovarian cancer. They did, after all, find the drugs to treat AIDS.

But still nothing. There are indeed more drugs available now than ten years ago, but the cancer remains nearly as deadly as it was. And my risk continues to grow.

I am now forty-eight and a half years old: I have reached that age when the women of my family began measuring their lives in months rather than whole years, as people do in the year or two after birth and in the short time leading up to death. By the time my mother was my age, she was dying. By the time her aunt was my age, she had ovarian cancer, though she didn't know she did. Studies show that in my generation women with the mutation develop their cancers on average seven and a half years earlier than did their female relatives of the previous generation. That would mean I've used up about seven and a half years of borrowed time already.

The phrase "borrowed time" comes from a book by Paul Monette, one of several men who wrote brilliantly about AIDS in the '80s and '90s. Their writing is permeated with a sense of rage and bitterness at the unfairness of their looming early deaths—a sense I very much shared at the time. Larry Kramer called the AIDS epidemic a holocaust. Vito Russo said in 1988 that if he was dying of anything, he was dying of homophobia and racism. Back then only a tiny, meek voice in my head objected, "But you are dying of a virus! People have been dying of viruses forever, and the only things exceptional about this plague are that it has come after a generation or so when people in the West weren't dying in pandemics, and also that it has affected people, many of whom are, but for their sexual orientation, so privileged they thought they had the right to live forever." When my mother died, at the height of the AIDS epidemic, in a year when I attended uncounted funerals, I don't remember thinking that she died of anything other than a randomly occurring cancer. Years later, I learned it wasn't exactly random: she carried the mutation. I wonder whether, if the hereditary-cancer activist community was, in its indignation and sense of entitlement, more like the AIDS activist community there would be a cure for ovarian cancer by now. As it is there are only excellent online resources for information and support.

Ovarian cancer specialists in Manhattan are few, scheduled months in advance, and highly selective about their patients. Most of them require a diagnosis of ovarian cancer before they'll agree to see you. This is obviously problematic: ovarian cancer is notoriously difficult to diagnose, so the chances of a non-specialist catching it early are less than negligible. Add that bit of Catch-22 to the long list of reasons to remove your ovaries. Things are a little easier across the Hudson: an ovarian cancer specialist there agreed to see me on a few weeks' notice in April 2015, and merely on the basis of my mutation.

Little had changed in the conversation in the more than ten years since I had last seriously considered my options. The doctor still used the standard phrase, a phrase that has driven me crazy, about how an oophorectomy is recommended "once a woman has completed her child-bearing"—as though child-bearing were the sole function of the woman parts. She used the other standard phrases too, about the cancer being virtually undiagnosable and generally incurable, about my risk for developing it being frighteningly high. She sounded almost desperate. And when I finally asked her to schedule the surgery, she thanked me. She touched me on the shoulder and said, "You are doing the right thing."

I think I am. What's changed isn't the role the ovaries play in the body—it's my risk. Most women with a mutation (mine is only the best-studied and apparently nastiest of a number of deliterious mutations in the BRCA gene) are diagnosed with the cancer in their fifties. I'm glad I didn't have the surgery when the doctors were recommending it a decade ago—my ovaries and I have had a good run—but my borrowed time has come to an end.

The doctor told me she could start me on hormone replacement thera-
py on the day of the surgery and promised that other patients who have
chosen that course "feel exactly the same" as they did before. I know I
will feel different, of course. I will have undergone surgical menopause—
which will instantly remove hormones from the body—and this will im-
mediately be alleviated by a constant stream of replacement hormones.
But I was enjoying my perimenopause. It's true. I started having hot flashes
a few months ago, and I found them weird and fascinating, if sometimes
inconvenient (as a cyclist, I often carry a fresh shirt in my bag anyway).
I wondered why women only ever complain about hot flashes. Come to
think of it, women generally complain about the bodily expressions of
being female, like having a cycle. When have you ever heard a woman
praise the first week or two after her period, all the energy and the feeling
of litheness that come then? When have you ever heard a woman say, "I
can't wait for the middle of the month, when everything feels like sex"?
It is as though women notice their bodies—or at least talk about noticing
their bodies—only when they are bloated and crampy.

Left to their own devices, my ovaries would have taken the next five years
or so to wind down. My period would have started coming at irregular
intervals. I'd have continued having hot flashes and any number of the
other unpleasant symptoms of perimenopause—the Internet supplies lists
of a hundred or so, including insomnia, depression, weight gain, gastro-
intestinal problems, and memory lapses. It would have been interesting to
go down that road and, with any luck, to experience some of the strange
and pleasant signs of natural menopause that no one bothers to describe.
Even after menopause ended, my ovaries would still have produced minute
amounts of hormones, which might or might not have had any bearing on
the way the body felt. But in my case, the change will be drastic: I will go
from perimenopausal to postmenopausal overnight, or over the course of
a few hours of drug-induced sleep, and then I will have to hope that the
pharmaceutical hormonal concoctions keep me from feeling too devas-
tated, or too different.

As I start the last complete menstrual cycle of my life, I can say that I've
liked having a body that produces hormones. I would have liked going
through their gradual decline, observing the tricks my body is capable of—
like constantly resetting its thermostat. But then, my chances of seeing that
to the end were never very good. My mother didn't live to see her natural

menopause; for that reason, I don't know at what age mine might have happened (genetics largely determine that age). I also don't know when I might go gray: my mother never did—by the time she was my age, she had lost her hair to chemo. If no cancer is found once my ovaries, fallopian tubes, and uterus are removed and dissected on June 22, I will have a good chance of seeing what I look like with gray hair. The nature of my transition seems to be this: I am taking a shortcut to an older age in an attempt to get to experience it at all.

The Body

BOSTON GORDON // MARCH 16, 2015

*Because people you know sometimes cut theirs /
off so as not to look like you.*

There is of course the cutting of the body.
Lean away from that for a minute. Stand
in the middle of a shack on fabric row
and browse the cardboard bricks wrapped
in lace and taffeta. You can feel the taffeta
like the bustle skirt thrown at you from stage
at the burlesque show. Where you sweat
under orange show lights and notice the ordinary
nature of breasts—watch the sequins swept aside.
The breasts are bags of wine. Your breasts
are hanging hunks that you often relate to cutting.
Because people you know sometimes cut theirs
off so as not to look like you. You being a bust
and ass and legs that make a man say *Ahem,*
miss what're you trying to tell me with those legs?
You're shocked because your boyfriend fucks
you like a real man, but everyone is looking
at your hormonal fat, your body like a melting
sculpture. So you tie your shoes or lock your bike
and look down and think about the cutting.
Think that even in another body, even after
that barter with the mud wasp and surgeon,
you would still not be settled. Not just this
body, but all body. So in the fabric store
the shears make that good sound like rubbing

two nickels together and you're back
to the six yards of burlap unfolding
on the countertop and the body steps away
from cut. Cut. It refuses to be just a body.

You, Disappearing

ALEXANDRA KLEEMAN // SEPTEMBER 15, 2014

The apocalypse was quiet. It had a way about it, a certain charm. It could be called graceful. It was taking a long time.

WHEN I WENT DOWNSTAIRS this morning and found Cookie missing, I knew that official emergency procedure called for me to phone all the information in to the Bureau of Disappearances. At the prompting of the prerecorded voice, I would enter my social security number and zip code. I would press "2" to report the sudden absence of an animal, "3" for "domestic animal," and then at the sound of the tone I would speak the word "cat" clearly and audibly into the telephone receiver. The woman's voice would then give a short parametric definition of a cat, and if this definition matched my missing item, I could press the pound sign to record a fifteen-second description. A three-note melody would let me know that my claim had been filed, and then that lovely prerecorded voice would read out my assigned case number, along with some instructions on how to update or cancel my claim.

Instead, I picked up the phone and pushed your number into it. I was always telling you about problems you couldn't fix, as though multiplying badness could dilute it.

"Cookie's gone," I said, and waited for your response.

There was a pause on the other end of the line.

"Have you phoned it in?" you asked. Your voice was casual, like it was someone else's pet entirely, a pet from a faraway land owned by people we'd never meet.

"I didn't," I said. "I'm kind of depressed," I added. I was often depressed, but now we all had better reasons to be.

"I'm sorry," you said back.

"Cookie loved to chew on wires," I said.

"I know," you said. You didn't say you wished you could be here. I didn't say it either.

There was nothing more to say. I hung up the phone. Sometimes I dialed you back right away just to hear you pick up and know that your hands were, at that very moment, resting on a chunk of plastic that threaded its way delicately to me over hundreds of miles of wire and cord. To know that even though your voice had disappeared, you had not yet. But recently I hadn't been allowing myself any callbacks. I was getting more afraid of the day when you wouldn't pick up.

The apocalypse was quiet. It had a way about it, a certain charm. It could be called graceful. It was taking a long time.

People prepared for an apocalypse that they could take up arms against, bunker down with. People hoarded filtered water, canned corn, dry milk, batteries. They published books on how to get things done in the new post-world, a world that they always imagined as being much like our own, only missing one or two key things. They might imagine, for example, that survivors would reemerge onto a planet stripped of all vegetable and plant life. First, the animals would grow vicious and then starve. It would be important to hoard as many of these animals as possible, pack them in salt and hide them away to keep. You'd want to have a supply of emergency seed to grow in a secure location, maybe using sterilized soil that you had already hoarded. Then you'd want to gather a crew. One muscleman with a heart of gold, a scientist type, an engineer, a child, and somebody that you thought maybe you could love, if you survived long enough to love them.

Nobody thought the apocalypse would be so polite and quirky. Things just popped out of existence, like they had forgotten all about themselves. Now when you misplaced your keys, you didn't go looking for them. Maybe you went to your landlord and asked for the spare set, took them to the hardware store and made two copies this time, an extra in case the disappearing wasn't a one-off but part of a trend. Or maybe you took this as a sign and decided to leave instead, walked out directionless into the world to find your own vanishing point, which meant moving to Chicago to stay with your brother, who still had the keys to his house and a spare set to give to you.

It was cute the way this apocalypse zapped things out of existence, one by one. It was so clean and easy, like clicking on a little box to close an Internet browser window. It had a sense of humor: a fat man walking down the street lined with small abandoned shops would look down and find that his trousers had vanished, baring his out-of-season Halloween boxers to the public. That kind of humor.

Videos of things like this used to show up all the time on the Internet, until the Internet went.

I thought I would visit the Ferris wheel at the pier before it vanished. I didn't know when it would go. I had the idea that I could try to be the last person ever to visit it, but that would require a lot of work, a lot of waiting around and watching, and there were things to do even in the time of last things. I put two apples in a plastic bag and headed out the door, which I didn't lock even though it would have been easy to do. I took the elevator down to the first floor and walked on East Jackson Drive to the edge of the water, then up along the highway holding onto the handrail with one gloved hand. A sedan full of teenagers drove by, and one of them shouted a blurry word at me that sounded like it had once been a taunt. It was winter, but it wasn't so cold. There was less weather, the same way there was less of everything. This day resembled the day before: sleepy air and wan blue sky, no clouds but a vague foggy white that might just have been a thinning of the atmosphere.

At the pier I saw the seagulls huddling together on the boardwalk, pressing their dirty white bodies up against each other. They seemed able to eat anything—crusts, rinds, paper napkins. They were made to survive, even in a fading world that was unthinking itself faster than we could fill it back up with our trash. One seagull worked to swallow a little plastic toy lion, snapping its beak down on it with blunt patience. The Ferris wheel loomed up big behind them at the end of the pier, though it wasn't as big as it had seemed the first time I saw it. The wheel was missing spokes at random, and some of the red seating cars had gone. It looked like the mouth of someone who had been punched over and over again in the face.

I walked over to it, right out in the open, but nobody saw me. When I reached the base the controls were all locked up. It had a big goofy lever that you could set to different speeds, like in a cartoon. I ducked the chain and climbed into the ground-level car, the one in starting position, and staggered from one side of the car to the other to try to make it swing, but it wasn't any fun. Then I sat facing the water and put down the guardrail. The lake licked at the shore the way it used to. When water disappears, other water rushes in right away to take its place, you never see any kind of hole or gap. Then when I reached into my plastic bag, I only had one apple.

This apocalypse disappears objects of all kinds, and it swallows memories whole too. I didn't want to be around you when you forgot me. I didn't want to watch it fall out of your head so easily, I was hoping to forget you first. But sometimes I second-guessed that. Then I called you and tried to be angry, as though you were the one who had been so afraid of being forgotten that you needed to move out of the apartment, out of the city and into another city where nothing had any familiarity to start with, or any familiarity to lose. I thought you might have forgotten who did what to whom, but you haven't yet.

When the first things began to disappear it had looked funny, like a continuity slip-up in a bad movie. You and I would make sound effects for them, shouting "poof!" or "boink!" as some flowers blinked themselves out of existence. This was how we'd make each other laugh. In those days the world still looked full, even though it was emptying fast. Then too many things vanished to keep making the sounds: we saw it was sad that anything in the world had gone and could not return. You joked around, saying there'd be fewer chores, our lives would clean up after themselves for a change, but still you went on doing the dishes, vacuuming the little spaces around and under the furniture, putting on a fresh shirt every day, making the bed. You folded cups out of paper for us to drink from when the glasses went away, and when the paper went you used the nice cloth napkins, which worked badly. You were the sort of person that keeps it all going, and I was the other kind.

This became clear two weeks after the first vanishings, when the news stations named it "The Disappocalypse." On the day they called it irreversible, I walked out of the office just before lunch. I didn't tell anyone where I was going, I didn't reply to the e-mails asking whether we wanted to cancel our health insurance and cash out retirement plans. I knew I wouldn't be coming back. The subway was shut down so I walked all the way to our apartment on Myrtle Avenue, across the Brooklyn Bridge to the Flatbush Extension. On that day the world still felt crowded. The sky above was pure undiluted blue, thick enough to mask how much emptiness lay behind it, out past the atmosphere. Cars were lined up on the bridge, bumper to bumper. Drivers honked sporadically, without aggression, like migrating geese.

When I got home it was late afternoon and you'd be back by six-thirty. I tried reading the newspaper but I'd read all I could stand about the vanishing, and the other sections had been thinning out, some with blank patches nobody bothered to fill where the color of the paper showed through grayish and soft. Then it was seven-thirty, and eight, and still you weren't around. I gave Cookie her dry food and refilled her water. I started crying and stopped again and then dragged eyeliner back over my lids so that I looked the way I had before. When you showed up it was close to nine, and you smelled normal: no sweat, no cigarettes, no liquor. Where had you been? You had been working late. Hadn't you heard? They said "irreversible," "imminent," "end of days." They used those words.

I put wet marks into your shirt as you held me. Then when I pulled away your chest looked back at me with two blurry eyes.

"Why did you do that?" I asked. "Why were you away so long?"

"I was working," you said. "A lot of people have left, you know that. Toby and Marianne and all of the interns. We're understaffed. I'm on two new building projects." Your back was warm and real under my hands.

"There's nothing to build," I said. "The world is going."

"I know that," you replied. "But there isn't anything we can do about it."

"That's what I'm saying," I said.

I looked at you looking at me. I heard that we were saying the same thing, though I didn't understand how it was possible for us to mean it so differently. Later that night I asked you to quit your job too, stay home with me during the days. We could get survival-ready, rent a garden-level apartment with barricadeable windows. We could walk around all day getting to know the things that wouldn't be there for much longer. But you wouldn't. You liked being an architect. You said it would make you happy to have added even one thing to a world now headed for total subtraction.

The walking path next to the highway passed under a bridge. In the cool dark beneath was a bench facing onto some empty lot full of broken glass from bottles that people had thrown, just because. When sunlight hit the broken pieces, the ground lit up like a reverse chandelier, a glittering patch of green and white. Now there was less each time I walked by. Also, no bench. I stood there facing the glass, eating my last apple.

There had been times when I thought I might be with you indefinitely, something approaching an entire life. But then when there was only a finite amount of time, a thing we could see the limit of, I wasn't so sure. I didn't know how to use a unit of time like this, too long for a game of chess or a movie but so much shorter than we had imagined. It felt like one of those days when we woke up too late for breakfast and lay in bed until it was too late for lunch. Those days made me nervous. On those days we fought about how to use our time. You didn't want to live your life under pressure, as though we'd run out, as though it were the last days. I'm not ill, you said. We aren't dying, we don't have cancer, you said. So I don't want to live like we do, you said. There are two kinds of people, and one of them will give up first.

When we fought, you got over it first. I'd watch you from the kitchen, through a rectangular space cut into the wall, and I could see you studying the newspaper, ducking your head down to read small details in the photographs. I saw how gracefully you fell back into whatever article you had been reading before. Even then I knew: whatever hollow I made in you if I left would heal up like a hole sunk into water, quick as water rushing to fill some passing wound.

This far from the pier I could still hear the seagulls fighting over scraps, crying out with their harsh voices. Sounds carried further these days, tearing through the thin air like a stone thrown as hard as you can toward the sea. The bitten-down apple core wettened my right-hand glove, while with the other hand I pressed on the bridge of my nose. There are two kinds of people: one will only weep when the possibility exists, however remote, that someone will hear them. I put the core of the apple down on the ground and looked at it. Poof, I said. I waited for something to happen. Then I went and walked back up the path toward the high-rise.

When I got home I collected all of Cookie's toys, her food bowl and water bowl, the little purple ball with a bell in it, the stuffed squeaking duck that was almost her size. I lined them all up on the mantle in the living room so that I could watch them disappear, one after the other.

Was the disappearing growing faster every day? No. Was it moving geographically from west to east, or east to west? Was it vanishing the world alphabetically, taxonomically, or in chronological order? It wasn't. As hard as we tried to understand it, there didn't seem to be much order to the disappearing at all. A week would go by with everything pretty much in its proper place, and then all of a sudden there was no such thing as magazines, not in your home or anyone else's, and nobody to bother making new ones. Did it work its way down from the biggest things to the smallest? Was there a plan? When you were in the right mood, when you were too tired to care much, it was beautiful—like watching the house across the street as someone walked through it turning each of the lights off in order, one by one, for the night.

I sat on the floor of my brother's empty living room and ate four chocolate-chip granola bars in a row. I had already called you once today, but I was working on a reason to call you again. Experts suggested that the things disappearing most quickly now might be intangible, metaphysical: concepts, memories, and modes of thought were just as vulnerable to erasure, they said, though they couldn't give any concrete examples. I thought I'd better call you to see if you still remembered that Cookie had gone.

I pushed the buttons in order. It rang twice, and then I heard you.

"Hello?" you said.

"It's me," I said.

"It's you," you said back to me.

"I just wanted to call to see if you still remembered Cookie," I said.

"Of course I still remember Cookie," you said.

There was silence on both our ends, a blur of static on the line between us.

"What do you remember?" I asked.

"I remember that you picked her because she bit you," you said, "and you decided it was important that you win this one animal over. I remember you didn't know how to hold a cat at the beginning so you grabbed her just anywhere. You grabbed her in the middle and tried to pick her up that way. You got bit a lot," you added.

"I have your number memorized," I said.

"That's good," you said.

And I said I should let you go, and you said goodnight, and we hung up on each other.

I missed you more now than I had when I lost you. I was forgetting the bad things faster than I forgot the good, and the changing ratio felt a little bit like falling in love even though I was actually speaking to you less and less. I used to play a game I called "Are We Going To Make It?" You were playing too, whether you knew it or not. It worked like this: you'd forget that we were going to see the movie together and you'd go by yourself instead or with a friend, while I waited at home. Or you'd stay at work until four in the morning and forget to charge your phone, and you'd wake me up on the couch where I had fallen asleep trying to stay up for you. Then I would ask myself: Are We Going To Make It? And the next thing, whatever thing you did next, would become the answer, a murky thing that I'd study until I was too tired to think about it anymore.

An "independent physicist" living in Arizona had become famous for his theories on how the Disappearing might be a sort of existential illusion, analogous to an optical illusion. He said the fact that we still remember what's been taken and can picture it in our minds is proof that it still exists. It's like how you only see the duck or the bunny at a given moment, never both, he said. Only imagine that instead of knowing the bunny exists alongside your experience of the duck, you believe that it's been irrevocably lost. It's all about vantage point, he said, temporal vantage point: the way you might lose sight of your house when you drive away from it, but find it again when you look for it from the top of a hill. To think your house was lost, he said, would be loony. Disappeared things were like this, he said, coexistent but obscured in time. This was his theory of spatiotemporal obstruction. Those who believed in it believed that there was one special place that offered temporal "higher ground." They made pilgrimages to a particular beach in Normandy where the cliffs were chalky white, the color of doves, and where it was rumored that recently disappeared things sometimes reappeared, soft-edged and worn and looking thirty or forty years older. In 1759, a twelve-year-old girl was said to have drowned herself there to avoid marriage to a much older man.

I sat on the floor and put the granola bar wrappers in a plastic bag. I put the plastic bag inside another plastic bag. Plastic bags were disappearing too, but my brother had had so many of them to begin with. Then I picked up the phone to call you back. I put your number in from memory.

Instead of you, I heard an error song and a recorded voice telling me my call could not be completed.

I dialed the Bureau of Disappearances. At the prompt, I pressed "1" for "person," then "1" again for "male." I pressed "3" to indicate "age twenty-one to thirty." Then I was supposed to press "3" for "friend," but instead I pressed "2" for "lover or significant other." I hoped you wouldn't mind. The beautiful female voice declared you a "male lover between the ages of twenty-one and thirty" and asked if that was correct. I pressed the pound key and then I described you.

I remember it was a bright morning in the fall and I woke onto your face looking in on mine. Some mornings when we woke together we pretended that one of us had forgotten who the other was. One of us had become an amnesiac. That one would ask: Who are you? Where am I? and it was the other's job to make up a new story. A good story was long, and the best stories could make me feel like I had gotten a whole second life, a bonus one. Yellow leaves outside the window threw yellowish light on the sheets as you told me not to worry. I was safe, I was with you. We had been living together since grad school, we met on the hottest day of the year, near the gondolas in the middle of the park. We were sitting on benches facing the pond and eating the same kind of sandwich, turkey and swiss in a spinach wrap.

"But that's what actually happened," I said.

"I know," you said, making a fake guilty face.

In the fall afternoon, leaves fell off whenever they fell off: it didn't depend on their color or weight or the force of the wind outdoors.

You added: "I just couldn't think of anything."

The disappearing when it started happening was everywhere, subtly, it hung on our days the way a specific hour does on a moment, dragging it down and reminding you of how much time you've let pass. It was a flavor you woke up with in your mouth, like the taste of blood on a dry winter morning. This made leaving easier in the moments before I had realized what I was planning to do. I stood outside of our building with no keys and I was calling you over and over on the cell phone even though I knew you were at work. Each time I got your voicemail I imagined that you had vanished, until one time I imagined that you had vanished and I didn't feel any way about it. It was like I had disappeared. I saw the things continuing without me, and I didn't mind. I went to the ATM on the corner and pulled everything out of my checking account. Checking accounts were still around then, existing invisibly somewhere. Possibly they exist still, even though the banks went. I took the cash and our car and got on the highway, driving on I-80 west toward Chicago. If it hadn't been the End of Days would we still be together? The most difficult thing about leaving you was discovering that I went on: that I had to be there sixteen hours a day watching myself live my own life, that I had to stay near myself all the time as I asked myself question after question, that I had to sit there in my body and watch the phone ring over and over next to me that night, after you had gotten home.

After the announcement, people did one of two things. Either they tried to care more, or they tried caring less. They decided to survive, to collect and hide and ration, or they decided to let the amount of time left in their lives work away at them. They tried to grow vegetables in their small backyards or they let the yard get overgrown, falling asleep drunk in the afternoon on a lawn chair encircled by weeds. For a while we did whatever we had chosen with dedication. But it was difficult to stay dedicated for more than a few weeks and eventually we middled, caring about things sloppily and in spurts. We poked at the dirt and then fell asleep feeling that we should have done more or maybe less. In the end, there was only one kind of person.

In the master bedroom I turned down the sheets. My brother wouldn't be back again, but I made the bed every day to be a good guest. I made it the hotel way, everything tucked in, the sheets stretched tight across the mattress and leaving no room to shift or wrinkle. Sleeping in it meant that you had to tear it apart. I yanked the pillows out from underneath the blankets, pulled the sheets down to the foot of the bed, let the comforter fall to the floor. Then I climbed in.

I have one of the last working phones, I said aloud.

I had started sleeping with the lights on: I wanted more minutes of seeing, more things I could see if I happened to open my eyes. Outside the window there was snow falling, falling like movie snow, all the dreamy fluffy bits drifting around in the light of a single streetlamp. I wished that I loved the woman on the Disappearance hotline so that I could call and hear her voice anytime I wanted, and feel that feeling that it didn't seem I'd be feeling again. Whoever loved her was lucky, if they were still around. I watched the snow slow down, thin out. Then it was two or three pieces at a time, falling reversibly, wavering up and down and up again like they didn't know where to go.

The light stayed on for a few minutes. I saw my reflection in the window. Then the bulb blanked out overhead. In the dark I could hear the cord swinging empty above, but I saw nothing. I knew from the mounting silence that other things were vanishing too. They say everything in the world vibrates at its own specific frequency, each thing releases a tiny bit of sound. But nothing, nothing doesn't vibrate at all. I felt the heat radiating from my body with no place to go. Dots of darkness that weren't really there drifted past my eyes. How would I know I was vanishing if there were nobody around to see me? What would tell me that I wasn't just falling asleep? In the darkness I couldn't see the disappearing any longer but I knew it was all going, going far, far away. Until gradually I didn't even know that anymore.

There was a woman in Lincoln, Nebraska, who claimed to be able to communicate with the disappeared. You could call her on the telephone and tell her who you were looking for, their full name, how old, how tall, how heavy. She would go out to the old well behind her house, a well that her grandfather had built decades earlier, and shout that information deep down into it. In the echo that came back they said you could hear whispers from the other side, your loved ones grabbing and molding the shouted words, distorting them to say what they needed said. You had to pay her in real gold, jewelry or bullion: it had to gleam. She wished we could hear their voices as she did, how happy they are, how they miss us. She said that everything that disappeared from our side went over to theirs, where they kept living normal lives waiting for the things still lingering with us to join them, and make the world whole once more.

Discrepancies Regarding My Mother's Departure

RACHEL ELIZA GRIFFITHS, GUEST-EDITED BY NICK FLYNN // SEPTEMBER 2, 2014

It's your turn, it's always your turn, / the night says.

Another time after she left
I saw a headless woman
hurrying after her like a jaguar.

She pried off her red mouth
like a scar. My father folded the window
so that it fit inside his silence,

pulled apart starlight
with his teeth. Then he ate the fruit
of his own wreckage

until he was full, discontented
where he slept beneath a bridge.
The bones beneath

that bridge disappeared
around him, annunciated
by neglect.

My mother often told me
about her dreams
where amnesia chased her,

where I could see the handle of the shovel
for myself. I could see
where she had buried us or him, how

she had dug up the bones,
twisting blood & metal, as she struggled
with the flesh of memory.

Waiting inside of the night,
I could make out the mound
& her eyes, the blank embrace

of innocence when she returned.
It's your turn, it's always your turn,
the night says.

Girl

ALEXANDER CHEE // MARCH 16, 2015

Sometimes you don't know who you are until you put on a mask.

HAIR
The year is 1990. The place is San Francisco, the Castro. It is
Halloween night. I am in my friend John's bathroom, alone in
front of the mirror, wearing a black turtleneck and leggings. My face glows
back at me from the light of twelve 100-watt bulbs.

In high school I learned to do makeup for theater. I did fake mustaches and
eyelashes then, bruises, wounds, tattoos. I remember always being tempted
then to do what I have just done now, and always stopping, always thinking
I would do it later.

This is that day.

My face, in the makeup I have just applied, is a success. My high cheek-
bones, large slanting eyes, wide mouth, small chin, and rounded jaw have
been restrung in base, powder, eyeliner, lipstick, eyebrow pencil. With these
tools I have built another face on top of my own, unrecognizable, and yet
I am already adjusting to it; somehow I have always known how to put this
face together. My hands do not shake, but move with the slow assurance
of routine.

I am smiling.

I pick up the black eyeliner pencil and go back to the outer corners of my
eyes, drawing slashes there, and, licking the edges of my fingers, I pull the
lines out into sharp black points—the wings of crows, not their feet.

I have nine moles on my face, all obscured by base and powder. I choose
one on my upper lip, to the right, where everyone inserts a beauty mark. I
have one already, it feels like a prophecy. I dot it with the pencil.

I pick up the lipstick and open my mouth in an O. I have always loved unscrewing lipsticks, and as the shining nub appears I feel a charge. I apply the color, Mauve Frost, then reapply, and with that, my face shimmers— a white sky, the mole a black planet, the eyes its ringed big sisters. I press my lips down against each other and feel the color spread anywhere it hasn't gone yet.

The wig is shoulder-length blond hair, artificial—Dynel doll hair, like Barbie's, which is why I choose it. The cap shows how cheap the wig is, so I cut a headband out of a t-shirt sleeve and make it into a fall.

The wig I put on last. Without it, you can see my man's hairline, receding faintly into a widow's peak. You can see my dark hair, you can tell I'm not a blond woman or a white one, or even a woman. It is a Valkyrie's head-piece, and I gel it to hold it into place. The static it generates pulls the hairs out into the air one by one. In an hour I will have a faint halo of frizz. Blue sparks will fly from me when I touch people.

John knocks on the door. "Girl!" he says through the door. "Aren't you ready yet?" He is already finished, dressed in a sweater and black mini-skirt, his black banged wig tied up with a pink bow. He has highlighted his cheekbones with rouge, which I forgo. He is wearing high heels; I have on combat boots. I decided to wear sensible shoes, but John wears "fuck me" pumps, the heels three inches high. This is my first time. It is Halloween tonight in the Castro and we are both trying to pass, to be "real," only we are imitating very different women.

What kind of girl am I? With the wig in place, I understand that it is pos-sible I am not just in drag as a girl but as a white girl. Or, as someone trying to pass as a white girl.

"Come in!" I yell back. John appears over my shoulder in the mirror, a cheerleader gone wrong, the girl who sits on the back of the rebel's motor-cycle. His brows rise all the way up.

"Jesus Mother of God," he says. "Girl, you're beautiful. I don't believe it."

"Believe it," I say, looking into his eyes.

I tilt my head back and carefully toss my hair over my right shoulder in the way I have seen my younger sister do. I realize I know one more thing about her than I did before—what it feels like to do this and why you would. It's like your own little thunderclap.

"Scared of you," John says. "You're flawless."

"So are you," I say. "Where's Fred?" Fred is my newest boyfriend, and I have been unsure if I should do this with him, but here we are.

"Are you okay?" Fred asks, as if something has gone wrong in the bathroom. "Oh my God, you are beautiful." He steps into the doorway, dazed. He still looks like himself, a skinny white boy with big ears and long eyelashes, his dark hair all of an inch long. He hasn't gotten dressed yet.

He is really spellbound, though, in a way he hasn't been before this. I have never had this effect on a man, never transfixed him so thoroughly, and I wonder what I might be able to make him do now that I could not before. "Honey," he says, his voice full of wonder. He walks closer, slowly, his head hung, looking up at me. I feel my smile rise from somewhere old in me, maybe older than me; I know this scene, I have seen this scene a thousand times and never thought I would be in it; this is the scene where the beautiful girl receives her man's adoration and I am that girl.

In this moment, the confusion of my whole life has receded. No one will ask me if I am white or Asian. No one will ask me if I am a man or a woman. No one will ask me why I love men. For a moment, I want Fred to stay a man all night. There is nothing brave in this: any man and woman can walk together, in love and unharassed in this country, in this world—and for a moment, I just want to be his overly made-up girlfriend all night. I want him to be my quiet, strong man. I want to hold his hand all night and have it be only that; not political, not dangerous, just that. I want the ancient reassurances legislated for by centuries by mobs.

He puts his arms around me and I tip my head back. "Wow," he says. "Even up close."

"Ever kissed a girl?" I ask.

"No," he says, and laughs.

"Now's your chance," I say, and he leans in, kissing me slowly through his smile.

MY COUNTRY

I am half white, half Korean, or, to be more specific, Scotch-Irish, Irish, Welsh, Korean, Chinese, Mongolian. It is a regular topic, my whole life, this question of what I am. People are always telling me, like my first San Francisco hairdresser.

"Girl, you are mixed, aren't you? But you can pass," he said, as if this was a good thing.

"Pass as what?" I asked.

"White. You look white."

When people use the word "passing" in talking about race, they only ever mean one thing, but I still make them say it. He told me he was Filipino. "You could be one of us," he said. "But you're not."

Yes. I *could* be, but I am not. I am used to this feeling.

As a child in Korea, living in my grandfather's house, I was not to play in the street by myself: Amerasian children had no rights there generally, as usually no one knew who their father was, and they could be bought and sold as help or prostitutes, or both. No one would check to see if I was any different from the others.

"One day everyone will look like you," people say to me, all the time. I am a citizen of a nation that has only ever existed in the future, a nation where nationalism dies of confusion. And so I cringe when someone tells me I am a "fine mix," that it "worked well"; what if it hadn't?

After I read Eduardo Galeano's stories in *Century of Fire*, I mostly remember the mulatto ex-slaves in Haiti, obliterated when the French recaptured the island, the *mestiza* Argentinean courtesans—hated both by the white women for daring to put on wigs as fine as theirs, and by the Chilote slaves, who think the courtesans put on airs when they do so. The book is supposed to be a lyric history of the Americas, but it read more like a history of racial mixing.

I found in it a pattern for the history of half-breeds hidden in every culture: historically, we are allowed neither the privileges of the ruling class nor the community of those who are ruled. To each side that disowns us, we represent everything the other does not have. We only survive if we are valued, and we are valued only for strength, or beauty, sometimes for intelligence or cunning. As I read these stories of who survives and who does not, I know that I have survived in all of these ways and that these are the only ways I have survived so far.

This beauty I find when I put on drag then; it is made up of these talismans of power, a balancing act of the self-hatreds of at least two cultures, an act I've engaged in my whole life, here on the fulcrum I make of my face. That night, I find I want this beauty to last because it seems more powerful than any beauty I've had before. Being pretty like this is stronger than any drug I've ever tried.

But in my blond hair, I ask myself, are you really passing? Or is it just the dark, the night, people seeing what they want to see?

And what exactly are you passing as? And is that what we are really doing here?

Each time I pass that night it is a victory over these doubts, a hit off the pipe. This hair is all mermaid's gold and like anyone in a fairy tale I want it to be real when I wake up.

ANGELS

John and I are patient as we make Fred up. His eyelids flutter as we try to line and shadow them, he talks while we try to put on his lipstick. He feels this will liberate him, and tells us, repeats, how much he would never have done this before. I realize he means before me.

"Close your eyes," I tell him. He closes them. I feel like his big sister. I dust the puff ball with translucent powder and hold it in front of his face. I take a big breath and blow it toward him. A cloud surrounds him and settles lightly across his skin. The sheen of the base is gone, replaced by powder smoothness. He giggles.

John pulls the wig down from behind him and twists it into place. He comes around beside me and we look at Fred carefully for fixable flaws. There are none. Fred opens his eyes. "Well?"

"Definitely the smart sister. Kate Jackson," John says and turns toward me, smiling. "I'm the pretty one, the femmy one. Farrah. Which one are you, girl?"

I shake my head and pull the lapels of my leather trench coat. I don't feel like any of Charlie's Angels and I know I don't look like one. I look more like a lost member of the *Faster, Pussycat! Kill! Kill!* gang. Like if Tura Satana had a child with the blond sidekick. Or just took her hair out for a ride one day.

"You're the mean sister," John says, with a laugh. "The one that makes you cry and breaks all your dolls."

Outside John's apartment 18th Street is full of cars, their headlights like footlights for the sidewalk stage in the early night. I can see my hair flashing around me in the dark as it catches the light. Doing drag on Halloween night in the Castro is an amateur, but high-level, competitive sport. Participating means doing drag in front of people who do drag on just about every other day of the year, and some of these people are my friends. I am most nervous at the thought of seeing them. I want to measure up.

According to the paper the next day, 400,000 people will come into the Castro tonight to see us. They will all try to drive down this street, and many will succeed. Some will have baseball bats, beer bottles, guns. Some of them hate drag queens, trans women, genderqueers. They will tell you they want their girls to be girls. If they pick you up and find out the truth they will beat, and maybe kill you. Being good at a blow job is a survival skill for some of my friends for this very reason—though men are unpredictable at best.

"Most men, when they find out you have a dick, well, hon, they roll right over." This is something a drag-queen friend tells me early on in my life here. "Turns out, their whole lives, all they ever wanted was to get fucked and they never had the nerve to ask for it."

I think about this a lot. I find I think about it right now, on the street, in my new look.

John, Fred, and I walk out in front of the stopped cars. They are full of people I will never see again. John swivels on his heels, pivoting as he walks, smiling and waving. He knows he is why they are here from the suburbs, that he is what they have come to see. I smile at a boy behind a steering wheel who catches my eye. He honks and yells, all excitement. I twirl my hair and keep walking, strutting. In the second grade, the boys would stop me in the hall to tell me I walked like a girl, my hips switching, and as I cross this street, and feel the cars full of people watching me, for the first time I really let myself walk as I have always felt my hips want to. I have always walked this way but I have never walked this way like this.

The yelling continues from the car, and the boy's friends lean out the window, shouting for me. John is laughing. "Shit, girl, you better be careful. I'm going to keep my eye on you." Fred is walking quietly ahead of us. From behind, in his camouflage jacket, he looks like a man with long hair. His legs move from his thin hips in straight lines, he bobs as he steps, and the wig hair bounces gently at his shoulders. He has always walked like this also, I can see this, and here is a difference between us. I don't want him to be hurt tonight, however that happens—either for not being enough of a girl or for being too much, not enough of a boy.

The catcalls from the cars make me feel strong, at first. Isn't beauty strong? I'd always thought beauty was strength and so I wanted to be beautiful. Those cheers on the street are like a weightlifter's bench-press record. The blond hair is like a flag, and all around me in the night are teams. But with each shout I am more aware of the edge, how the excitement could turn into violence, blood, bruises, death.

We arrive at Café Flore, a few blocks from John's apartment. We run into Danny Nicoletta, a photographer friend. He sees us, and does not recognize me. I see him every day at this café, I have posed for him on other occasions. He has no idea who I am. I wave at him and as he looks at me, I feel him examine the frosted blond thing in front of him. I toss my hair—I already love the way this feels, to punctuate arrivals, announcements, a change of mood with your hair.

"Hi Danny," I say finally.

He screams.

"Oh my God, you look exactly like this girl who used to babysit for me," he says. He takes out his camera and snaps photos of me in the middle of the crowded café, and the flash is like a little kiss each time it hits my retinas.

We leave the café and I move through the Halloween night, glowing, as if all of the headlights and flashes have been stored inside me. I pause to peer into store windows, to catch a glimpse of myself. I stop to let people take my picture, and wave if they yell. I dance with friends to music playing from the tower of speakers by a stage set up outside the café. A parade of what look to be heavily muscled prom queens in glistening gowns and baubles pours out into the street from one of the gyms nearby. They glow beneath the stage lights, their shoulders and chests shaved smooth, their pectorals suitable for cleavage. They titter and coo at the people lining the streets, affecting the manner of easily shocked women, or they strut, waving the wave of queens. As they come by, they appraise us with a glance and then move on.

This power I feel tonight, I understand now—this is what it means when we say "queen."

G I R L

My fascination with makeup started young. I remember the first time I wore lipstick in public. I was seven, eight years old at the time, with my mother at the Jordan Marsh makeup counter at the Maine Mall in South Portland, Maine. We were Christmas shopping, I think—it was winter, at least—and she was there trying on samples.

My mother is a beauty, from a family of Maine farmers who are almost all tall, long-waisted, thin, and pretty, the men and the women. Her eyes are Atlantic Ocean blue. She has a pragmatic streak, from being a farmer's daughter, that typically rules her, but she also loves fashion and glamour—when she was younger, she wore simple but chic clothes she often accessorized with cocktail rings, knee-high black leather boots, white sunglasses with black frames.

I had a secret from my mom, or at least I thought I did: I would go into her bathroom and try on her makeup, looking at myself in the mirror. I spent hours in front of my mother's bathroom mirror, rearranging my facial expressions—my face at rest looked unresolved to me, in between one thing and another. I would sometimes stare at my face and imagine it was either more white or more Asian. But makeup, I understood; I had watched the change that came over my mother when she put on makeup and I wanted it for myself. So while she was busy at the makeup counter, I reached up for one of the lipsticks, applied it, and then turned to her with a smile.

I thought it would surprise her, make her happy. I am sure the reddish-orange color looked clownish, even frightening, on my little face.

"Alexander," was all she said, stepping off the chair at the Clinique counter and sweeping me up. She pulled my ski mask over my head and led me out of the department store to the car, like I had stolen something. We drove home in silence, and once there, she washed the lipstick off my face and warned me to never do that again.

She was angry, upset, she felt betrayed by me. There was a line, and I had thought I could go back and forth across it, but it seemed I could not.

Until I could. Until I did.

I was not just mistaken for a member of other races, as a child. I was also often mistaken for a girl. What a beautiful little girl you have, people used to say to my mother at the grocery store when I was six, seven, eight. She had let my hair grow long.

I'm a boy, I would say each time. And they would turn red, or stammer an apology, or say, His hair is so long, and I would feel as if I had done something wrong, or she had.

I have been trying to convince people for so long that I am a real boy, it is a relief to stop—to run in the other direction.

Before Halloween night, I thought I knew some things about being a woman. I'd had women teachers, read women writers, women were my best friends growing up. But that night was a glimpse into a universe beside my own. Drag is its own world of experience—a theater of being female more than a reality. It isn't like being trans, either—it isn't, the more I think about it, like anything except what it is: costumes, illusion, a spell you cast on others and on yourself. But girl, girl is something else.

My friends in San Francisco at this time, we all call each other "girl," except for the ones who think they are too butch for such nellying, though we call them "girl" maybe most of all. My women friends call each other "girl" too, and they say it sometimes like they are a little surprised at how much they like it. This, for me, began in meetings for ACT UP and Queer Nation, a little word that moved in on us all back then. When we say it, the word is like a stone we pass one to the other: the stone thrown at all of us. And the more we catch it and pass it, it seems like the less it can hurt us, the more we know who our new family is now. Who knows us, and who doesn't. It is something like a bullet turned into something like a badge of pride.

Later that night we go to a club, Club Uranus. John and Fred have removed their wigs and makeup. I have decided not to. Fred was uncomfortable—a wig is hot—and John wanted to get laid by a man as a man. I wasn't ready to let go. As we walked there, we passed heterosexual couples on the street. I walked with Fred, holding his arm, and noted the passing men who treated me like a woman—and the women who did also. Only one person let on that they saw through me—a man at a stoplight who leaned out his car window to shout, "Hey, Lola! Come back here, baby! I love you!"

My friend Darren is there, a thin blond boy done up as Marie Antoinette in hair nearly a foot tall and a professional costume rental dress, hoopskirts and all. On his feet, combat boots also. He raises his skirts periodically to show he is wearing nothing underneath.

Soon I am on the go-go stage by the bar. On my back, riding me, is a skinny white boy in a thong made out of duct tape, his body shaved. We are both sweating, the lights a crown of wet bright heat. The music is loud and very fast, and I roll my head like a lion, whipping the wig around for the cool air this lets in. People squeeze by the stage, staring and ignoring us alternately.

I see very little, but I soon spot Fred, who raises his hand and gives me a little wave from where he is standing. I want to tell him I know the boy on my back, and that it isn't anything he needs to worry about, but he seems to understand this. I wonder if he is jealous, but I tell myself he is not, that he knew what he was getting into with me—when we met, he mentioned the other stages he had seen me on around town. Tonight is one of those nights when I am growing, changing quickly, without warning, into new shapes and configurations, and I don't know where this all goes.

I feel more at home than I ever have in that moment, not in San Francisco, not on earth, but in myself. I am on the other side of something and I don't know what it is. I wait to find out.

R E A L

I am proud for years of the way I looked real that night. I remember the men who thought I was a real woman, the straight guys in the cars whooping at me and their expressions when I said, "Thanks, guys," my voice my voice, and the change that rippled over their faces.

You wanted me, I wanted to say. You might still want me.

Real is good. Real is what you want. No one does drag to be a real woman, though. Drag is not the same as that. Drag knows it is different. But if you can pass as real, when it comes to drag, that is its own gold medal.

I'm also very aware of how that night was the first night I felt comfortable with my face. It makes me wary, even confused. I can feel the longing for the power I had. I jones for it like it's cocaine.

The little boy I used to be, in the mirror making faces, he was happy. But the process took so much work. I can't do that every day, though I know women who do. And that isn't the answer to my unhappiness, and I know it.

When my friend Danny gives me a photo from that night, I see something I didn't notice at the time. I look a little like my mom. I had put on my glasses for him—a joke about "girls who wear glasses"—and in that one picture, I see it all—the dark edges of my real hair sticking out, the cheapness of the wig, the smooth face, finally confident.

I send a copy to my sister and write, *This is what I would look like if I was your big sister.*

I can't skip what I need to do to love this face by making it over. I can't chase after the power I felt that night, the fleeting sense of finally belonging to the status quo, by making myself into something that looks like the something they want. Being real means being at home in this face, just as it is when I wake up.

I am not the person who appeared for the first time that night. I am the one only I saw, the one I had rejected until then, the one I needed to see, and didn't see until I had taken nearly everything about him away. His face is not half this or half that, it is all something else.

Sometimes you don't know who you are until you put on a mask.

A few months after Halloween, a friend borrows my wig. He has begun performing in drag on a regular basis. I have not. I bring it into the bookstore where we both work and pass it off to him. It looks like a burned-out thing, what's left in the wick of a candle after a long night.

I go to see my friend perform in the wig—he has turned it into the ponytail of a titanic hair sculpture, made from three separate wigs. He is beautiful beneath its impossible size, a hoopskirted vision, his face whited out, a beauty mark on his lip. Who was the first blond to dot a beauty mark on her upper lip? How far back in time do we have to go? It is like some spirit in the wig has moved on, into him.

He never gives me the wig back, and I don't ask for it back—it was never really mine.

Terrorists Speak in Strange Languages

ASEF HOSSAINI, TRANSLATED FROM THE PERSIAN DARI BY
FARZANA MARIE // FEBRUARY 2, 2015

*I lock my tongue / even though I've prayed /
in Persian for a thousand years.*

Time burst and we emerged
to begin our lives,
we tied our shoes and ran away.
The street was full of worried eyes,
we
were full of the street—
our hands have been cobblestoned
and our heart valves opened
like cheap cabarets.

I don't know why or where or how
I put your temptation away inside a book
I don't know why or where or how
my eye slipped on the buttons of your dress
I don't know why or where or why
                my eyelid pulsed—
Now you're gone
and life in my brain's gray cells
is a replay of our days together.
The Sahara is expanding in my chest
and yet seven seas beyond that
acid rain intoxicates the dead

of Dasht-e Leili.[1]

Do you remember, darling?
We were suffering
while the government in the Arg[2]
flourished
we were suffering
and a woman in Badakhshan was dying
we were reciting poems
and a man was butchered
in the south.

Do you remember?
I was in Mullah Omar's heartland
reciting love poems
I said: the prayer beads mature in the tavern
and love matures in fear.

Everything is fine here.
"No clouds, no wind, I sit next to the pool."
Just a song is enough to complete
the Attan dance
and the looting of my father's land
even outdoes the Mongols.

Everything is fine:
the disaffected brother
smokes shisha and cuts off ears in the evenings,
cuts off the nose so his wife
will not smell the opium
and people's steeped brains.
He cuts off ears so that
we will be domesticated,

1 Dasht-e Leili refers to a desert located in Jawzjan province in the north of Afghanistan. The place is famous for the massacre of Taliban fighters there in 2001, but prior to that, in the summer of 1998, when the Taliban captured Mazar-e Sharif, its fighters brought hundreds of men to the desert and killed them.
2 The Arg refers to the Afghanistan presidential palace.

he is so religious
that he impregnates eleven hours every night
and in the morning, goes to the Arg
to sharpen his artificial teeth.

But I still worry
about your dress
because my eyelid pulses constantly.

My darling,
the weather is cold
and many babies are being aborted
and we,
standing in a line
of one hundred and twenty thousand prophets
are still thirsty, still hungry…but we voted.
We cannot change the world,
sing songs, and be happy;
just let me squeeze the map
into the space of a cage
so that our lands will mate.

The police say: terrorists
speak in strange languages.
I lock my tongue
even though I've prayed
in Persian for a thousand years.
In solitary confinement
I continually confess
and at night
when I stretch out my bones in the corner
I pray your name
seventy two times and no more.

You sit in far-off longing
and all of my roads to your arms
are blocked today
           —They say an explosion happened out your way—
Do you remember

190
Venice, where the Mediterranean came up
and pulled your ankle to the ocean?
I said: this is enough for the sea fairies
to find their lost way.
You laughed, what a pity
how quickly we have been lost.

My longing is so deep
that three hundred and sixty five miners
have died in it.

Berlin, 26 November, 2010

Household Gods

JOHN BENDITT // DECEMBER 15, 2014

The house of the Memory God is filled with junk in piles. It started innocently enough, the way a blizzard starts: a flake here, a flake there.

THE SUNSET GOD

The house of the Sunset God is empty. Someone has swept it *broom clean*, as it says in rental agreements. Though not perfectly. There is a stipple of dust along one wall at the baseboard, drawn with blue evening pencil. The house of the Sunset God is empty, there are no shadows left. They have been packed in the right containers along with everything else. The Sunset God works with professionals, and the departure wasn't done in a hurry. There's nothing left to finger: no notebooks open to the spot where the black scratch stopped, no child's cup or plate, no fork. Just surfaces, an insanity of them, twisting this way and that, hungry for contact. A pencil rattles in an empty drawer, booming hexagonal as it rolls. The Sunset God has packed himself up and departed, leaving nothing but advice: *Draw a line under everything, in memory blue. Sum up!* Imitate the Sunset God, his infinite subtlety, his legacy, the way everything changes, imperceptibly, to darkness.

THE DOORKNOB GOD

The Doorknob God walks down the hallway of his life touching everything. Not just doorknobs, though G_d knows there are enough of those. Walls, side tables, lamps, sconces, molding. Everything an institutional gray-green, anonymous. The molding has a lovely hand. Not a real hand, silly. *Hand* is what tailors call the feel of the cloth. The Doorknob God feels the *hand* in everything, reaching out to tap, touch, finger, suggest, remind, insist, nudge, pinch. The Doorknob God is caught. He must keep moving. He comes to things he's seen before, though they look different now. Why is that? A different light? A different time of day? There are no windows.

A hotel corridor undergoing eternal renovation, every room numbered, key-carded, exact. Perhaps the difference is that he touched them on his previous circuit. The Doorknob God is a toucher, not a counter, a cleaner, or a checker. He has no illness. Instead, he has Time, flowing through his veins like the perfect drug, simultaneously stimulant and depressant, moving him down the gray-green carpet, the signature of his feet worn in, signing deeper with each round, the doors beginning with 1 and ending with 365, the peepholes into which he must not look on pain of disappearance.

THE GOD OF ANXIETY

The God of Anxiety has long since been turned out of his own home. He is long and white; his skin has an odd texture, as if he's come up from a long time underground. Most people don't see him, but they feel him like cool moisture in the air and turn away. When they get home and take off their coats, they feel clammy, as if something has brushed up against them without their knowing. Later on, they get in bed and pull the covers up, trying to read, but the words blur and run, sentences spill over their boundaries. They begin thinking of something that happened a long time ago in school, something they wish hadn't happened. If only they hadn't said that one thing, they think. But that wasn't really where it started. It started long before that, with something in the family that got turned inside out and projected onto the big screen of the world. Yes, something happened. And before each thing, another and another, until the first light is crawling through the bedroom blinds while the thread of thought is still being pulled. And you don't want to go to work. You just lie there, watching each hurt, each matched retaliation, unwinding deeper into darkness.

THE GOD OF LINES

The God of Lines disappears into his work. Worships Saul Steinberg. His favorite paper is gridded like a French schoolgirl's notebook. *Havin' it both ways,* he calls it. He's a wag, the God of Lines. His boat: J class, America's Cup. His favorite time of day: any time the horizon is visible. His suit: Armani Classico, the one with the black label. His horse: Man o'War. His bet: over and under. His shoes: two-tone oxfords, like the pair the Babe wore the day he nailed Lazzeri's cleats to the clubhouse floor. Lazzeri dumped a bucket of ice water on his head. The Babe just kept right on walkin' in his two-tone oxfords. His drink: anything with a swizzle stick—but hold the umbrellas. Starting: right where he finishes, every time. His favorite place: the equator. Says *he just feels comfortable there.* The last time he went to the track? He's there right now as a matter of fact, underlining entries in *Racing Form*, using a code only he understands. The only thing he won't bet on: whether the sun will come up tomorrow. *Depressin'*, he says, puttin' on the accent of a toff from the Nineteen Thirties. And the place where parallel lines intersect?

Shhh, follow me…

THE MEMORY GOD

The Memory God lives in a part of the city you find only by chance. You can never find it when you want it. But if you give up and wander, then sometimes, only sometimes, you're there. The Memory God comes home after a long day (all his days are long), takes off his overcoat, and flings it on a pile in the corner where it must wait until he picks it out again the next morning. His hair, what's left of it, is bristly, standing up around the great dome where everything is stored. The house of the Memory God is filled with junk in piles. It started innocently enough, the way a blizzard starts: a flake here, a flake there, dropping silent through the evening air. Then it got deeper, piling up until it was *serious business*. The Memory God's house is like that place up in Harlem where the two brothers lived (remind me of their names again), their world mapped by paths growing finer and finer until things crashed in around them and they rotted, losing first their outline, then their form, finally their substance. *Cause of death: forgetting.* Or being forgotten, I can't remember which. The Memory God decides to create systems. Finally, everything will make sense. Anything that's in a pile belongs in that pile and in no other, for ever and ever. The problem is, the systems don't work. In theory, they're wonderful. In practice, there's *too much of it*. No system can hold it, even the most ingenious, the most flexible, the most German. They are the play of a child compared to the depth, the texture, the variety of the mess in the Memory God's house. He has come to believe, grudgingly, against his will, that each thing is unique. Each thing is unique! Can you imagine what that means? It means no system is possible; each thing must be apprehended as it is: infinite. In the end, the brothers in Harlem (their names again?) lived on despair, having exhausted oranges, peaches, and oatmeal. After a night of dreams resembling a triptych by Francis Bacon, the Memory God leaves his house for a walk, trying to forget the mess inside, humming an old song about *buttoning up your overcoat when the wind blows free.* And taking good care of yourself. Away from his hoard, the Memory God is free. And he will have no trouble finding his house in the evening. But you will, you always will. You will find it only by chance and then it will be as if you are there for the very first time.

THE GOD OF SEX

The God of Sex lies on his woman like a snake, undulating slowly as he deposits. Stretched out above her, he feels the power roll up in him, surging from tail to triangular green head. When he is finished, he leaves a stinging wetness: lacerations, seeds with tiny hooks buried in the cuts. As he rolls off, spent, he realizes he has been used again. The unborn are always making use of those who are already born. But the God of Sex is as old as the universe. He knows tomorrow is another story. He lies there panting, summoning the energy to begin again: to do, to undo, to do, to undo…

THE GOD OF MELANCHOLY

The God of Melancholy is never seen, is sensed in things. A long empty street, shadows of houses on the sidewalk, popular songs from decades past whispering in their angles. The God of Melancholy has a fascination with money. He piles it up, rarely spends it. *There is something so deeply sad about money,* he thinks. The masculine beauty of banknotes with the profile of Apollo, cigarettes. Someone said the pleasure of smoking comes from the fact that when you smoke you control death, mastering it a puff at a time. I am the master of death each time the smoke drifts into me and out again. Dust on windowsills in the low-angled winter light of late afternoon. Blazing dust, golden dust, changing, as the moon rises, to silver, a wisp, elusive. The smell of brick after spring rain before anyone has come outside again. The barking of a puppy, forlorn, inside a house down the street. Dirt piled against a wall, footprints in the mud. A last raindrop falling into water, the sound of it clear and ringing. Everywhere we turn, something is leaving and leaving us behind. When we reach out to grasp it we feel again the presence of this god, without whom no household could ever call itself complete.

THE GOD OF MADNESS

The God of Madness fails to recognize the rooms of his own house. He wanders into the bathroom thinking it's the kitchen. *I cooked a meal here once,* he thinks, *but that was long ago and it seems to have become something else.* There is an odd smell in the air, as of regret, or remembrance, or even lilacs. The floor is an organized perversity, black and white, extending to forever, expanding and contracting. *Everything is alive,* he thinks, *everything breathes.*

Expansion and contraction is all there is. Indivisible, from Beginning to End. He looks out the window. The cars flow down the street, moving forward to touch their neighbors and back again, while still remaining parked. It is an odd spring, this, unlike the others. The trees speak to one another in Greek. The layers of me peel off like old clothes, which I set aside, planning to donate them to charity, if charity will have them. *The less I have, the more I am.* I am learning every day, removing and removing until I reach the glowing center, of stillness and silence. By then I am fully metabolized and flowing, draining to the city underneath the street, frightened by my too-adult face in the mirror, the emptiness behind it filled with shelves.

THE GOD OF RECONCILIATION

The God of Reconciliation has been out all night, is worse for wear. It's always like this, the coming home. He's promised himself, so many times, he'll never do it again. He knows there are programs. Even for gods, there are programs. Infinite-step programs. The God of Reconciliation has decided to enter one, sworn he will never again come home tattered, wet, ripped, forlorn, filled with self-loathing. Yet deep down he knows his nature cannot be changed by any program, even one with an infinite number of steps. Until the end of time he will be sitting in a basement, coffee mug in one hand, cigarette in the other, under neon lights clicking like moths, thinking about the highs, the lightness, the sureness, how bright the colors are, how beautiful the women are *when he is there.* Knowing, as he sits on a folding chair in a basement stuffed with farts, that everyone else is thinking the same thing. It's not for the God of Reconciliation. He'll stick to what he is. Tattered as that might be, at least it's genuine. He'll find his way home on shaky legs, pants wet down the front. At the bus stop he'll prop himself up. He'll flag a taxi, find he lacks the fare. He'll dial a number, let it ring regardless of the hour, knowing no one will pick up. He'll see a city bus, outlined in black, rolling through the quiet streets, and let it pass. He'll take his time, the God of Reconciliation, knowing he must reach his bed at just the right moment, fall into that crevice fully clothed, a mountain climber roped to every living soul on this planet, bringing them together in one soft brief moment of *yes* before sleep erases everything again.

THE NEEDLE GOD

The Needle God sets out daily from his neatly packed house, a place of tasks finished and done. He roams the streets, approaches strangers one by one, handing each of them a tiny folded paper. Not many refuse. The

Needle God seems benign, his town not big enough for hostility. His neighbors bend over to unfold messages written in a minute hand, with the letters leaning forward. The writing is the color of venous blood, the blue of return journeys, each note an invitation drawing strangers together. He never invites them to his home. The destination is different every time, often a trolley ride away in a different neighborhood. The guests accept, drawn by the stranger's calm, precision, uprightness. Through him they think they see their better selves. Off they go, to a nondescript working-class bar, a union hall, a threadbare church. The pastor at the lectern is startled to see his black-and-white linoleum covered by strange feet. The people meet, discover each is holding a tiny invite in a spidery blue hand. At last they're where they're meant to be, in the company of those whose lives they're meant to be bound up with. By the time they are joined, the Needle God has slipped away and disappeared, returning to his home, unfound, catalytic, himself.

THE GOD OF IRONING BOARD

The God of Ironing Board has a passion for neatness. He sees a world divided into things clean and unclean. His doctor says: *You have an illness.* The God of Ironing Board knows he has no illness. He has *a passion:* that the world be different and better than itself. The God of Ironing Board knows more than any doctor. He has seen the world before the Beginning and after the End, and he is on the side of rebirth, of order, of cleanliness and health. He walks the streets faultlessly pressed. His suit is in three pieces, brilliant seersucker, his tan brogues bespoke, furled umbrella in the crook of his arm, poking its tip into hidden places. For the God of Ironing Board, everything is always in the balance. The future is not ordained. A soul is not a given, it must be made. Soulmaking is the work of a lifetime. Death is a choice. The universe may run up or down, depending on the choices made in the Here and the Now. The God of Ironing Board is a presence, encouraging us to choose the running up to order, rebirth, not the running down, to chaos. But like any god, he has no infinite power. Instead, he has influence: a wisp, a scent, an inclination to one direction, evanescent, strong. Every day he walks the world beautifully pressed to spread his message of liberation. But now a dot of mud the size of a Liberty dime has landed on the tip of his handmade brogue, soiling the perforated toecap, and he must home to change and safety.

THE GOD OF KITCHEN DRAWER

The God of Kitchen Drawer is small and tidy. He and his wife sleep spoon fashion in monogrammed pajamas with green and white stripes. Verticals make them look taller—even to themselves. The god and his wife live on similar schedules, hold the same views, go in and out at the same time from their house on a street where all the houses look like theirs. They have no children, and their friends are in agreement. At evening, when the lamps are lit, the God of Kitchen Drawer and his wife stroll arm in arm through the streets, looking in the windows at families performing their nightly rituals. They are not sad when they do this, nor are they envious. They are merely interested in the chaos of others. They have no reason for envy. They have each other, and they fit.

THE GOD OF WOODEN SPOON

The God of Wooden Spoon answers to no one, but has an answer for everything. He has a degree in aeronautical engineering from MIT. He didn't get it because he had a practical use for it, but simply to have mastered the subject. He was interested in propellers, how air flows around them, the turbulence they create and live within. Propellers are *of his tribe*, though they are inanimate and he is not, being all spirit all the time. The God of Wooden Spoon walks down Mass Ave. in sunlight, full of himself, knowing MIT is the best in the world, that he has secrets even from them. He keeps a low profile, mingling with Indian students, Koreans, Chinese. After getting his degree, having no need for an income, he retires to the country and builds a house, very snug, everything in its place. He has a way of making things come alive that is unusual, even for a god. He sees the chair in the tree, the bowl in the log. He sees these things then brings them out, one by one, from where they are hiding in the grain. He places them around his house in circles spreading out across the Pennsylvania countryside, not far from General Eisenhower, from where the Union was torn apart and reassembled. It is the right place. The wood sends messages all the livelong day, and he is content.

THE OVEN GOD

The Oven God is voraciously fat. Nothing he eats is ever enough. He sits on a hot dusty street in the angle of a wall, shadow covering him part of the day. His belly is large and greasy, a showplace. Around his neck, a scrap of rag with which he wipes his bald head. The Oven God is fond of ghee. Actually, he doesn't need to beg. He has enough for a house. But he begs anyway. In the Oven God is a hunger so deep nothing he owns could ever satisfy it. So he waits for strangers to come and fill the hollow place within. People give scraps of thread, crumbs of food, tiny birds. The birds are brightly colored. They die of longing before the Oven God can bring himself to eat them. He buries them in boxes carefully inscribed with names and dates. The date he received the bird. The day it passed over *into other hands.* On the edge of the hot city, where the unruly plain begins, stands the house of the Oven God, filled with tiny cardboard boxes not yet labeled, waiting for the next story to begin.

THE WIFEBEATER GOD

The Wifebeater God doesn't beat his wife. He's the god of a shirt called the wifebeater. Brando in *Streetcar.* Working-class underwear for men, turned at some moment of fashion history into outerwear for women. The Wifebeater God sits home unshaven, beer cans piling, saucers filled with butts. Sometimes when he goes out, he wears a shirt that says: *I forgot to get married.* He thinks people will laugh. They don't. They turn aside, thinking: *Who would marry him?* Pity is what they feel. He doesn't want to know that. Who would? Would you? Around him in the air are wiggly lines drawn by a manic cartoonist. His eyes are dark and shiny. When you see him coming, you don't want to start a conversation with him. Or let him start one with you. The Wifebeater God is the hero of his own lifestyle. All the stuff piling up—it's good, reassuring. So what if it smells? There ain't no life without smells. One reason the stuff piles up is that he decided to fire his housekeeper a couple of months ago. Just like that. Didn't need her. *Fuck women,* the Wifebeater God thinks. Not literally. It's a metaphor. Like Travis Bickle, when he says he's waiting for a *real rain, to wash away the scum on the streets. The cheaper the hood, the gaudier the patter,* somebody said. The smaller the person, the bigger the metaphor, says I, right here from within this white ventrilo-box.

In Defense Of

JEAN STEVENS INTERVIEWS LYNNE STEWART // APRIL 15, 2015

The "people's lawyer" on her most controversial criminal defense cases—including the one that sent her to prison.

DURING AMERICA'S CIVIL RIGHTS and women's liberation movements of the 1960s and '70s, hundreds of activists who challenged state repression and surveillance faced arrests and criminal convictions. Many such activists sought legal defense from "movement lawyers," those who understood and sympathized with their social justice aims.

By the late 1970s, Lynne Stewart emerged as one of the movement's leading defense attorneys, fiercely representing members of the political left—most notably, leaders of the Black Panthers and the Weather Underground. And in 1993, Stewart represented defendant Sheik Omar Abdel Rahman, an Egyptian Muslim cleric, in one of the nation's first terrorism cases. That role ultimately resulted in her own conviction, disbarment, and incarceration, which lasted from 2009 to 2013.

Stewart, now seventy-five, was born to a white working-class family in Brooklyn and grew up in Queens. She began on a path of challenging the status quo while working in the '60s as a school librarian in Harlem, where she discovered a movement for greater access to education led by parents, teachers, and organizers in the neighborhood. There, she also met her future husband, Ralph Poynter, who became her lifelong champion.

In the '70s, Stewart discovered her true calling—law. After studying at Rutgers School of Law, she advertised her services as a legal advocate, and, she says, "took anything that came across my doorstep." However, she felt most compelled by defense work, especially the defense of those facing incarceration for struggling against "institutions which perpetuate capitalism, racism, and sexism," as she told the *New York Times* in 1995. A self-described "people's lawyer," she not only took on the cases of high-profile clients facing political prosecution, but also low-income clients without access to a proper defense, as well as unpopular, controversial defendants, like Sammy Gravano of the Gambino crime family. Regardless of how provocative the case, as Stewart contended in a recent interview with Chris Hedges, progressive attorneys should "fight like hell" to defend their clients against increasingly powerful state repression.

In the aftermath of September 11th, about ten years after she represented Abdel Rahman, former US attorney general John Ashcroft charged Stewart with aiding terrorism. The case hinged on her relaying documents on her client's behalf, allegedly conveying messages from him to his supporters. The *American Criminal Law Review* wrote that Stewart's guiding principle was to defend those whose actions could be considered anti-imperialist: "While these views were considered radical when she expressed them in the '90s, as seen through the lens of 9/11, they were judged by many as bordering on the seditious." While preparing for court in her home one evening in 2002, she was arrested. Two years later, she was arraigned, convicted, and sentenced to twenty-eight months in prison. During these proceedings, Stewart was diagnosed with stage IV breast cancer and spent three years out on bail for medical treatment. Despite her ill health, in 2009, prosecutors appealed her sentence. She was re-sentenced to ten years in federal prison.

Mumia Abu-Jamal, the National Lawyers Guild, and other activists and social justice organizations considered Stewart a political prisoner. Her most avid supporters—led by her husband, Poynter—organized a campaign calling for Stewart's compassionate release and assembled a zealous legal defense team. They sought review from the Supreme Court and, in 2013, argued in federal district court that her sentence be reduced and concluded given her previous time served. Several months later, on New Year's Eve, Stewart was released on the grounds that her terminal condition and short life expectancy warranted a shorter sentence. Newly free, she alighted at LaGuardia Airport, where an enormous crowd of family, friends, and journalists greeted her. When asked what she felt in that moment by *Democracy Now* host Amy Goodman, Stewart replied, "Beyond joy."

I spoke with Stewart and her husband—who occasionally added context and color to our interview—over coffee at their home in Brooklyn, where she is currently resting, seeking treatment for her ongoing illness, and sharing her lessons and life experiences with the next generation of people's lawyers.

—Jean Stevens for *Guernica*

Guernica: How did your upbringing lead you to a life of activism?

Lynne Stewart: It's very simple. I grew up in white, working-class Bellerose, Queens. There were no black people to be seen—Bellerose is still pretty white. I went to an all-white school, had all-white friends, all-white everything. Through chances of fate, a marriage that went on the rocks, a baby, in 1962, I found myself in [Harlem].

I got a job as a children's librarian at PS 175 in Harlem, and that changed everything. That was an epiphany. I didn't know Harlem existed. I didn't know there was such a place, because I grew up in white Queens, where five miles is 100 miles. So I went to the school and, being a smart cookie—as they called us in those days—I had a million questions. How did this place exist? How come I didn't know about it? Why are people living like this? Do they want to live like this? To show you how singular I was, I said to the principal, "Well, I was a Spanish minor in college, so that might be useful to me." He looked at me and said, "We don't have anyone who speaks Spanish at this school. This is an all-Negro school."

Why wasn't I told about this? How could I have been the valedictorian, the smartest, and never known Harlem existed? As a result, I began a lifelong learning experience, because I could not accept what the party line was with education—that these people want to live like this, these people don't have ambition, they don't want to work. You know, all the usual bullshit. I met Ralph there probably within the first month. We were both there in September of '62.

Guernica: How did you meet?

Ralph Poynter: I was teaching at another school at 8th Avenue and 141st Street and they asked me to go to a troubled school if I didn't mind.

Lynne Stewart: That was, and still is, a typical Board of Education ploy—put the strong, masculine figure in a school with tough kids and you have a certain control. It's very demeaning to the kids and very demeaning to the tough, black guy, but that's how they worked it. So he came to PS 175, and the principal decided to interview him in the library. And the rest is history! [*laughs*]

Guernica: You worked at the school through the '60s, through Vietnam and the civil rights movement. What were those years like, and how were you involved in activism there?

Lynne Stewart: I stayed at PS 175 through an early and very telling political action around community control of schools, which was to become my main focus for the rest of the '60s—along with the Vietnam War and other things. It was to reclaim schools for the community, and to have the community have a first say in the schools. Of course, the leadership of that was Ralph. He went out, he was in the streets, Ralph was organizing in Harlem—the people, the parents. You name it, he was out there. I was not exactly the girl in the office, but I was still learning. It was a very, very highly fraught battle. It ended up that we did not win, and I ended up teaching on the Lower East Side, close to where we were living. Then I ended up organizing on the Lower East Side till the spring of '71.

Guernica: After nearly ten years of library work and organizing around education, you shifted your focus to law. What led you to that transition?

Lynne Stewart: I was teaching at a very large public elementary school in the Lower East Side and we had our usual monthly teacher/principal conference. The principal got up and made a ten-minute speech about how the school was improving so much, that the kids were all reading, how we were doing such a great job. When he finished, I got up and said, "That sounds very good on paper, but I'm the librarian. I see every kid in this school. My observation is they still can't read. They're in sixth grade, and they're still reading *Hop on Pop* and *One Fish Two Fish* because it's easy and they can do it. But nobody's reading *Huckleberry Finn* or *Tom Sawyer*." So there was a moment of silence, and then the meeting went on as if I had never spoken. But that's because I was known. I was a radical. I had opened up the schools during the Shanker strike [by New York City's United Federation of Teachers in 1968]. I was speaking out for kids in the community. But that day, for some reason, just grabbed me.

Ralph had, by that point, been to jail and lost his teaching license. He had opened a small motorcycle shop right around the corner from the school. I left the school that day and went over to his shop. I was expecting a baby. I said to him, "I am going to end up like one of those shopping bag ladies on the subway because [the administration is] going to make me crazy." It's one thing to be in the opposition, it's another thing to be ignored. He said to me, "What'd you want to do?" And I said, "You know, I always wanted to go to law school." So he looks at me and he does not say, "Well, if you could teach another year we'd be in a much better position," or, "Could you go part time?" He said, "I guess you'd better go." So when people say, "What do you look for in a partner?" I say, "That's what you look for." So I went to law school, I had the baby, and he continued working in the shop.

Guernica: Legal education at that time was fairly regimented and traditional, yet you developed a sense of law as a tool for social justice and radical change. Was it something about Rutgers that inspired your thinking on legal work?

Lynne Stewart: I went to Rutgers because they gave me a free ride, because that year they were very progressive and very anxious to have a freshman class with over 50 percent women. All of that [tuition] money was a fortune in those days.

Ralph Poynter: After the first day of orientation, she came back directly to the shop, took the first bus across town, and she said, "I met the most wonderful man who lectured us on the law. His tie was down to his knees, but when he opened his mouth, the sky opened up." It was [civil rights attorney] Arthur Kinoy. From that moment on, Lynne wanted to be Arthur Kinoy.

Lynne Stewart: To a certain extent, in law school, I always had an attitude. I had been in the movement for ten years, I had kids, I had worked with Ralph. I was there to get through, to take the bar, and to get to work. But along the way, I met some remarkable professors, one of them being Arthur Kinoy, whom I remained in touch with until he died. I always said, no award is greater than when Arthur said, "We have to defend Lynne. She is a people's lawyer." To him, that was the goal, to be a people's lawyer.

Guernica: What does being a people's lawyer mean to you?

Lynne Stewart: It means that you're working not for the corporate interest, not for the government interest, not for your own self-interest. You have a higher calling. Your goal is to make a better world through the work you do. It's not always possible, and you have to earn a living. We certainly had to earn a living; we had all these wonderful children. But, basically, you're not looking to join the country club.

Ralph Poynter: [*laughs*] I couldn't even pick up golf balls at the country club!

Guernica: Your interpretation of being a people's lawyer seems to center on criminal defense work, for which you developed an enormous reputation. How did you begin?

Lynne Stewart: My anti-authoritarian instincts let me directly to criminal defense work. I worked for a couple years for one of Ralph's customers, whom he met through the Hells Angels. It was private work. I was originally advised that I should work as a prosecutor because they say, "If you make a mistake as a prosecutor, your mistakes go home, whereas if you make a mistake defending, they go to jail." It never worked out, anyway. I was told by Frank Hogan, who was a legend of prosecutors then, "We don't hire women." He just said it right out. Well, what am I doing here then?

I went from there and hung out my shingle [as a legal advocate]. I've been asked by young people, "How do you become a lawyer?" You make yourself available to the movement. At that point, for example, battered wives were not on the top of anybody's list. It was, "What did you do to provoke him? Why would he do that to you?" Stuff like that. I called the hotline, and I said I was available to help get orders of protection. I would help do whatever needed to be done, serve their papers. Many times, they'd go to court, get their papers, and then be afraid to serve them on the guy. So that was one source of income. But I took anything that came across my doorstep. I started getting a reputation.

Guernica: Your first major political case was representing the May 19th Communist Organization. What was the genesis of that?

Lynne Stewart: It was probably one of the most white radical groups out there, mainly radical women. They were organizing around the Springboks rugby team that came over [to New York City] from South Africa to play [in 1981]. They organized a demonstration outside Kennedy Airport, and after the demonstration, things got rowdy and ended with some acid being thrown. The Port Authority claimed the acid was thrown in the eyes of one of their cops. Seven or eight people were arrested, and I had let them know that I was available if they needed lawyers. They called me, and I went to represent one of the people who actually threw the acid, Donna Borup, who's still wanted.

Guernica: How did you feel about taking such a high-profile case and representing these clients?

Lynne Stewart: I was just afraid I'd get passed by! It seemed like it was an industry for [a few] movement lawyers, and they were not anxious to let anybody else in. But I was friends with some people who were very close to [the May 19th Communist Organization] and I knew they needed lawyers. And see, I was non-organizational. I was not a member of May 19th, or a socialist party, or any of these organizations. I was not one of their house lawyers.

We've never been card-carrying communists. We have a Marxist view, but it's not doctrinaire. We're not waiting for the working class to rise up, we're not waiting for the unions. That's gone, that passed, that didn't happen back in the '30s, and it's not going to happen now. But we still ally ourselves with organizations that strongly believe it will happen.

Guernica: Your reputation was cemented when you represented David J. Gilbert of the Weather Underground in 1983 for his role in the Brinks robbery and subsequent shootings. At the time, the Weather Underground was increasingly under surveillance, and public support for their work had dwindled. Gilbert had been spotted shooting at the scene. What was your approach to that case?

Lynne Stewart: A group [involved with the Weather Underground] came to see me and said, "We need a lawyer for David Gilbert, and we'd like to know, how would you represent him?" Well, he was caught at the scene with money, with everything right there. And I said, "Well, there was a guy who represented himself at a trial and he said in his defense that 'history will absolve me.' I guess we'd start it from there." They said, "You're the one! That's it!" But I'm no fool: caught at the scene, dead cops, Weather Underground background—everything was working against him. There was not much hope for the case. But I'm committed, and I'm particularly committed to the political people who needed defense. I understand that they're fighting a bigger war than just, "Let me go get some money for cocaine tonight." They're out there fighting the government on behalf of everybody.

But of course, the judge had promised that everyone would be paid from government funds. The three lawyers who had been on the case from day one were paid. They were all male; they were all white. My two co-counsel [a woman and African-American man] and I had a six-month trial, but we were paid no money. I said to him, "I just want you to know, they're turning off the phone in my office tomorrow. I have a son in college, and we get phone calls every day because we haven't paid tuition yet." And at this point, he turns around and says to another guy, "She has children?" So we never got paid. I'm happy to say I became an enemy of [that judge] for the rest of my life.

Guernica: Have you ever turned down a case?

Lynne Stewart: I would never take a case that had to do with abusing children. They're the true innocents. All of the rest of us, we have smears and stains, but they're helpless. I couldn't add my talent, which is prodigious, to a defense of someone even accused of hurting a child. I would never defend a cop—though I did on a few private cases, when cops were acting not as cops but as private citizens. Other than that, I represented everybody who came by. It made me somewhat of a pariah, with some people like the National Lawyers Guild, which didn't think we should be representing drug dealers and cases like that. They thought that we were representing people who didn't deserve high-class representation.

Guernica: So others within the legal left did not always support you?

Lynne Stewart: I've always been knee-deep in trouble, I guess, but the only incident I really remember was when I was given a subpoena by the special narcotics prosecutor to come in—this was in the late '80s—and tell him who had brought money to me in a certain drug case. I said, "I can't testify to that, it's privileged." I raised all the issues. In the end, I was ordered to speak. I went before the grand jury and refused. The judge held me in contempt and actually indicted me. It was then that both the Center for Constitutional Rights and the Guild said they couldn't help me because it involved drugs. I must say, I had contempt for them. Come on, we're in this because we're lawyers and we believe [that people have a right to] a certain level of representation. And what is this? Now I am going to get tarred? My son Geoffrey wrote a motion to release me, and he won.

Guernica: You represented Egyptian cleric Sheik Omar Abdel Rahman against charges of conspiring to commit terrorism, for which he was convicted in 1995, a case that resulted in your arrest and eventual incarceration. How did you become involved in his case?

Lynne Stewart: I got a visit from [a colleague of former US attorney general] Ramsey Clark to see if I'd be interested in doing the sheik's case. After a certain number of years, doing the same kind of cases, I had a sense that Muslims were the new target of the government and [the state] was going to really come down on them. Ramsey was very anxious to get a high-level, high-quality movement lawyer because this man probably had more prestige than any Middle Eastern person who's ever been on trial in this country. He was a doctor from Al-Azhar University. He was highly respected all over the Middle East. There was a sense, a true sense, in my opinion, that he was being railroaded. So when Ramsey Clark asked me to go down and interview the sheik, I did, of course. To many people's amazement, we hit it off very well, and he indicated to Ramsey that he wanted me to represent him.

I had a couple of problems. Here was a mountain of material I hadn't even seen or contemplated, it was not my usual milieu of the American left, or even the mob, for whom I'd done some cases. I was your typical living-room liberal. He, of course, was a very different kettle of fish. He was arrogant, he was brilliant, he went by his own rules. It was difficult for him to have a woman lawyer.

Ralph Poynter: He wanted to get my permission to allow Lynne to do the case. So he got on the phone with the interpreter and called me. He said, "This is an important case. Your wife could have problems doing it." I said, "My dear sheik, I am guilty of the most serious crimes you can be guilty of in America: I was born poor and black, and you are just small potatoes." I could hear all the translation, I could hear a roar of laughter, and he got on the phone and said, "Small potatoes!" And that was the joke from then on. He'd introduce himself as "small potatoes."

Lynne Stewart: During the course of the trial, my daughter got chicken pox on her honeymoon. I told the sheik, and he said, "You're the mother, you should be home with her." I said, "I should be home with her? Sheik, who's going to try your case?" He laughed. He got it right away. We were very, very close. He said things that still tear my heart at this point. We were, of course, completely cut off as part of my ongoing punishment. You know that question: What do you do when you think the client's guilty? The real question is: What you do when you think a client's innocent?

I really believe he was innocent. And "innocent" is a word I don't use. They manufactured a case against him because it was in the interest of the United States government, and the Egyptian government, and they came at him from both sides. They both worked on this to make sure he went to jail and he was off the scene in Egypt, because Egypt was, and is, the tinderbox of the Middle East. Our most important ally.

Guernica: Many lawyers, organizers, and activists within the movement face severe burnout. Given the pressure around your cases, how did you work against fatigue?

Lynne Stewart: I always had a variety of cases, so while I was representing [Larry Davis, acquitted of shooting six police officers] in the Bronx, with the entire press corps of New York showing up, I also was representing Jose Diaz, who lived down the block from me. The variety was good.

Ralph Poynter: You always said you took your job seriously, and I thought you always took it too seriously. She took on responsibility, and it just never left her.

Lynne Stewart: I loved the work. I missed it for years after I was arrested. I couldn't drive past 100 Centre [New York City Criminal Court], that whole area, without crying, seeing people going to court and knowing I couldn't do that anymore. I still do miss it. I don't think I could ever go back. Maybe I could consider second-seating my son or someone else whose work I respect. But I could not take on any responsibility. I'm out of step; I haven't kept up.

Guernica: How do you think the role of movement lawyers has changed since you tried your biggest cases?

Lynne Stewart: Today, it's not the same playing field as when I first became a lawyer in 1977, where the government had been restricted by our wonderful [Supreme Court Justice] Earl Warren's court rulings. Now it's all going the other way, the flow is against the defendant, against anything that could really help a client. But you still fight it, you do what you can do. It's all there is.

Lawyering is very individualistic. There are lawyers who are going to be that persistent bird dog, they're never going to give up on the client, they're going to defend people. A good recent example is Ben Rosenfeld, who defended the "eco-terrorist" [Eric McDavid] who just [was released]. Ben is of the old school. He is a fighter, and he's young. There are lawyers who believe in client-centered representation and who are dedicated on that level, the same level I feel I was dedicated.

My son does criminal defense work. I get the war stories from him, and I see it is harder than it was [for my generation], much harder. The law has basically restricted the playing field so that the prosecution makes all the important decisions: what's charged, how much is charged, whether you can get a decent offer. Every [defendant] becomes an informant today.

I feel for young people today. When I came out of law school, yes, we were broke, we had these kids, we had problems. But it was straightforward. I didn't have to say, "My God, I am $80,000 in debt, I have to get a job, I have to pay it back, my life is ruined otherwise." We were able to go forward and work toward building something new, and that's what we did. Today many lawyers are unable to feel free to be advocates.

Guernica: What advice do you have for movement lawyers and organizers today?

Lynne Stewart: First of all, think creatively. Think, "How can we deal with this particular case in a way we haven't dealt with similar ones in the past?" Second, don't be afraid of the people who are willing to defend your client. I find too many lawyers say, "Keep that defense committee away from me!" If it weren't for my defense committee, I'd be sitting in [federal prison in] Texas today. And the press! You've got to learn to handle the press because God knows the government does all the time.

The night they announced the verdict in Ferguson, there should've been some spokesperson that was not Al Sharpton to have responded to that, to raise the movement or progressive position, and to raise the question that the use of the grand jury by a prosecutor is hardly something that is legally sacrosanct, and we should question it. On a certain level, we don't try enough cases. We should try more cases before juries and let jurors decide. On grand juries, my position is the grand jury should be eliminated, but there are creative ways a lawyer can use a grand jury if they have a client with a sympathetic cause who has been wronged by the police.

Guernica: Reflecting back on your organizing work in the '60s around community-based education, do you think there's a role for social justice lawyers and advocates in other movements besides criminal defense?

Lynne Stewart: I'd say there's a role in all. [Ralph and I] were discussing not long ago that in the '60s, everybody had their own niche. We had people who did housing, people who did anti-war, people who did schools. Everyone operated in their own niche, but not separately. We all were together on certain issues when it was important. Everybody was active in the '60s. I feel that there's a lot of active radical thought today but not much action.

Guernica: Why do you think so?

Ralph Poynter: I think people are afraid. I remember when we'd have discussions in the '60s among people who were active. We'd say, "Well, people are afraid," and the answer to us was, "If you're afraid, you know you should be doing something." People are afraid today, but they're not doing anything.

Lynne Stewart: I spoke in front of a huge gathering in Seattle, and someone got up and said, "I'm just so afraid." I said, "The only way not to be afraid is to join with other people who are also afraid." There's a great poem, ["The Low Road"], by Marge Piercy that says, "Alone, you can fight...but two people fighting can...cut through a mob." The only thing we have is each other.

How to Be a
Woman in Tehran

HABIBE JAFARIAN, TRANSLATED FROM THE PERSIAN BY
SALAR ABDOH // MARCH 16, 2015

I stay because, as my mother never stopped repeating,
I am my own woman, but also my own man.

WHENEVER MY MOTHER would talk to me about her thirty-five years of marriage to my father, she'd end on a familiar refrain: "I was always my own woman. And I was always my own man too. You see, I had to carry my own weight every day of every year, and I mean every bit of it."

I understand what my mother says. Iran: it's the country I was born in, went to school in, and have worked as a professional journalist in for twenty years; a country where authority, religion, and fate would have it so that even someone like my mother had to pull a permanent double shift as both a woman and a man throughout her entire adult life. I can't say if, as a country, Iran is unique in this way, but I do know it is one place on earth that is emphatically this way—a place where women are in every measure equal to men, and in every measure not.

I had to dig deep into my backpack before I found the acetone polish remover and cotton pad that would save the day. My nail polish was hardly head-turning. After many days of dishwashing and cooking, the color was like a faded stain. I wasn't going to tempt any man to his doom with seductive fingernails, but I was headed to see a cleric for an official interview at the Armed Forces of the Islamic Republic of Iran's Division of

Topography. Neither the cleric nor the Division of Topography would be amused at the sight of any color on me, faint or not. So I rubbed those nails with everything I had and then stuffed the sharp-smelling cotton in a pocket of my backpack. Next I put on a proper hijab; there was no way they'd let me in with a simple shawl. I secured it over my head so that no hair would show. As I prepared myself, the rest of the passengers in the taxicab barely gave me a glance. This, after all, was not an unfamiliar scene.

As I'd expected, the Topography Division had separate entrances for males and females. I took a deep breath and stepped inside. A woman wearing a *chador* asked what my business was there. I told her. She asked if I was sure that Haj Aqa was in today. "This is not a day he usually comes in." I repeated that I had a 10 a.m. appointment with Haj Aqa and it was already getting late. The woman gave me another once-over. Then she said, "Your *manteau* is too short. You also have makeup on. No, you can't go inside." My *manteau* came below my knees and I wasn't wearing any makeup. I looked at her. My cell phone rang; it was Haj Aqa himself. He wanted to know if I'd arrived. He was flying to Mecca later on that day and couldn't afford any sort of delay. I told him that I was stuck downstairs at security and they weren't letting me in. "They say I don't look proper." He was surprised, then became angry. He told me to wait right there and in a minute he was downstairs.

Until then I'd only known Haj Aqa from the articles he'd written. He seemed like a well-educated fellow, pragmatic and sensible, which was why I'd called to secure an interview with him. Now I watched as he turned to the woman at security: "This lady is coming upstairs with me." The woman immediately sprang to her feet. "But Haj Aqa, her hijab is not proper. Her *manteau* is too short and she's wearing makeup."

This time he didn't even bother looking at her as he commanded, "Come with me!"

The woman's voice followed us out of security: "Haj Aqa, if anything happens, the responsibility is your own."

What could "happen"? I wondered to myself as I followed the cleric to his office. What possible ignominy could a woman reporter standing a little over five feet two inches, looking positively average in a pair of gray sneakers, a dark green *manteau*, and a black headscarf, wreak on the Topography Division of the military of the Islamic Republic of Iran?

When we were in his office I didn't mince words. I asked the cleric, "Why are women treated this way at government offices? I mean, just because I'm not wearing a *chador* I'll turn this place into a den of immorality?"

He was quiet for a minute, then said, "You know, the other day my car was stolen near Argentina Circle. I went to the local police station to put in a report. I could hear people behind me in line whispering among themselves. Would you like to hear what they were saying? 'Whoever steals from a *mulla* is a saint!' This is what they said behind my back. And I had no answer to that. Know why? Because people are angry at us clerics and they have every right to be angry. We haven't been fair to them. Actually, we haven't been fair to this country ever since the Islamic revolution. So to you I say, 'You too have every right to be upset.' But… don't expect me to repeat any of this during our interview."

"Haj Aqa, I doubt there's going to be an interview at this point." I was looking at the puckered carcass of my professional voice recorder. Somehow the acetone pad that I'd stuffed in the backpack's side pocket had eaten right through the gadget's microphone. The thing was useless now, but I asked my question anyway: "You teach social psychology at the university. Let's say I arrived for an interview at the college wearing pink nail polish. What would you think of me then? Would they treat me there like they treated me here today?"

He regarded me for a long time. It was as if he was trying to tell me something—*I just tried to convey to you, a reporter, my honorable intentions as a man of the cloth and an official of the Islamic Republic. And still you have to be stubborn with me?*

I met his gaze and thought, *What do you expect from a woman, and a reporter at that, in this town? Any way you look at it, it's this town that taught me to be ruthless. It's this country that forces me to act as I do and ask the questions I ask.*

He adjusted his turban a little. "If two years ago you'd come to my office wearing pink nail polish, I wouldn't have thought well of you."

Two years ago signified 2009, the year of the Green Movement, a time of vast street demonstrations and arrests. I pretended not to catch the significance of this and asked, "What's happened since that time that's made you change your mind?"

"Two years ago is just a number," he said, playing along. "What I mean is that I've traveled a lot over the years. I've seen a bit of the world by now, but, more importantly, I've been reading a lot of history. I'll tell you something, studying history clarifies a great many things." He stared at my cell phone, which had begun vibrating without sound on the table.

"Haj Aqa, if the phone is a bother, I'll put it in my bag."

"You can go ahead and answer this one."

It was my boss at the paper. He wanted to know when I'd be back at the office. With more than a hint of irritation I told him I was in the middle of an interview. He sounded apologetic, and said he knew where I was but he'd been forced to call me anyway. There was a pause and he added, "There's a woman here. Says she won't leave until she sees you. Says…"— another pause before he mumbled awkwardly—"She says you've been with her husband."

I was born in the city of Mashhad, Iran's most religious city—arguably more religious than the seat of clerical power in Qom because one of the twelve revered imams of the Shia is buried in Mashhad. Mashhad is a major pilgrimage center for Shia from around the world and a place where I never felt at home. Rather, it was Tehran, the capital, that I yearned for since the age of eleven when I read Somerset Maugham's *Of Human Bondage* and discovered in my older brother's biology textbook where babies came from. By the time I was fifteen, I had a map of the city that I'd stare at for hours. I would spread that map out on the floor of the barely 600-square-foot, blue-collar apartment our family of eight lived in and I would try to learn each twist and turn of the Iranian capital by heart.

When I finally arrived in Tehran for university, it was as if I'd always known the place. The museums, the spots our poets had written about, the neighborhoods where film sequences had been shot: they were mine now. This was my city. I quickly got a job at a no-name journal where I could make some pocket money and I walked everywhere.

My father, always afraid for his daughter, would telephone and say, "Please don't go anywhere by yourself!" When inevitably he didn't receive a response from me, he'd add one of the expressions he repeated often: "A man cannot drive a nail into a stone." Then he'd quote a famous saying from the first Shia imam, Imam Ali: "Fearfulness, which is the worst of traits in a man, is indeed the best of traits in a woman." And then, "A woman, unlike a man, should have fear. But you have no fear, my daughter, and so I have fear for you."

"I fear for you, Habibe."

My boss at the paper told me this as he stood up and closed the door on all of the prying eyes, people eager to know more about the woman who had barged into our office claiming that I'd had a relationship with her husband. The woman had not been wrong, but the husband she spoke of was a man I'd seen for the last time under the Seyyed Khandan Bridge over two years earlier. I'd met him that day to tell him I didn't want to see him anymore because, among other things, he had lied to me about not being married.

I didn't have to explain any of this to my boss, but I did. After I was finished, he said, "Be that as it may, you can't go around trying to vindicate yourself to all the people this woman has been poisoning against you. Do you understand? People will judge you because that is what they do and because this is Iran. Don't forget! I think it's best if you don't come to work for a week. Give it some time for people to forget about all this."

I stood up. "I'm going to follow up on the report I have to turn in tomorrow and," I paused, "I'll be here at the office bright and early in the morning."

My boss repeated, "I fear for you, Habibe."

Walking back to my desk, I could feel the weight of the "judgment" my boss had spoken of. My fellow reporters buried their noses into their notes and computer monitors, but their silence hinted at unasked questions: *Why are you still here? Why aren't you crying? Where is your embarrassment?*

My desk was next to Miss Ahmadi's, our photo editor, though what she mostly did was to "improve" the kinds of pictures that officials deemed "improper." I knew Miss Ahmadi lived alone, but despite her meager salary, she was also the sole supporter of her mother and younger sister. As I sat down I saw that she was busy using Photoshop to add a collar to Nicole Kidman's exposed neck and shoulders. I patted her back. "In addition to your work with Photoshop, you could go into business as a tailor. Think of all the sleeves, collars, and pants you've created out of thin air for famous women all these years!"

She smiled and changed one pair of glasses for another. "You wouldn't believe it, Habibe. Nowadays whenever they send photos my way, what I immediately notice are all the uncovered ankles, chests, upper arms, and shoulders that I have to 'edit.' I swear to God, it's like I've become another one of those lecherous guys on the streets who see nothing but flesh everywhere." She zoomed in a little closer on Nicole Kidman's gorgeous figure to make sure she hadn't missed a body part.

I gave her a thumbs up. "Your handiwork is perfect."

She turned back to me. "Perfect? As what? As some horny guy fixated on women's bodies?"

We both laughed.

It was the first time I'd laughed that day.

"But this is no laughing matter, Habibe."

I was digging, as always, in my backpack for a cigarette. I knew my silence was getting on my friend Shahrzad's nerves. Back from Paris for two days of Christmas vacation, Shahrzad had left Iran five years earlier. She was the third of my closest friends who had done so in the last half-decade. At first she'd left to study anthropology, then she'd stayed, which is pretty much what they all do; leave to "study" and then never return. I found a cigarette at last and asked the young waiter at the café to give us an ashtray. He looked at me a bit hesitantly and admitted, "They don't allow ladies to smoke in the café. If the Bureau of Public Places finds out we allow it, they'll close the place down." I reminded him that it was true the Bureau had gotten tough for a few months, but they'd relaxed things a bit lately. He thought some more and then relented, "All right then." He pointed to a table that was hidden away from the entrance. "Sit over there."

Shahrzad's shawl slipped off her head. Next to her, on a narrow column, was the café management's notice to customers: *For your own peace of mind, and ours, please control your emotions. Do not smoke (it is bad for you anyway). And please, please make sure that your Islamic head-cover is proper.* Shahrzad grimaced reading the note. I laughed and lit my cigarette. She swatted at the smoke between us. "You're laughing again? I just can't understand why you stay in this country. Why?"

"Actually, I'm going away," I said. Her eyes flashed at the news and she waited for me to elaborate. "I'm going to Lebanon," I went on. "On assignment. I'm going to interview the family of Imam Musa Sadr, the original architect of the Hezbollah of Lebanon. I've accepted a job to write his biography. I'm going to Beirut and to the deep south. They're taking me right up to the border where Hezbollah and Israel clash."

Shahrzad pulled her shawl tightly back over her head. "Habibe, don't you have any fear? You don't, do you? But I do. I have fear for you."

But of course I have fear. In fact, I've been afraid all my life. I was afraid when my brother told me that now that my studies were over I should leave Tehran and return to Mashhad. I was afraid at Tehran airport's investigation unit—the woman who asked me where I was heading, and when I said, "Paris," leaned in skeptically and responded, "Paris? And who, pray tell, is accompanying you to Paris for two weeks?"

I was afraid when I saw my name on the list of female reporters who could not come back to the newspaper until they corrected their "improper" hijab. I was afraid in 2009 when I watched a soldier beat demonstrators at random with his baton in 7th-Tir Square. And I was even more afraid when he suddenly turned on me and barked, "What are you gawking at?" I was afraid in Maroun al-Ras, Lebanon, when I watched several peaceful cows grazing on the other side of a barbed-wire fence and my guide told me, "That's Israel over there. We're at the border." Yes, I've always been afraid, but I've always carried on. I've always tried to suppress my quiet frustration with compatriots who've made Europe, Canada, and the United States their homes, but choose to, over their vacations back in Tehran, admonish people like me for our decision to stay.

I've chosen the harder path. Which means: not running off to another world as soon as life gets tough. It means staying in your own country and engaging in its discourse, even if you have to be cross-examined now and then at the Armed Forces of the Islamic Republic of Iran's Division of Topography. The harder path means reporting from here (rather than reporting about Tehran from London or Washington); it means intimately knowing Tehran's back alleys and countless addicts, its impossible traffic, its unbearable pollution, its corruptions, its day-to-day humiliations.

For all of this, I feel I should be respected and not pitied, because what I do for a living, journalism—journalism in Iran—is of special consequence. I stay because, as my mother never stopped repeating, I am my own woman, but also my own man. Not only do I have to compete, neck and neck, with men in Iran as a single woman; not only do I have to sometimes stay until 11 p.m. at the news desk to meet a deadline; not only, on my way home on those late nights, am I followed and accosted, because a woman should not be out so late by herself; not only, when I visit, say, a real-estate office to rent an apartment, will the agent's attitude change immediately when he finds out that I'm on my own; not only do I inevitably get a variety of offers on such occasions (mistress, temporary wife, second wife); and not only, when I politely decline, will the same fellow's "kindly" offer suddenly turn into outright hostility; but also, on the other side of this societal split, I find myself being censured by my own milieu for bothering to stay at all, for bothering to fight it out. Because this is a fight. And if women like me don't stay then nothing will ever change.

I don't mention much of this to all those friends who vacation in Iran, or to those "writers" who take their Grand Tour of the country before writing their memoirs about us "poor folk" here. Because, truly, it is not their fight; it is not their issue. Instead, when expatriate friends ask why I don't leave Iran, I lie and tell them I don't have the patience to speak in any language other than Persian. This I heard from the lips of one of my professors a long time ago, and I decided then that it was the perfect answer. Why? Because it is an answer that's neutral, an answer that does not force one to qualify the reply with one's gender.

God suspected my heart was a geode but he had to make sure

LAYLA BENITEZ-JAMES // DECEMBER 15, 2014

God said, I took clouds and planted them / in soft, red clay.

No fissures of light shine from inside
but He has seen fresh fish bellies—all cream
and copper—slip from my hands back into the water.
He has seen the flint gray tide slink out and hide.

He thought he heard a car backfire,
but He could not be sure. This was good,
the house was silent, a sick mountain
lion crept into town, this was good.

Rabbits wriggling through wire fences good,
slipping out of their skins under blades
and thumbs good, coats soaking red good,
my knees gulping mud, sun sparking on water—

good, God said, *I took clouds and planted them
in soft, red clay. I watered them with spiders' threads
until they sprouted a stream translating into river
into rapids, good, lace-capped sliding good*—my back

to the woods good.

A Dangerous Language

VINEET GILL INTERVIEWS MANO KHALIL // MAY 15, 2015

The Kurdish filmmaker on deploying a camera rather than a gun to fight for his community.

IN OCTOBER 2014, the Kurdish filmmaker Mano Khalil arrived in Dharamsala, a northern Indian town inhabited by thousands of Tibetan exiles, for a screening of his recent documentary, *The Beekeeper*. Edward Said once wrote that to be an exile is not to feel alienated from the idea of home, but to be reminded every day of your life "that you are in exile, that your home is not in fact so far away." Though the film screening marked Khalil's first visit to the city—the site, also, of the Dalai Lama's residence—he is intimately familiar with states of exile: he has lived in Switzerland for over twenty years, since escaping the Baathist regime in Syria, his place of birth.

There are close to 30 million Kurds living in the contiguous area that now lies divided between Syria, Turkey, Iraq, and Iran, making them the world's largest stateless ethnic group. Kurds are also among the most persecuted minorities in the region. "It was enough to say that one was a Kurd to be imprisoned," Khalil said during our interview, which took place in Dharamsala a day after the screening. He spoke from firsthand experience. As a film student in former Czechoslovakia in the late 1980s, Khalil mentioned his Kurdish identity in a magazine interview. Upon his return to Damascus, he was jailed for the offense.

For Khalil, filmmaking is as much a political act as a creative pursuit. He told me he'd picked up a camera instead of a gun to "continue that fight"—the fight for Kurdish statehood, the fight against mass repression, and the fight to restore the Kurdish identity both politically and culturally.

The documentary *The Place Where God Sleeps* is the only film Khalil has shot in Syria. Released in 1993, the film tracks the lives of Kurdish community members living between the borders of Syria and Turkey. It was well received, winning first prize at the Augsburg Film Festival in Germany. But following the film's international reception, Khalil said, "the doors of hell opened" for him and his family in Syria, and he fled the country for Switzerland, where he later became a citizen.

For more than twenty years, through both feature films and documentaries, Khalil has continued to explore themes central to the Kurdish experience, including ethnic repression, displacement, and loss. His 2005 documentary, *Al-Anfal: In the Name of Allah, Baath and Saddam*, was an investigation into the holy war Saddam Hussein waged against the Kurdish population of northern Iraq in the 1980s. *David the Tolhildan*, released in 2007, follows Swiss citizen David Rouiller as he gives up a life of Western privilege to join the Kurdish liberation movement.

That particular narrative arc is reversed in *The Beekeeper*, which explores a Kurdish refugee's life in Switzerland. In the film, Ibrahim Gezer pursues his passion for rearing honey bees while coming to terms with the loss of his family: some left behind in war-torn Turkish Kurdistan; others, including his son, killed fighting alongside the Kurdistan Workers' Party.

When the film opens, Ibrahim has already spent seven years in hiding in the mountains following his arrest and torture by Turkish forces. In Switzerland, as he rebuilds his life from scratch at the age of sixty-four, beekeeping—a childhood enthusiasm—is his only contact with the past. "I love it when they sting me," Ibrahim tells the camera at one point. This "hobby," as the Swiss authorities disparagingly call it, becomes a symbol of normalcy and continuity.

Khalil grew up speaking Kurdish and Arabic, later becoming adept in Czech, German, Swiss German, and English. He spoke with me in fluid English, though he routinely apologized for his lack of fluency. Twice after the interview, he contacted me to say that he wanted to have another go at what he thought he'd failed to convey earlier. At times I wondered if a camera, which conveys truths through the manipulation of light rather than words, might have proved more comfortable.

—Vineet Gill for *Guernica*

Guernica: You were born in the Syrian part of Kurdistan. Tell me about growing up as a Kurd in the shadow of Arab nationalism.

Mano Khalil: My mother came from Turkish Kurdistan and my father was from Syrian Kurdistan. When they got married, there was no border between Syria and Turkey, and people could move freely between the two countries. Then, around sixty years ago, the border was set up, and my mother just couldn't go back to her family. She was stuck in Syria.

I was born in a small village in Syria where Kurdish was spoken: a language absolutely different from Arabic, which is a Semitic language. Kurdish belongs to the family of Indo-European languages. We were forbidden in Syria to speak Kurdish. This was of course a time of Arab nationalism—of Assad's Baath party in Syria and Saddam Hussein in Iraq. In these countries, if you were caught selling ten kilos of heroin, you could be imprisoned for a year; if you killed someone you'd get a three-year prison sentence. But if you wrote a poem or a small article in Kurdish, you'd spend over ten years in jail and may even have ended up being killed. Kurdish was seen by the authorities as a dangerous language.

My brothers and I were all sent to Arabic schools, where speaking Kurdish wasn't allowed. Imagine six-year-old Kurdish kids walking into these schools without knowing a word of Arabic. The teachers would start hitting the kids, saying, "Why do you speak Kurdish?" We started asking ourselves, "Why are we being treated like this? Why is it that my mother sings Kurdish songs to me at home, and at school they say that it is a bad language?" Very quickly we learned what it meant to be a Kurd. We had no rights. It was enough to say that one was a Kurd to be imprisoned. Which was exactly what happened to me.

Guernica: You were imprisoned for saying you were Kurdish?

Mano Khalil: Yes. I was studying filmmaking in the former Czechoslovakia. In 1988, I was interviewed there for a magazine, and the introduction to that piece said, "Mano Khalil, a Kurdish student from Syria, studying film direction in Czechoslovakia." The interview was about why I had chosen Czechoslovakia for my studies. In 1992, I returned to Syria and was arrested on arrival. Then they showed me a copy of this Czech magazine that carried my interview. They asked me, "Why did you say you were a Kurd when you know there are no Kurds in Syria?" Remember that this was a time when there was no Internet or e-mail. The regime still managed to get copies of this article, and my name was all across the country's borders and airports as a wanted man. So I was sent to prison in Damascus. Thankfully, it was only for a short time. We paid some money and I was allowed to go free.

Guernica: When and how did you decide to become a filmmaker?

Mano Khalil: This was before I went to Czechoslovakia to study film-making. We were young and we were all thinking of liberating the world through socialism. We were reading the works of Che Guevara, Mao, and Lenin. After school, I went to Damascus to study law and history, which I didn't really like. I didn't like history, in particular. In Syria, the regime was trying to present to us a distorted version of the past. Assad was shown as the father of history.

So I decided to shift to film, which was something I had always loved as a teenager. For instance, we had hundreds of Bollywood movies in Syria. I would walk into the cinema ten minutes after the film started, as it was cheaper. Ticket prices were halved a few minutes into the movie. And sitting in the darkness of the cinema, I got to see another world. This imaginary world was a refuge for many of us. Of course, the films were controlled and censored by the regime. But I still thought, around this time, that maybe making films would be good for me. I thought of expressing myself through this medium, and of doing something for the Kurds. The options were clear: either I'd work as a lawyer under the Baath regime or make movies independently.

Guernica: Is there any particular filmmaker from the region whose work inspired you when you were starting out?

Mano Khalil: There was a Kurdish filmmaker named Yılmaz Güney. In 1982, he won the Palme d'Or at Cannes. This inspired great hope in us. We got a movie out into the world that spoke about the Kurdish people! The name of the film, *Yol*, means "the road." It's a story of five Kurdish prisoners in Turkey who are going back to their families.

For the first time we saw the word "Kurdistan" written there on the screen. I watched that and said to myself, "If my friends are going to the mountains with guns to fight, I will continue that fight, not with guns but with a camera." So I decided first to go to Moscow, but when I couldn't get there due to lack of paperwork, I went to Czechoslovakia instead in 1986.

I dreamt of making films about my people, about the fate of this nation of 30 million people who had no right to have a single school in the Kurdish language.

Guernica: So when you returned to Syria after studying filmmaking, you made a movie about the Kurdish people?

Mano Khalil: Yes. I finished school, returned to Syria, and made a movie. Unfortunately, this is the only film I've made in Syria. It's called *The Place Where God Sleeps*. It is a short movie, about thirty minutes in length: a documentary about Kurdish people living at the border between Syria and Turkey. I see it as a mosaic, the life of one family in Kurdish Syria at that time. The film won first prize at the Augsburg Film Festival in Germany.

Soon after, the doors of hell opened for me and my family. The regime was very aggressive toward us. They wanted to know who had financed the film, who had helped me make it. How did I shoot the film in Syria without their knowledge? For me, it was becoming impossible to stay in Syria. I decided to go to Switzerland in 1996, and I've never returned since. Now I meet my family in Iraqi and Turkish Kurdistan. At the Turkish-Kurdistan border, my family walks across some ten meters to this side of the border and we see each other.

Guernica: You studied fiction filmmaking, yet your focus has been on documentaries. Do you find the sense of urgency in documentaries lacking in feature films?

Mano Khalil: It's difficult to make movies. For me it was easier, as a refugee in Switzerland, to make documentary films, because I didn't need a lot of money for it. The way I tell my story or my opinion would be very similar in both fiction and documentary forms. But I found I could speak more effectively to convey this brutal reality through documentary than I could through fiction. With fiction, you are creating an imaginary world. And it can be a very mechanical process. In a fictional film, you create the characters who become "real people" when facing the camera. When you stop shooting, they change their costumes and become someone else. And people tend to believe in documentary more than fiction. Even if the fiction is based on a true story, everybody will say, "Oh, they're only actors."

Guernica: This wariness with which some audiences approach works of fiction may have to do with a difficulty in understanding how close to reality good fiction can get.

Mano Khalil: Exactly. Most people look at a feature film and say, "It's just a movie." For me there is no border or wall between fiction and documentary filmmaking. In documentaries, you have to deal with real people and their real feelings—you are working with real laughter, happiness, sadness. To try to reflect the reality is not the same as reality itself. That's why I think that making a good documentary is much harder than making a good feature film.

Documentary has been a way for me to establish myself as a filmmaker. It's my way of proving that I have a language, that I can say something through film. Now, after a couple of successful documentaries, including *The Beekeeper*, it's become a little easier to get some more money and work on fiction. My latest movie, *The Swallow*, is a work of fiction based in Iraqi Kurdistan.

Guernica: Could you talk a little more about *The Swallow*? How much of the film did you draw from real events?

Mano Khalil: *The Swallow* is a story of a 28-year-old Swiss girl who travels to Iraqi Kurdistan in order to find her father, a man she's never before met. Equipped only with an old letter and a faded photograph, she leaves Switzerland on a journey that will change her life. This movie is a work of fiction, but the way it's shot makes it seem more like a documentary. Of course there was a script with dialogue and scenes, and everything was planned. But we shot the film mostly with a hand-held camera, barely using the tripod or artificial light. Some of the long scenes were completed in a single shot. We had actors who knew exactly what to do and say. But there were times when these actors were talking to people in villages and in the streets, as in a documentary. The most important aspect of this movie is how it is rooted in contemporary reality—words like "Peshmerga," "ISIS," "Yazidis," themes of war crimes and revenge.

Guernica: I'm curious to hear about the rapport you share with the subjects of your documentary films.

Mano Khalil: In all my documentaries, I have great respect for the people I work with. Really, I love them. And it's very important for me that when I finish a movie, they stay my friends. It's important that they won't feel that

I in any way manipulated them or showed them in a bad light. I want to show them in all their reality—not as subjects but as people with flesh and blood—but I want to do this with all my respect.

Guernica: In *The Beekeeper*, there comes a point where Ibrahim, the protagonist, doesn't forget about the camera so much as he befriends it. There are scenes in which the camera is his only companion and he exchanges brief knowing glances with it.

Mano Khalil: Some months ago, a friend of mine, a Swiss filmmaker, told me he was going to make a movie about this person. And he started speaking about her very negatively. He said, "Oh, the subject is so fat, and she stinks," and so on. I said, "Hey, your movie is going to be bad." Why? Because you don't like your protagonist. When I am making a film about you, I have to like you. Even if you make a movie about a criminal locked up in prison, you may not support him as a criminal, but you have to like him on some level. You have to love your protagonist and respect him. He will only open his heart to you when he believes that you are treating him with respect, with love. Only then will there be no more walls between the filmmaker and the protagonist. I acted the same way with Ibrahim, whether or not the camera was on. I was eating, sleeping, laughing, and crying with him. We built a life together. And this brought out a very intimate reality.

Guernica: You said that you picked up a camera instead of a gun. Are you interested in influencing politics with your art?

Mano Khalil: Yes, I hope so. I never think of myself as a Buddha or a Christ figure saving humanity and so on. But the fact that this film, *The Beekeeper*, was screened in India, and that people saw the story of Ibrahim here, means a lot to me. When I see that people are touched, and they feel solidarity with him, I say to myself, "I made a little change." We went to Turkey with this movie. The film was screened at a film festival there. I was concerned that the audience there would see the story of Ibrahim [whose son dies fighting for the PKK, the Kurdistan Workers' Party] as somehow connected to terrorism. But I brought this film to Istanbul, and people said, "Our government did all this to him?" They told me, "Ibrahim is such a nice person. He is so lovely." The film has changed people's perspectives. That sort of change is small, but it has power. It would be nice if we could resolve all our political problems through cinema.

Guernica: Do you ever think about returning home?

Mano Khalil: I dream about going back, but I know that it isn't easy. Thirty years of being in Europe has changed my life. I am not the Kurd from Syria anymore as I was before. Kurdistani Syria developed somewhere, and I developed elsewhere. I think we will not find each other easily again. If I go back I will be a foreigner in my own country now. But of course it remains a dream to make another movie in Syria, and I am waiting for that opportunity.

Guernica: What are your views on the ongoing campaign against the Islamic State in Iraq and Syria? Has the current crisis impacted the push toward a free and sovereign Kurdistan?

Mano Khalil: The problem of ISIS is not recent. Ever since the Second World War, people in this region have been, and are today, living under brutal dictatorships governed by nationalistic fervor. As for the Kurdish question: nobody from the Arab world is serious about fighting ISIS. It's only the Kurdish people who are standing firm against ISIS. And I think Europe, the United States, and most other democratic countries of the world are beginning to look at the Kurds in another way. The Kurds are really becoming their partners in the region.

Guernica: Do you see Kurdistan becoming a political reality?

Mano Khalil: I do believe Kurdistan is becoming a reality. When we shot our movie in Iraqi Kurdistan a few months ago, it became clear that there is a country called Kurdistan there. Nobody knows about it, but there is a border between Arab Iraq and Kurdistan. It's not easy for a man from Baghdad to go to Kurdistan. You have to have a sort of visa for that. The border is controlled. There are now Kurdish forces there for security, too.

Also, now the world believes in Kurds, as they have become partners in that region. The West doesn't believe in the Iraqi government—not in Maliki before or Abadi today. It doesn't believe in Syria in any way, nor in Iran. So the Kurds could maybe work together with the Western world to bring stability to the region. It's a nice change, coming as it is after hundreds of years of the struggle of the Kurds. I am not saying that the Kurds are angels, but they have suffered too much. These people have a right to live in their country. The right just to be where they are, in freedom. And now the world has started believing in this. Kurdistan is coming. In some five years, I hope, we will have a flag in New York, hanging with all the other flags.

CONTRIBUTORS

SALAR ABDOH was born in Iran, and splits his time between Tehran and New York City, where he is co-director of the creative writing MFA program at the City College of New York. He is the author of the novels *The Poet Game*, *Opium*, and his latest, *Tehran at Twilight*. His essays and short stories have appeared in various publications, including the *New York Times*, *BOMB*, *Callaloo*, *Guernica*, and on the BBC. He is the recipient of the NYFA Prize and the National Endowment for the Arts award. He is also the editor and translator of the anthology *Tehran Noir*.

JOHN BENDITT had a distinguished career as a science journalist. He was an editor at *Scientific American* and *Science* before serving as editor-in-chief of *Technology Review*. He has written poetry, prose poems, and fiction. His debut novel, *The Boatmaker*, was published by Tin House Books in February 2015.

REBECCA BENGAL is completing a collection of short stories and a novel. A former editor at *DoubleTake* magazine, her writing has appeared in the *New York Times*, *The Paris Review* Daily, *The New Yorker* online, Vogue. com, and elsewhere. "Outlaw's Territory" was written during a fellowship at the MacDowell Colony.

LAYLA BENITEZ-JAMES is a graduate of the University of Houston's creative writing program in poetry. Her poetry, interviews, reviews, and flash fiction have appeared in *Acentos Review*, *Matter*, *The San Antonio Express News*, *The San Antonio Current*, and *Gulf Coast*. Translations into Spanish appear in *Revista Kokoro*. She is currently living in Murcia, Spain, where she is translating the works of Madrid poet Óscar Curieses and teaching English in Torre Pacheco.

ANNE BOYER's most recent book is *Garments Against Women*. She is an assistant professor of the liberal arts at the Kansas City Art Institute.

KHALYM KARI BURKE-THOMAS is an MFA candidate at the University of Wyoming. His work has also appeared in *Vol. 1 Brooklyn*.

LAURA BYLENOK is the author of *Warp*, winner of the 2015 T.S. Eliot Prize, and the hybrid prose chapbook *a/0* (DIAGRAM/New Michigan Press, 2014). Her poetry has appeared in *Best New Poets, Pleiades, North American Review*, and *West Branch*, among other journals. She is currently pursuing a PhD in literature and creative writing at the University of Utah. She lives in Salt Lake City.

MONIKA CASSEL is acting chair of creative writing and literature at New Mexico School for the Arts in Santa Fe, where, with the support of the Lannan Foundation, she is developing a major in creative writing for high school students. She was raised bilingual in English and German. Her chapbook, *Grammar of Passage*, won the Venture Poetry Award and is forthcoming from flipped eye publishing in 2016; her translations have appeared or are forthcoming in *Asymptote, Michigan Quarterly Review*, and *Structo Magazine*, and her poems have appeared in *The Laurel Review* and *Stone Canoe Journal*.

ALEXANDER CHEE is the author of the novels *Edinburgh* and *The Queen of the Night* (Houghton Mifflin Harcourt, February 2016). He is the recipient of a 2003 Whiting Award, a 2004 NEA Fellowship in prose, and a 2010 MCCA Fellowship, and residency fellowships from the MacDowell Colony, the VCCA, Civitella Ranieri, and Amtrak. His essays and stories have appeared in *The New York Times Book Review, Tin House, Slate, Guernica*, NPR, and *Out*, among others. He lives in New York City.

INGRID ROJAS CONTRERAS is a recent Bread Loaf Bakeless Fellow and recipient of the San Francisco Foundation's Mary Tanenbaum literary award. Her writing has been published in the *Los Angeles Review of Books*, and has been anthologized in *Wise Latinas* and *American Odysseys: Writings by New Americans*. Currently, she is working on a nonfiction book about her grandfather, a medicine man who could move clouds. She lives in San Francisco with her books.

J. MALCOLM GARCIA has written on Pakistan, Sierra Leone, Chad, Haiti, Honduras, and Argentina, among other countries. He is the author of *The Khaarijee: A Chronicle of Friendship and War in Kabul* and *What Wars Leave Behind: The Faceless and the Forgotten*, and a recipient of the Studs Terkel Prize for writing about the working classes and the Sigma Delta Chi Award for excellence in journalism. His work has been anthologized in *Best American Travel Writing, Best American Nonrequired Reading*, and *Best American Essays*.

ZACH ST. GEORGE is from Anchorage, Alaska. He studied at the UC Berkeley Graduate School of Journalism, and lives in New York. He has written for *High Country News, The Atlantic, Bloomberg Businessweek*, and elsewhere.

MASHA GESSEN is a Russian-American journalist and the author of several books, including *The Man Without a Face: The Unlikely Rise of Vladimir Putin* and *The Brothers: The Road to an American Tragedy*. Her award-winning work has appeared in *The New Yorker*, the *New York Times, Slate, Vanity Fair*, the *Washington Post*, and elsewhere. A longtime resident of Moscow, she now lives with her family in New York City.

VINEET GILL is a journalist based in Delhi. He has written on books, arts, and culture for publications like the *Times of India, The Hindu, Open*, and *The Sunday Guardian*, among others. You can stay up to speed with his sparse but classy Twitter feed by following the handle @vineetgill.

BOSTON GORDON is a poet and writer living in Philadelphia, PA. Boston earned their MFA in poetry through Lesley University. They have previously been published in *Amethyst Arsenic, Word Riot, Bedfellows*, and more.

RACHEL ELIZA GRIFFITHS is a poet and visual artist. Her most recent collection of poetry, *Lighting the Shadow* (Four Way Books), was published in 2015. Currently, Griffiths teaches creative writing at IAIA and Sarah Lawrence College. She lives in Brooklyn.

JENNIFER HAIGH lives in Boston. Her stories have been published in *The Atlantic, Granta, The Best American Short Stories 2012*, and other places. She is the author of four novels and the story collection *News From Heaven*, winner of the 2014 Massachusetts Book Award. Her new novel, *Heat and Light*, will be published by Ecco in May 2016.

S. ASEF HOSSAINI was born in northern Afghanistan. When he was one year old, his family emigrated to Iran due to the Soviet invasion. He completed his primary and secondary education there. After the fall of the Taliban, Asef returned to Afghanistan at age twenty-two to study philosophy and sociology at Kabul University. In 2005, as a student and a leader of the Afghanistan Student Movement, Asef ran for a seat in Afghanistan's first parliamentary election. His poetry collections, *These Walking Shoes, Four Planets in My Room and I*, and *Affected by the Lunar Eclipse*, have been published in Kabul, Tehran, and Germany.

HABIBE JAFARIAN was born in the city of Mashhad in northeastern Iran. As a writer and journalist, she has worked at such magazines and newspapers as *Jam-e-Jam, Hamshahri Javan, Mostanad, Zan-e-Ruz, 24*, and *Dastan*. Her work in the series titled *According to the Wives* includes the biographies of three of the major Iranian commanders of the Iran-Iraq war: Mostafa Chamran, Ibrahim Hemmat, and Hamid Bakeri. Her latest books are: *Being With the Camera*, about the life and times of the legendary Iranian war photographer Kaveh Golestan, who was killed in Iraq, and the biography of Imam Musa Sadr, the original creator of the Hezbollah of Lebanon, who disappeared under suspicious circumstances in Gaddafi's Libya. Currently Jafarian is staff writer and senior editor for the documentary section of the monthly journal *Dastan*. She lives and works in Tehran.

MANO KHALIL was born in 1964 in Syrian Kurdistan. Between 1981 and 1986, he studied history and law at the Damascus University in Syria. Then, from 1987 to 1994, he studied fiction film direction in the former Czechoslovakia (Vysoká škola múzických umení-filmova a televízna fakulta). During the first half of the '90s, he worked as an independent film director for the Czechoslovakian and later the Slovakian Television. He has been living in Switzerland since 1996, where he works as an independent film director and producer. In 2012, he established his own film production company called Frame Film.

ALEXANDRA KLEEMAN was raised in Boulder, Colorado, and currently lives at the tip of Staten Island. Her work has been published in *The Paris Review, Zoetrope: All-Story, Conjunctions, n+1*, and *The Guardian*. She is the author of the novel *You Too Can Have a Body Like Mine* and *Intimations*, a story collection (Harper 2016).

ARIEL LEWITON is director of marketing and publicity at Sarabande Books, interviews editor at *Guernica*, and adjunct faculty at the University of Iowa. Her writing has appeared in the *Los Angeles Review of Books*, Vice.com, *The Paris Review* Daily, *Tin House* online, and elsewhere. She lives in New York.

SARA MAJKA's stories have been published in *A Public Space, The Gettysburg Review*, and *The Massachusetts Review*. *A Public Space* and Graywolf Press recently published her debut story collection, *Cities I've Never Lived In*. She lives in Queens.

FARZANA MARIE is a PhD candidate in Persian literature at the University of Arizona and president of the nonprofit Civil Vision International. She grew up in Chile, California, and Kazakhstan, later spending years in Afghanistan as a civilian volunteer and Air Force officer. She is the author of the nonfiction book *Hearts for Sale! A Buyer's Guide to Winning in Afghanistan* (Worldwide Writings, 2013), the poetry chapbook *Letters to War and Lethe* (Finishing Line Press, 2014), and a forthcoming book of poetry in translation, *Load Poems Like Guns: Women's Poetry from Herat, Afghanistan* (Holy Cow! Press, 2015). She's on Twitter @farzanamarie.

MAGGIE NELSON is a poet, critic, scholar, and nonfiction writer. She is the author of nine books of nonfiction and poetry, including *The Argonauts*, *The Art of Cruelty: A Reckoning* (a 2011 *New York Times* Notable Book of the Year), *Bluets*, and *Jane: A Murder* (a finalist for the PEN/Martha Albrand Award for the Art of the Memoir). She has been the recipient of a 2012 Creative Capital Literature Fellowship, a 2010 Guggenheim Fellowship in Nonfiction, a National Endowment for the Arts Fellowship in Poetry, and an Andy Warhol Foundation/Creative Capital Arts Writers Grant. She currently teaches in the School of Critical Studies at CalArts and lives in Los Angeles.

HENRY PECK is a writer based in New York. He has contributed to *Guernica*, NPR, the *New York Times*, Almirah Radio, and other outlets. He works for the office of the General Counsel at Human Rights Watch.

RICHARD PRICE is a novelist (*Clockers, Freedomland, Samaritan, Lush Life*) who has written for the HBO series *The Wire*. His new novel, *The Whites*, was released under the pen name Harry Brandt by Henry Holt in February 2015.

DANA RANGA was born in Bucharest, Romania, and emigrated to Germany in 1987, where she studied at the Free University of Berlin. Her first book of poetry, *Stop*, was written in Romanian. Ranga is the director of the award-winning documentaries *East Side Story, (Astronaut) Story, Cosmonaut Polyakov, Oh, Adam*, and *I Am in Space*. *Wasserbuch*, her first book of poems in German, was published by Suhrkamp in 2011 and was awarded the Adelbert von Chamisso Promotion Prize in 2014. Ranga's Romanian poems have been translated into numerous languages; this is her first German poem to appear in English translation.

CLAUDIA RANKINE's most recent book, *Citizen: An American Lyric*, was a *New York Times* Best Seller and winner of the National Book Critics Circle Award, *Los Angeles Times* Book Prize, NAACP Image Award, and PEN Open Book Award, as well as a finalist for the National Book Award. She is the author of four previous books, including *Don't Let Me Be Lonely: An American Lyric*. She currently serves as chancellor of the Academy of American Poets and is the Aerol Arnold Professor of English at the University of Southern California.

MEARA SHARMA is a nonfiction editor for *Guernica* and an artist, writer, and dancer. She has contributed to the *New York Times*, NPR, the *Squaw Valley Review*, *Matador*, and elsewhere. By day she works as a producer for the public radio program *On the Media*, in New York City.

JEAN STEVENS is a freelance journalist and public interest attorney based in Brooklyn. Her work has appeared in publications including RHRealityCheck.org, *Guernica*, *Bitch* magazine, and *Dissent*. A graduate of the S.I. Newhouse School of Communications at Syracuse University, Jean has also worked as a staff reporter and contributor to daily newspapers including the *Herald/Record* of northern New Jersey and the *Telegram & Gazette* of Worcester, Mass. She received her JD from the City University of New York School of Law and represents indigent tenants in eviction proceedings in Brooklyn.

LYNNE STEWART is a radical human rights attorney who has devoted her life to the oppressed—a constant advocate for the countless many deprived in the United States of their freedom and their rights. Lynne has been falsely accused of helping terrorists in an attempt by the US government to silence dissent, curtail vigorous defense lawyers, and install fear in those who would seek to help Arabs and Muslims being prosecuted for free speech. She was arrested in April 2002 and arraigned before Manhattan federal Judge John Koeltl, who also presided over her trial in 2004. She was convicted and received a twenty-eight-month sentence in October 2006. However, she was free on bail until 2009, when the government appealed the sentence. In late 2009 Lynne was re-sentenced to ten years in federal prison. Lynne was freed from prison on December 31, 2013, and is now home with her family.

BEN WIZNER is director of the Speech, Privacy & Technology Project at the American Civil Liberties Union. He has litigated numerous cases involving post-9/11 civil liberties abuses, including challenges to airport security policies, government watchlists, targeted killing, extraordinary rendition, and torture, and he is a legal advisor to NSA whistleblower Edward Snowden.

WENDY XU is the author of *You Are Not Dead* (Cleveland State University Poetry Center, 2013) and several chapbooks, including *Naturalism* (Brooklyn Arts Press, 2015). In 2014 she was the recipient of a Ruth Lilly and Dorothy Sargent Rosenberg Fellowship from the Poetry Foundation; her work has appeared in *The Best American Poetry*, *Boston Review*, *Poetry*, *jubilat*, and widely elsewhere. Born in Shandong, China, in 1987, she currently lives and teaches in Brooklyn.

About *Guernica*

Guernica is an award-winning magazine of literature, politics, art, and ideas. We give equal weight to reportage, polemic, and criticism of domestic and international affairs, alongside first-person narrative, fiction, poetry, and visual art by established and emerging artists.

Guernica contributors come from dozens of countries, write in nearly as many languages, and offer original, at times radical, takes on global issues. They include acclaimed writers like Chimamanda Ngozi Adichie, Bei Dao, J. Malcolm Garcia, Mark Dowie, Ariel Dorfman, Richard Price, Margo Jefferson, Jonathan Steele, George Szirtes, Victoria Redel, Norman Solomon, Richard Howard, Julian Rios, Edith Grossman, Sasha Polakow-Suransky, Tom Engelhardt, Tariq Ali, Susie Linfield, Pierra Bayard, Horacio Castellanos Moya, Alimorad Fadie Nia, Marie Monique Robin, Shelley Jackson, Alexandra Kleeman, Alexander Chee, Anna Badkhen, Alan Lightman, Lidia Yuknavitch, Chika Unigwe, Scott Cheshire, Peter Manseau, Deb Olin Unferth, Porochista Khakpour, Mark Binelli, Josh Weil, Jesse Ball, Sadanand Dhume, Monica Ferrell, Ayana Mathis, Kiese Laymon, Catherine Lacey, and Laura van den Berg. *Guernica* guest fiction editors have included Claire Messud, Brenda Wineapple, Sam Lipsyte, George Saunders, Francisco Goldman, and Ben Marcus.

Guernica is published twice monthly, on the 1st and 15th, *Guernica Daily* is updated every weekday, and the magazine produces four special themed issues per year.

For our submissions guidelines, please visit:
http://www.guernicamag.com/information/contact

Guernica magazine is a volunteer-driven 501(c)3 organization and reader support makes this work possible. If you would like to make a contribution, please visit: **www.guernicamag.com/donate**

With special thanks to:

Lorraine Adams

Anthony Arnove

Jonathan Binstock

Hillary Brenhouse

Caroline Casey

Alexander Chee

Coffeehouse Press

Community Bookstore

Creative Time

Electric Literature

Europa Editions

Julie Fain

Toni Fay

W. Ross Foote

Katharine Freeman

Roxane Gay

Graywolf Press

Jacqueline Grindrod

Lauren Groff

Nadxieli Nieto

James Hannaham

Phil Klay

Knopf

Reggie and Leslie Lucas

Megan Lynch

DeShay McCluskey

New York Review of Books

Classics

OR Books

Duvall Osteen

Elliot Peters

Random House

Riverhead Books

Helen Rosner

Sackett Street Writers' Workshop

Rebecca Saletan

Sarabande Books

Rosie Schaap

Kamila Shamsie

Nalini Sharma

Luke Simpson

Rob Spillman

Erica Wright

And to each and every individual donor who made this book and our magazine possible with their contributions, large and small.

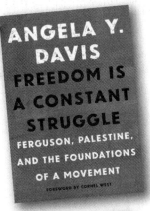

Angela Y. Davis, Edited by Frank Barat,
Foreword by Dr. Cornel West

Freedom Is a Constant Struggle
Ferguson, Palestine, and the Foundations of a Movement

In these newly collected essays, interviews, and speeches, Angela Y. Davis illuminates the connections between struggles against state violence and oppression throughout history and around the world. Davis challenges us to imagine and build the movement for human liberation. And in doing so, she reminds us that "freedom is a constant struggle."

Keeanga-Yamahtta Taylor

From #BlackLivesMatter to Black Liberation

In this stirring and insightful analysis, activist and scholar Keeanga-Yamahtta Taylor surveys the historical and contemporary ravages of racism and persistence of structural inequality such as mass incarceration and Black unemployment. In this context, she argues that this new struggle against police violence holds the potential to reignite a broader push for Black liberation.

Edited by Kevin Coval,
Quraysh Ali Lansana, and Nate Marshall

The BreakBeat Poets
New American Poetry in the Age of Hip-Hop

This is the first poetry anthology by and for the Hip-Hop generation. It is for people who love Hip-Hop, for fans of the culture, for people who've never read a poem, for people who thought poems were only something done by dead white dudes who got lost in a forest, and for poetry heads. This anthology is meant to expand the idea of who a poet is and what a poem is for.

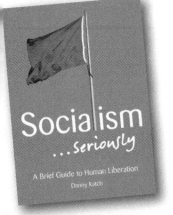

Danny Katch

Socialism . . . Seriously
A Brief Guide to Human Liberation

Danny Katch brings together the two great Marxist traditions of Karl and Groucho to provide an entertaining and insightful introduction to what the socialist tradition has to say about democracy, economics, and the potential of human beings to be something more than just bomb-dropping, planet-destroying, racist fools.

haymarketbooks.org